COMES A RECKONING

COMES A RECKONING

QUINCY HARKER, DEMON HUNTER VOL. 8

JOHN G. HARTNESS

FALSTAFF
BOOKS
WWW.FALSTAFFBOOKS.COM

For Puck, my best buddy.
2004 - 2021

Events in this book take place immediately following *Blaze of Glory*.

1

The sun came up over the Queen City and found me waiting on my balcony again, Irish coffee in hand, trying to drink away my guilt and the recriminations of the dead. It wasn't working. It never does. The more I drank, the clearer the faces became in my memory, the sharper their voices got.

I don't remember everyone I've killed. I don't know that humans, or mostly humans, or whatever I am, are meant to be able to keep that many people in memory. My body count numbers in the hundreds, most of them monsters from other planes of existence, but a good number of monsters from right here on Earth, too. Vampires, lycan-thropes, demons, half-demons, rapists, murderers...my human death toll is probably well into the triple digits, too, and that's without remembering all the Nazis I killed when I was a little insane.

I can't keep track of all of them, and I don't really give a shit. Human or monster, they were evil, and somebody had to take out the trash. By sheer luck, weird mystical genetics, and a thoroughly shoddy upbringing by my parasitic uncle, I was elected sanitation engineer for humanity. Whatever. Like I said, somebody has to do it. If not me, then it would probably fall to some poor schmuck even more ill-suited to the task than I am. But I don't remember the bad guys. Don't even try.

I can't remember the bad people I've killed, but I can't forget the good ones. The ones who died at my hand, or died because I wasn't in the right place, or because I made a mistake. The ones who died because I wasn't good enough, because they trusted me to keep them safe, because I failed them.

Cassie, who died because I wasn't fast enough to knock Watson aside. Stupid, beguiled Watson, the one-legged man who kicked my ass and murdered the woman Luke loved. Dennis, who died because in my hubris I thought that nobody would ever come after my friends to get to me. Christy, who died because she was in the wrong place at the wrong time when my maelstrom of shit whirled past and swept her up. Renfield, who died because a half-demon bastard thought it would be deliciously ironic to bring his dear old dad to Earth by killing someone I cared about. Joe, the priest and maybe more who gave his life to rescue a piece of evidence for my fight. And Gabby. That one stung the most, and not just because it was the freshest. It hurt because it was so stupid, so goddamn *random* that I finally, for the first time in a long time, found myself believing there really was a God because he was obviously a fucking prick.

"Out here praying, cursing, or just drinking?" Faustus said from the sliding glass door behind me. I turned and found the usually dapper demon wearing his human suit, but barefoot in a pair of jeans and a Lady Gaga t-shirt. He held out a handle of Bacardi 151, but I shook my head.

"Pass. It's barely worth it to try and get drunk, my metabolism is so fast."

"Oh, I know," he replied, coming to lean next to me on the balcony railing. Faustus was a good-looking man in his human form, brown hair with a little stubble, piercing blue eyes, and a cleft chin. I could see why he never had much trouble convincing people to sell their soul to him. "I haven't been able to get drunk since I stopped drinking Prohibition hooch. None of this legal stuff has enough alcohol and sin attached to it. But sometimes it's the only solution to a problem." He took a long pull from the bottle, then hurled the rest out onto the lightening sky.

"Goddammit, Faustus!" I snapped, firing off a purple blast of raw energy and shattering the bottle before it crashed down onto the busy South Boulevard below and caused a ten-car pileup.

"Sorry," he said, without an ounce of regret in his voice. "Demon. Old habits die hard."

"You okay?" I asked. Not a question I ever thought I'd ask a demon, but these were pretty uncharted waters we found ourselves in lately.

"No," he replied. "You people have fucked me up. I'm a demon, for Lucifer's sake! I'm supposed to be sowing havoc and reaping souls, reveling in the suffering of humanity. But instead, I..."

"Give a shit?" I finished, walking over to one of the heavy metal chairs and sitting down. "Sucks, doesn't it?"

"Yes! It really does." Faustus sat across from me and looked chagrined. "And now I want a drink, but I threw my booze away."

"I would tell you to go get something off my bar, but I'm pretty sure that's where the last one came from."

"Oh, yeah. That was totally your liquor you blew up." We sat there for a second looking at each other, then I snickered. Then Faustus snorted a little, then it grew into a laugh, and before I knew it, the two of us were sitting across my patio table from each other, laughing until tears rolled down our cheeks. Somewhere along the way, they stopped being tears of laughter, and then we were just sitting there crying. I leaned forward and patted him on the shoulder, the way you do when you kinda want to hug somebody, but neither of you are the hugging type, but you feel like some kind of contact is needed.

"I really liked her," he said. He was still looking down, his gaze locked on his hands, which were clenched on the table. I could see his knuckles turning white, like the effort of holding his hands together was the only thing keeping *him* together, and I squeezed his shoulder again.

"I know." Faustus and Gabby had an on-again, off-again relationship. One of those things where people have a lot of sex and really like hanging out, but know that if they're around each other too much, eventually they'll have all the sex they want to have with each other and then one of them will probably murder the other in their sleep.

"And I fucking *trusted* him." Now we were into the guts of it. Not a week before Gabby got herself turned into a kabob by a piece of debris in an explosion, Jack Watson, one of my allies and quite possibly Faustus's first real friend in, well, *ever*, betrayed us all and killed Cassie while trying to murder Luke. Luke then reminded all of us exactly what they used to call him on the battlefields of Wallachia and left Watson's corpse in the middle of a high school football field.

"Yeah," I said. "People suck."

Faustus looked up at me, his yellow demonic gaze burning through the illusion of his meat suit. "You don't get it, Harker. I was raised in Hell. Betrayal is a fucking art form to me and mine. I've been around since the Fall, and I've never trusted *anyone*. But I trusted Jack. I trusted that prick, and he killed Cassie, and now because of him killing Cassie, Gabby's dead, and all because I—"

"No." I cut him off short. He glared at me, but I kept talking. "You don't get to hog all the blame. We all trusted Jack. And you might be older than the rest of us, but we've all seen enough shit to know who we can and can't trust. Most of the time. But he snowed us all. And yeah, if he doesn't kill Cassie, then Luke doesn't go dark, and maybe doesn't end up in that building where Joe and Gabby got blown up. But that's not on you. It's not on you, it's not on me, it's not on Luke. None of us. It's on Jack, and Director Shaw, whoever she really was, and this Master prick who's behind all this bullshit. And you know what?"

"What?"

"Every one of those motherfuckers is dead except for the 'Master.' So now we've got one job."

"Find the Master?"

"And send him down to Hell to catch up with all his friends. Now do you want to sit here in the corner and cry, or do you want to get the fuck to work and go find this son of a bitch?"

"Let's get to work." He stood up and ran his hand across his face. It instantly dried, with no red eyes, no runny nose, nothing. I guess there's something to be said for having an illusory countenance.

"Go find Luke and translate that goddamned grimoire. It's in a dialect of German that I can't figure out."

Faustus snapped off a salute and went inside, moving with a purpose. *That was well done,* Becks said through the telepathic link we shared.

How long were you listening?

You woke me up when you were laughing. That sent some really weird signals through your head.

Sorry.

It's fine, she replied. *It was better than the numbness you've been sending. I was starting to get worried.*

I'm okay, I said.

I felt her laugh inside my head. *You're so far from okay, you're not even in the same time zone. But you're functional, and that's enough to get us started. Now get in here and let's get a shower. Everybody else will be here in an hour, and I want breakfast before we start our grand planning session.*

I haven't lived over a century by not learning a thing or two, and one of the new lessons I learned over the past few years was that when the woman who shares your bed and your psyche tells you to do something, you should do it. So I carried my coffee cup inside, closed the sliding glass door, and gave one look back at the sun as it crested the horizon, bathing the city in crimson. *Red sky in the morning, sailors take warning,* I thought. Sailors, Masters, whatever. Anybody who wanted to mess with my family should look to the sky and take the warning. It was time to fight back.

2

I stood at the head of the conference table and took a moment to look at the remnants of us. Jack's chair beside Faustus sat empty, and I suppose I was a little bit grateful that neither the demon nor I had thrown it off the balcony, because that would have been difficult to explain. And because I can't vouch for me having the presence of mind to open the sliding glass door first. Becks was at my right hand, as always, but instead of the sensible cop wear I'd grown accustomed to seeing her in, she was looking more like the yin to my guardian angel Glory's yang these days.

Becks left the Charlotte-Mecklenburg Police Department after a disagreement with department leadership over their willingness to commit ridiculous levels of brutality against their own citizens, all to make sure their bloated budget kept getting approved every year. Nowadays, she was a Deputy Director of the Department of Homeland Security's Paranormal Division, working for our ally Regional Director Keya Pravesh. Because working for the federal government was such a step up from working for the local cops. Either way, Homeland's dress code was a lot less slacks and sport coats cut to hide your sidearm and more Lilith Fair t-shirts and jeans with a Glock clipped to her waistband for all the world to see.

Glory was across the table from her at my left elbow, kicked back in her chair with her feet up on the table and her hands behind her head. I smacked her purple Docs onto the floor and grinned as she sat up involuntarily. She glared at me from under a curtain of blond curls that spilled down onto the shoulders of the white Def Leppard tee she wore. Or conjured, more likely. Like Faustus, I wasn't sure where Glory's clothes came from, but I was pretty sure it had more in common with fairy dust than the clearance racks at Goodwill.

The foot of the table was reserved for Luke, my uncle, mentor, and, oh by the way, the most famous vampire in history. Gabby Van Helsing managed to rescue him from a bunch of DEMON's assholes before they got themselves blown up, killing Gabby in the process. Next to him sat Jo Henry, the muscular great-granddaughter of the legendary John Henry and daughter of Cassandra Harrison, Luke's most recent Renfield. Also, and not even a little coincidentally, the most recent woman my uncle fell deeply in love with. When she died at the hands of Jack Watson, Luke went over to the dark side for a little bit. I wasn't completely convinced he was all the way back. I knew for damn sure Jo wasn't.

"So...hey," I said, then stood there staring at them all like a blithering idiot. Or I guess a not blithering idiot, since I didn't even say anything.

"God, Harker, you suck at this," Becks said. "Sit down and let's talk about where we go next. You look like a general without any idea who the enemy even is, much less how to find them and kick their ass."

I did as she said and sat down. "I wish there wasn't any truth in that, Becks. I *don't* have any idea who this 'Master' asshole is, how to find him, if he can even be killed, and what the hell his beef is with me and mine."

"Well, what do we know?" Becks asked. I allowed myself a little smile as she slipped right back into the role of detective. Good thing, because we definitely needed somebody driving this bus who knew how to solve a mystery.

"We know he's after me, and he's not afraid of killing the people I care about to get at me," I said.

"Not only is he not afraid of it, it's kinda his whole plan," Glory said. "Watson had specific instructions to kill Luke in the hopes it would push you over the edge."

"Yeah, I sense a theme here," I said. "That was Mengele's goal, too. Torture me until I go all code red on everyone around me. When Becks pulled me out of that, the Master had to change plans."

"Because obviously going at you directly was hazardous on his henchmen's health," Glory said with a smirk. I shot her a look, and she shrugged. "What? You literally ripped that dude limb from limb. Then you beat his torso into pieces with his own severed arms. It was the kind of savagery that people make slasher movies about, only most horror directors don't have the imagination for that kind of ass-kicking."

"He was a Nazi," I replied. "I should have t-shirts printed up. Quincy Fucking Harker, Killing Nazis since 1939."

"He wasn't just a Nazi," Becks said. "He was *Josef Mengele*. One of the most famous murderers in history. The guy who led the SS experiments on prisoners at Auschwitz. And he was still alive in the twenty-first century, and looking closer to fifty than ninety, so there was something weird going on with him."

"The Nazis were into a lot of different shit," I said. "They had a whole Occult Division looking for artifacts, spell books, potions, cryptids—anything they thought would help them achieve their goals, they were into. Luke spent a lot of the forties either swapping the stuff they were looking for out with harmless fakes or just killing any Aryan fuckhole who got too close to anything with real power. But a few things slipped through the cracks."

"Most notably the Spear of Destiny," Luke said.

"Yeah, that wasn't our most shining moment," I said. "Letting the spear that pierced the side of Christ on the cross fall into the hands of *Der Fuhrer* was a pretty epic fail, but he killed himself before he managed to unlock any of the Spear's powers."

"Or so we think," Faustus added.

A whole lot of eyeballs suddenly zeroed in on the demon at the table. "What exactly do you mean by that, Faustus?" Becks asked.

"Well, we don't *think* Hitler managed to get the Spear to do anything, because he still lost the war and offed himself in his bunker. But we don't *know* that he didn't get it to work. And we certainly don't know if any of his henchpricks managed to unlock some of its power."

"But an Implement in the hands of the wrong person could certainly instill longevity in a human, or perhaps even immortality," Luke said. The Spear of Destiny did double duty as the divine focus of the Archangel Azrael, the Angel of Death. It was his Implement. All the Archangels had one. I know, I'm the one who had to collect them like they were fucking Pokémon a couple years ago.

"Mengele wasn't immortal," I said. "I killed the shit out of him."

"There's a difference between immortal and invulnerable, Q," Glory said. "Mengele wouldn't die of natural causes, but you are anything but natural causes."

"Makes sense," I agreed. "Okay, so Mengele, or some other Nazi fuck, managed to unlock the power of the Spear of Destiny, or at least some of it, and it made him immortal. You think this Master was part of that deal? Was he a Nazi shitbag, too? Or just a regular shitbag?"

"Harker, have you ever used the word 'Nazi' as a noun without having a profanity associated with it?" Becks asked. "I'm just curious."

I thought about it for a second. "I can't say with one hundred percent certainty about my entire life, because I had to deal with a lot of Nazi cockwrinkles in Europe in the forties, but I can guarantee you that I have never called anyone just a 'Nazi' before. They're always 'Nazi insert insulting and probably profane term here.' I really don't like Nazis," I said.

"Oh, I am very aware of that," Becks said. "I'm inside your head, remember?"

"That must be a truly terrifying place to be," Faustus said. "And I grew up in Hell."

"Faustie, you have *no* idea," Becks replied.

"Okay," I said, holding up both hands to try and regain a tiny bit of order. "So we know there are Nazi assclowns involved, and we know they want to turn me back into a psycho killer and turn me loose on the world."

"We know they're interested in taking the sliver of the demon Skyffrax out of Luke and setting *him* free upon the world," Glory added.

"Is that even possible?" Becks asked.

We all looked at each other, the vampire, the magician, the angel, the demon, and the humans. After a pause that I found a lot longer than was comfortable, Faustus shrugged and said, "Maybe. I mean, you two are kind of an anomaly. There have been a lot of deals made with demons over the centuries. I should know. But no one has ever taken a piece of one of us inside themselves and kept hold of it for this long. Most people would have succumbed to possession before the first century was up."

"I always said you were stubborn," I told Luke with a wry smile. He didn't return it.

"The first several decades were very difficult. It wasn't until I accidentally had the blood of an enemy run into my mouth on the battlefield that I realized the blood quieted the demon inside me."

"Wait, so you don't have to drink blood to survive?" I asked. Fireworks were going off inside my head as everything I'd known for more than a century started to rewrite itself.

"No," Luke said. "Blood is the conduit for my ongoing survival, and by this point, it has mutated into a hunger that is physical. If I go too long without it, I weaken and begin to starve. And as I weaken, Skyffrax becomes stronger. Thus my...lack of discretion when I have not fed for a time."

I love my uncle's gift for understatement. That had to be the most refined way of saying, "I'll eat anyone in sight like the Tasmanian devil going after a turkey leg if I get hungry enough." I'd seen Luke blood-starved. It was some scary shit. I could certainly see a demonic component to him in that situation.

"Is that why they took you?" I asked. "When I was in Memphis and DEMON and Mengele kidnapped you. Were they trying to cut Skyffrax free?"

"I don't know, Quincy," Luke replied. "We did not have much opportunity for conversation. They kidnapped me, locked me in a cell, and left me to starve. I was not given the chance to question their motives."

"And they were a little dead by the time you got loose," I said. "I remember. So let's assume that was the plan. They talked about someone called the Chancellor pulling Shaw's strings. But the guys from the warehouse were talking about The Master."

"Are they the same person?" Glory asked.

"Fuck if I know," I said. "Seems like, and this dickhead does have a penchant for using multiple names to sow confusion. Case in point, the half dozen Director Shaws we've put in body bags." A slight exaggeration, but not through any fault of mine. I would have happily gone on murdering DEMON Directors as often as I was given the chance. I had a feeling Pravesh might object. Maybe.

"Okay, if the Chancellor and the Master are the same person, then we're back to Nazis. Sorry, Nazi shitheads," Becks said.

"So, if we just pretend that I've never been much on politics, would somebody explain the connection?" Faustus asked. We all stared at him for a moment. "Look, I make deals, and I take souls. While I appreciate the opportunity for greater volume of soul-stealing that politics gives one, I've always favored a more personal approach. I'm not saying I didn't have plenty going on in Nazi Germany, I just never paid much attention to titles."

"Hitler was Chancellor of Germany," I said. "Among other titles. A lot of other titles, if I recall."

"You don't think this Chancellor, or Master, or whatever, might be a sawed-off little house painter with a penchant for titles, do you?" Becks asked, her eyes flashing wide.

"No," Faustus said, his tone definitive.

At the exact same moment, Glory said, "Not a chance."

I raised an eyebrow at my guardian angel, and she said, "Oh, he's in Hell. I promise you he's in Hell. Shit, I wouldn't be surprised if Lucifer built a whole new wing just to torment that little fuck. Right, Faustus?"

"Oh, not just Lucifer. He's the plaything of every major demon in the place. He gets passed around more than a bottle of cheap bourbon at a high school bonfire. It's not often someone gets tossed down and the only directions from on high are 'Do whatever you want with them,' so everyone gets really excited for their turn torturing Hitler. I hear a guy on the Fourth Circle actually came up with a weapon so excruciating that he got promoted all the way down to the Seventh Circle for it."

"Okay, so it's not Hitler," I said, trying once again to herd the kittens. I was starting to feel a tiny bit of sympathy for Flynn having to keep me on task. But just a little. "Then we need to figure out who it is, where they are, and how to kill the motherfucker."

Jo stood up, the first time she'd moved or even really seemed engaged in the discussion since she'd sat down. "All that sounds great, and it's real important, but you're going to have to do it without me. I only came this morning to tell you that my stuff is all packed. As soon as Ginny gets out of school, we're headed back to Phoenix. I can't do this anymore. I can't *be here* anymore. I'm out."

And with that, she laid her great-grandfather's hammer on the conference table and walked out of my apartment.

3

I shook loose the paralysis that Jo's bombshell gripped me with and chased after her. I caught her arm as she turned into the hallway toward her apartment. She stopped and looked at me.

"You really want to let go of my arm, Harker." Her voice was low and steady, but her eyes were brimming with rage.

I did as she asked and let go. "Okay," I said, stepping back. "No grabbing. Got it. But can we talk about this?" I reached out across our mental connection for Becks, but got nothing, just a vague sense that she was paying attention, but she certainly wasn't contributing. I was on my own for this one.

"There's nothing to talk about. I'm done. I'm taking my little girl and I'm getting as far away from this shitshow you call a life as I can, while she's still young enough to maybe forget some of the insane stuff she's seen, and maybe, just maybe, grow up to be a normal, well-adjusted woman who doesn't feel the need to swing a magic hammer at every problem in her life. Shit, maybe I'll even try to rebuild a bridge with my in-laws so she can have *one* set of grandparents, at least."

That hit home. I knew what had been taken from Jo. Hell, I'd been there for most of it. Her father, killed by a werewolf who then came hunting her later. Her husband, ripped to shreds by something we never even managed to identify. Her mother, who died right in front of her at the hands of someone we thought was a friend. It wasn't pretty, the wreckage this life left in its wake, the scars it left on the survivors. "Okay."

A look of shock came over Jo's face. "What?"

"I said okay. You're right. Ginny deserves the chance to grow up without all this shit around her. Without wondering when somebody who isn't me tucks her in at night if Mommy is coming home. Without buying new funeral clothes every year when she buys her new school clothes, because death is just something that happens around us. She doesn't need to be around that. And neither do you. You both deserve better."

"But you should take this anyway," Glory said as she stepped up beside me. Angels are sneaky, just in case you didn't know that. Way sneaky. She held out John Henry's hammer like it weighed nothing. We all knew better. That thing had a heft to it that was a lot more than the nine-pound iron-and-silver head.

"I don't want it," Jo said. "I've never wanted it."

"I don't think it cares," I replied. "Remember what happened the last time you tried to leave it behind?" That had been the night Jo and I met, when she was attacked by the same werewolf that killed her father. It had been drawn by some kind of mystical bond between it, the Harrison family, and the hammer. When Jo touched the hammer for the first time as an adult, it rang like a bell through anyone with a drop of magical ability within a hundred miles.

"I remember. I remember we killed that furry bastard, so there shouldn't be anyone else looking for me," Jo said.

"Yeah, except for the rogue government agency we're in the middle of disbanding, the demons we've fought, any of the monsters DEMON or Homeland Security has battled in the past decade, or just some random asshole who's heard about you and your connection to me and Luke online and decides that coming at you is a good way to get to us. Not to make it all about me, but there a *lot* of people in several dimensions who really don't like me, and they'll take a shot at anyone they can if they think it will hurt me. And it would."

"Would what?" Jo asked.

"It would hurt me, you asshole!" I kept myself from yelling, but only because Glory stuck an elbow in my ribs. "You think I like seeing my friends die? No. It tears out a piece of what little soul I have left every time something shitty happens to one of you. That's why I went to Memphis when we got back from Hell, so I could try to keep you all safe. And we see how well *that* worked out." Which is to say, not at all. Turns out, being ten hours away in a different time zone is not enough distance to deter a bunch of psychos from kidnapping one's family.

"I know," Jo said with a little half-smirk. "I just wanted to hear you say you gave a shit. You're not such a dick after all, Harker. You play one pretty well, but we know what's up."

"Oh, for fuck's sake, don't encourage him," Glory said. She turned to look at me. "She's full of shit. You're a total dick."

"Thanks, G," I said. I still found it unnerving when an angel dropped f-bombs in my presence, but as I'd been recently informed, I seem to have a deleterious effect on the vocabulary of those who spend significant time with me. Although I'm pretty sure Robert "Bubba" Brabham has never used the word "deleterious" in his life.

I turned my focus back to Jo. "If you want to go, I won't stop you. I think you've made it pretty clear I couldn't if I wanted to. But if you need us, for anything, you just call. We'll be there. You're family. We love you." I took a minute, then I reached out and hugged her. It was a little awkward, because we're both more punchers than huggers, but after a second, she wrapped her arms around me and gave me a good squeeze.

Jo pulled back, and I saw a glint of moisture in her eyes. "I love you, too, Harker. I love all you bastards. I just…can't be around you. Not and keep my baby safe." But she took the hammer. Then she went into her apartment and closed the door, on the hall and on this chapter in her life. I put my hand on the door for a second, silently wishing for the best for Jo and for her daughter and hoping that they could stay out of this life, stay safe, forever.

Then I turned to go back to the team. We had a war to fight, and the bad guys weren't very big on giving us time to mourn our fallen.

"Is that a tear in your eye, Q?" Glory asked, her tone teasing.

"Blow it out your halo, angel," I growled. "Let's get this shit show on the road."

LATER THAT NIGHT, AFTER A COUPLE MORE HOURS OF CIRCULAR guessing and no real progress, Becks came out to find me in my favorite thinking spot, leaning over the balcony railing watching the traffic on South Boulevard.

"You know, if I thought it would kill you, I'd be afraid you'd jump," she said, wrapping her arms around my waist and laying her head on my back, right between my shoulder blades.

"I've lived through worse falls than this," I said. And I had. I'd been tossed off a taller building just a couple miles away when I crossed paths with an asshole wizard way back when Becks still wanted to arrest me every time she saw me. For the record, I was only guilty of something worthy of arrest about half the times she saw me.

Becks stepped back and sat in one of the patio chairs. "No booze?"

My ever-present whiskey glass wasn't present, and Becks noticed, of course. She paid attention to details like that. I was usually focusing on other details, like whether or not someone was trying to murder me. "Between me and Faustus, we've either drank or exploded everything in the joint. And the liquor store doesn't deliver."

"Well, that's just inconsiderate of them," she said with a smile. "Have you thought about lodging a complaint with management?"

"Well, since liquor stores in North Carolina are state-run, and I haven't paid income tax in, well, ever, I don't think I have a ton of stroke with the revenuers, as they like to call them around these here parts."

She laughed. "I'm pretty sure not even Bubba calls them that anymore."

"Yeah, probably not. He's alright, for a giant hillbilly."

"He'd probably say you're alright, too. For a potty-mouthed wizard." Her expression turned sober. "You've got a plan, right? To end this?"

"Only in the loosest sense of the word. Right now, I'm kinda hoping that Faustus and Luke find something in that grimoire Gabby gave her life getting out of the explosion. Because if not, I don't know where to go from here. Any suggestions?" She was a detective, after all. I didn't have to go looking for my problems all that often. Most of the time they found me.

"Well, this is obviously personal, so we can rule out following the money. I guess we start with the people in town with the most reason to hate you and try to follow that thread back to the source. If I didn't know the territory, but I knew someone I hated was there, I'd start by recruiting people who also hated that person."

"The enemy of my enemy and all that?" I asked.

"It's a cliché for a reason, Harker. So, who hates your guts in Charlotte?" She looked at me expectantly, and after a second, I just laughed.

I sat in the other patio chair and propped my feet up on the small round table where booze normally sat. I was definitely going to have to make a whiskey run. And a tequila run. And a rum run. "Babe, do you really think I have a *list*? Shit, the list of people who don't hate my guts is shorter. Like, the people in this apartment building and Pravesh, most of the time. That's about it. Almost everyone else I know in this city has tried to murder me at least once, or seriously considered it. I think the only reason Mort has never taken a run at me is because he's still kinda tied to the Lords of Chaos and they think keeping me around is good for the universal mayhem quota or something."

"You do have a way of antagonizing people," Becks agreed. Her gift for understatement was yet another reason I loved that woman. I thought for a second, trying to put my finger on the exact moment I fell for her. I don't think it was the last time she arrested me. It was almost certainly before that. But not too much before. It was definitely one of the times she arrested me. Something about the way she put the handcuffs on me...

"Please stop that, I am trying to think," she said, blushing. It was just a slight darkening of her cheeks, almost unnoticeable unless you knew what you were looking for, but I spotted it. "I'm in your head, remember, and it is *very* distracting in there right now."

"Then let's go inside and I'll try to take your mind off all the people who want to kill me. We could concentrate on enjoying life for a few hours instead." I stood up and held out a hand.

She took it, giving me a sharp smile. "A few hours, huh? I like the sound of that. Let's see you put your stamina where your mouth is."

So I did.

4

I lay in my bed, with a beautiful woman curled up asleep beside me, her warm body stretched out against mine, feeling the sweat drying on our skin as she snored softly into the bend of my elbow. I stared up at the ceiling, thinking about these people, these wonderful, messy, impossible people who had wormed their way into my life, into my soul. I thought I was done with that after Anna. I thought when I staggered out of the Arizona desert in the Forties with no memory of the past four years, that I would never let anyone back in like that again. It felt too dangerous. Not to me, but to everything around me.

And here I was again, all wrapped up with a woman way too good for me, with a group of friends literally willing to go to Hell and back for me, and no more deserving of them than I'd ever been.

"Penny for 'em, Harker," Becks said, smiling up at me. I hadn't even noticed she was awake.

"Just thinking about mistakes I've made, and family."

"Well, if you don't learn from your mistakes, you're doomed to repeat them," she replied.

"That sounds like something my sister Maddy used to say—that no one was more doomed to repeat their history than me, because no one more steadfastly refused to learn from their own mistakes. Maddy was always a big thinker, if a little wordy."

"Maddy? Was that her name? You never talk about her. Even less than your brothers."

"I barely even think about her. Not for decades. Probably not since a few years after she walked out of mine and Luke's life in Chicago in 1929." I lay there in bed with my fiancée and started telling her about a chapter in my life I thought long forgotten—the story of my sister, Maddy.

MADELINE JUSTINA HARKER. MADDY WAS YOUNG, BUT FIERY. SHE'D taken a lot of punches in her young life. Our mother died when she was just two years old, then Father followed two years later. Both our brothers died in the flu pandemic in 1918, so I was left with an eight-year-old baby sister and a whole lot of growing up to do very quickly. I lasted a year before I hunted down Luke, Maddy trailing along behind me looking like a very dingy rag doll with a bird's nest where her hair should be, and asked for help.

"I am not in the habit of tending to children, Quincy. I think you would understand this, given what you know of me." Luke's circumstances had never been a secret from me. I was born the year before his eponymous book was published and my family was thrust into a wholly unwanted celebrity. When my mother died, I was sixteen years old, and I sat by her bedside as she told me the entire, true, story of her and my father's acquaintance with Uncle Luke, Vlad Tepes, Count Dracula. Stoker got most things right, or close to right, depending on perspective. And since he was working from the notes of, as Luke called him up until his death, "that fat shite Van Helsing," there was a certain bias to be expected.

So, seeking refuge on his doorstep on a rainy night in London near the turn of the century was the most extreme of last resorts. I'd always got on well with Luke—he seemed to tolerate my wit better than my brothers' roughhousing or Maddy's dolls. But there is a great distance between getting along well with someone for a few hours at a time and living with them, and that is what I was asking.

"I know, Uncle," I replied, brushing wet hair back from my eyes. My own hair was only slightly less unkempt than Maddy's, having grown far longer than was fashionable or convenient. "But we have nowhere else to go. You're the only family we have left."

That was the most terrifying moment in my life, standing on that front step in the rain. Not sitting by my father's bedside as he drew his last breath. Not screaming at the doctors to help my baby brother when his lungs were so full of fluid it sounded more like he was gargling than coughing. Not even standing in the cemetery holding Maddy's hand as our last brother was lowered into the ground was more frightening than asking Luke for help that night. He had always been kind to us, yes. But he was still *Dracula*, the monster featured in so many stories since Bram Stoker had published his "novel."

He opened his mouth, I'm sure to tell me that we were not family, that we had no blood ties in fact, when a savior in a tailcoat came to the door and roughly shouldered Luke aside.

"Come in out of the rain, you little idiots," Renfield said, stretching out a hand to both Maddy and me. "Get in here where it's dry. I'll fetch some towels and put some tea on. I'll put a big spoonful of honey in yours, young lady, and we'll get you all warmed up. Then I'll make up the guest rooms on the second floor for you, and tomorrow when the sun is shining bright again, we'll go to your house, get your things, and move you all right in here." He was smiling when he said it, this spidery-limbed servant of my uncle's, but his gaze brooked no argument. Luke, for his part, simply stepped back and nodded.

"As you wish, Renfield. Welcome to my home, children. Please think of it as your own. I must go out for a bit, but if you are awake when I return, we can discuss your situation further."

Part of me thought I knew what he was going out to do, but the greater part of me didn't want to think about it in the least, not with my little sister preparing to bed down under the same roof. I swore then that as long as we remained under his roof, I would mirror Luke's schedule. If he slept, I would sleep. But if he was awake, no matter how late the hour, I would not let my eyes close at any cost. I never wanted the responsibility of raising my sister, but after reading so many tales of the depravities of Luke's "wives," I felt obligated to keep her from becoming some sort of succubus or other creature.

Obviously, I learned in years to come that succubi aren't something you can turn a human into, and that Luke's "wives" were not some type of bizarre harem that he kept for sexual gratification, but rather three female vampires who were under his protection from both human and supernatural dangers. I did not learn, nor did I ever attempt to learn, the true nature of my father's dalliance with the women in question. He was not my father when that happened, nor was he my mother's husband at the time, and some information is far better lost to history.

In other words, I did *not* want to know if my dad boned three vampires and donated more than blood to them. I know they fed on him, and that he drank from them as well, as is evidenced by my oh-so-twisted DNA. Not all my weirdness is demon transference from Luke passed down through my mother. Dear old dad's youthful indiscretions had some effect on my genetic code as well. We know this to be true because neither Luke nor his "wives" were celibate, or even indiscriminate. But my parents were the only time someone Luke had bitten married and made babies with someone that his "wives" had… dallied with. *Viola!* Quincy f'n Harker.

Luke seemed surprised to see me awake, if barely, in his den when he came home several hours later. He walked into the room as if he were coming home from the opera rather than sucking the life's blood out of some poor unwitting victim and stopped cold when he saw me sitting by the fire with my feet up on an ottoman and a copy of *Great Expectations* open on my lap. I had a blanket over my legs and had changed into a pair of Renfield's pajamas, which were a bit long for me, but did the job well enough.

"Hello, Quincy," Luke said as he hung up his hat and coat. He had given up his penchant for long flowing cloaks by the time I was old enough to remember, but he still enjoyed an ankle-length coat. "I thought you would be asleep in one of the guest rooms by now."

"I stayed up to speak with you," I replied.

Luke sighed. "Ah. It's to be one of *those* conversations. Let me at least take the edge off the night with a drink before we get on to the tedious bits. Would you care for something?"

This was not how I expected things to go. But I was young and adaptable and knew my uncle to have a taste for the finer things in life. I assumed this extended to his whiskey. "Yes, please."

"Scotch or Irish?"

"Irish, if you have it."

He nodded and walked over to the small bar. He took two glasses down from a shelf and poured a finger of amber liquid into each, then paused and added another two fingers. He handed one glass to me and sat in the other armchair in front of the fire, holding out his hands to warm himself. At that moment, fresh from feeding, his skin was tinged pink, and he looked more alive than I'd ever seen him. I could almost believe he was just an ordinary man, until he turned to look at me, and sat with such perfect stillness that he seemed more statue than living creature. Which of course, he wasn't.

"Threats or bargains?" he asked.

I blinked at him a few times, thoroughly confused by the question. "Huh?" I wasn't terribly eloquent as a young man. To be frank, with the exception of a modicum of skill in poetic profanity, I'm not all that eloquent as an old man.

"Do you plan to bargain with me for your sister's safety, or just threaten me with some heinous demise should I hurt her in any way? It's certain to be one or the other, and knowing both your parents as well as I did, I would expect your natural inclination to be to threaten. But it is a different age, and one that considers open violence gauche, so if you are truly a product of your environment, then perhaps you plan to offer me something to keep her safe."

"Neither," I said, taking great pleasure in the look of surprise on his face. Through the decades, one of the great joys of my life has been surprising Luke. When someone has lived as long as he has, and seen all that he has seen, he tends to think there are no surprises left. I see it as my job to prove him wrong as often as possible.

"Oh?" He raised an eyebrow. Lucas Card could give Dwayne Johnson eyebrow lessons, I swear. "Am I at least correct that you stayed awake to discuss your sister with me?"

"Yes," I replied. "But I have no intention to threaten you. I doubt it would do any good. If even half the stories told about you are true, there is very little left in this world that frightens you, and I'm fairly certain that a bankrupt twenty-three-year-old Londoner does not have access to any of those things."

"I am certain of that as well. But you said bankrupt? Your parents were fairly successful, I thought. And there was money in your mother's family..."

"There was. They were. But they have been gone for five years now, and running a household in London is not an inexpensive proposition, nor is boarding and educating three siblings. Especially when one has, shall we say, not applied themselves with much dedication to either education or employment."

"So, you're an impoverished wastrel who now comes looking for me to rescue you and your sister from the poorhouse?"

"Her, at least," I said. "I can make my own way if I need to. But I can't raise her in any decent flat in the city and keep a job to pay for it. I don't have any skills, Uncle. Father barely kept things afloat after Mother died, and when he passed, it was everything I could do to keep us all clothed and fed. Then the boys got sick last year, and..." I spread my hands, as if laying the litany of my failures out on a table before him. "I can't take care of her like she needs, and I can't lose her. So please, Uncle. If any of the things Mother said about you are true, help me take care of Maddy."

He looked deep into my eyes, and for the first time I understood why people claimed to be mesmerized by him. The uncanny stillness, mated with his chiseled features and deep brown eyes created an arresting tableau. Finally, after studying me for a full minute or more, he nodded. "Yes. I will make sure no harm befalls her, and to such extent as I can prevent it, you either. We shall be a family, Quincy. Or as much of one as a motley group such as ourselves can be."

I let out a breath and took a long sip of whiskey. "Good," I said. I drew out the wooden stake I had been holding down by my right leg. "I'm glad to hear it. Now we can move on to the part where I tell you if I see even so much as a mosquito bite on my sister's neck, I'll shove this stick through your heart by way of your arse, I swear on my dead mother's grave."

5

And we were a family, albeit a strange one. Me, Maddy, Luke, and Renfield. This was the second Renfield, not the one that eventually got himself turned into a vampire and came back to try to murder Luke and me. This Renfield was less a companion and more a manservant, but he doted on Maddy, so he was fine in my book. It was a pretty good trick, keeping Luke's true nature from Maddy, but we managed somehow.

She wasn't a stupid child, far from it. But she was, for the most part, a very practical one, and grew into a practical young woman. And practical young women didn't believe in vampires, regardless of their last name. So, it was relatively simple to explain that Luke had a rare skin condition that forced him to avoid sunlight, lest he be horribly burned by its rays, a fiction closer to the truth than we cared to admit. And Luke moved his hunting to later in the night, after Maddy was asleep. It made finding donors more difficult, but he never seemed to be short of vigor, and I didn't ask too much about his methods of procuring meals, at least not in those days.

We stayed in London for another few years, then moved to America. Chicago, to be specific. Luke had long since mastered the art of changing locales before it became too noticeable that he didn't age like the rest of the population, and we were just getting to the point where my own ever-youthful appearance was becoming noticeable. I still aged, but much more slowly once I reached my mid-twenties. In fact, we left London just as I was beginning to understand that I wasn't exactly what most people would call "normal."

I was twenty-six when the first real, outward manifestation of my...differences occurred. I was crossing a busy street with my nose stuck in a book, a mystery published the year before by a young woman named Agatha Christie. The book was *The Mysterious Affair at Styles*, and it introduced me, as well as the rest of the world, to a fascinating detective by the name of Hercule Poirot. Having spent many nights in Luke's library reading the journals of the real Dr. John Watson, I was a huge fan of the genre, and Christie's book had me so wrapped up in Poirot's exploits that I never heard the truck coming until the sound of squealing brakes yanked me back into the real world. My world became both real and painful seconds later when the bumper of a delivery truck slammed into my thigh, fracturing my femur with a loud *crack*.

I think that was probably the first time I had ever gotten truly inventive in my swearing. I'd dabbled in cursing before that day, but it was strictly on an amateur level. But lying there on the cobbled street with a broken thighbone and an absolutely pulverized dignity, I composed an aria of such vile epithets that I'm amazed I wasn't committed to Bedlam on the spot.

"Are you hurt, young sir?" The driver fairly flew out of the truck and dashed to my side.

I glared up at him and was honestly a little startled when he staggered back, as if my look terrified him. I've grown accustomed to it in the century or so since, but at the time, I still thought I was a normal human being. "No, I'm perfectly well, thanks. I just had a truck slam into me and knock me to the ground, breaking my bloody leg, but I'm right as rain, thanks for asking! Give me a hand up, you idiot."

"You shouldn't try to stand," he said, gesturing to my leg. I ignored him, trying to get to my feet without his help. It went almost exactly as well as you'd expect, given that the largest bone in my damn body was broken. I dropped flat on my back and shouted more curses up to the heavens, then took a deep breath and looked to the driver, who was standing over me wringing his hat in his hands. "How about you help me over to the curb and we see about getting an ambulance, alright?"

He motioned to some bystanders, and after several excruciating attempts, three of them managed to hoist me up and carry me, cursing with every step, over to the curb. The driver sent one of the Samaritans into a nearby bookshop to call for a doctor and turned back to look at me. "Look here, mate, I'm dreadfully sorry you got all bunged up, but you should have been paying attention where you were going. You're lucky to be alive."

I opened my mouth to inform him exactly how unlucky I felt at the moment, when I realized two things. One, that he was right, and I was a moron who'd walked into the street without looking where I was going, and thus deserved everything I got and more. And two, that my leg was already feeling some better. Not good, mind you. It still hurt like a son of a bitch. But it wasn't the blinding pain of a moment before. So, either I was healing magically fast, or I was going into shock.

Or both. I was certainly going into shock, and by the time an ambulance arrived, I had passed out. The paramedics, or whatever we called them back then, managed to revive me and bring me somewhat back to myself, and I noticed with a marked lack of surprise that the lorry driver was conspicuous by his absence. They carted me off to a nearby hospital, which was *not* Bedlam, where my leg was set, more profanities were invented, and I passed out again.

I awoke in an uncomfortable bed in a smallish ward where most of the six beds were unoccupied. There was one old man snoring at the far end of the room, four empty beds, and me. Moonlight streaked in the windows, and I became immediately frantic with worry. It was early afternoon when I left our house, and if it was already full dark, Maddy would be out of her mind with worry. I pushed myself up into a sitting position, felt the lightning bolts of pain shoot down my leg and up to my groin, and collapsed back with a groan.

"That looked like it hurt," came a voice from my left side. I turned my head as far as I could and saw Maddy sitting there, my Agatha Christie novel open on her lap.

"It hurt very much, thank you," I replied. "How did you get here?"

"I took a taxi."

"That's not what I meant, you little smart aleck. I meant, how did you know what happened?"

"Oh, that." She smiled, a dimpled grin that always reminded me of our mother. Maddy took after her so much that it almost hurt to look at her sometimes. They had the same hair, the same eyes, the same upturned nose. Even the same sense of humor, which was surprising given how young Maddy was when Mother died. "The man from the bookstore sent a boy to tell Renfield that you were hurt and what hospital you were taken to. He wanted me to wait until Luke was awake, but I told him I wasn't waiting a single minute while my brother rotted away in a hospital bed." She smiled at me, but there was a quiver in her voice. It was just four years hence that our brothers James and Orly had been admitted to the hospital with influenza. Like so many in that dark year, they never returned home.

"I'm fine, duckling," I said, reaching up to pat her knee. "I'm just stupid is all."

"And while that is not normally a terminal condition, you seem determined to make it so." Luke's voice came from the doorway at the far end of the room. The snoring man started awake and drew in a breath to scream. Luke reached out and tapped him on the forehead and said, "Sleep." However hard he struck the man, it was hard enough, as his eyes rolled back in his head, and he collapsed once more to his pillow.

Luke crossed the room to stand at the foot of my bed. "Are you hurt badly?"

"I suppose this is the time I should lie and put a brave face on it?" I asked.

"No, this is the time you should be completely truthful with me so I know if Renfield and Madeline will be able to tend to you while you recover, or if I shall need to hire a nurse." Luke didn't *look* concerned, but he was standing at my hospital bed offering to hire a nurse to tend me, so he apparently wasn't *unconcerned.*

"It's pretty bad," I said. "My femur is broken, and before I passed out, I think the doctor said something about my walking being impaired. I don't know how long they expect that to be the case."

"Forever, Quincy," Maddy said. I twisted around to stare at her. "I spoke to a nurse. She said you would walk with a cane for the rest of your life, and that's only after you spent the next several months in a wheelchair until that leg can bear any weight again."

"Well, fuck," I said, lying back.

"Quincy!" Maddy gasped.

"Oh, piss off, Mads," I snapped. "It's nothing you haven't heard before." That was probably unfair as well as unkind of me. Maddy was a precocious child in many ways, but her parents, and then I, had worked hard to keep her as sheltered as possible.

Luke cleared his throat, cutting off any incipient argument before it could get going. "I suppose our first step will be to move your bedroom down to the first floor, and near to the lavatory."

"Yes," I agreed. "Being able to use the bathroom without help would be nice."

"And will likely take some time to accomplish," Luke, ever the ray of hope, said. "Have you been given any timetable on your release into our care?"

"No," I said. "I was asleep, or unconscious more like, until just a few minutes ago. Maddy, did you ask anyone how long I would be here?"

"They don't know," she said. "Said it would be at least a few weeks, until they could make sure you didn't get an infection from the surgery and teach you how to move around in your wheelchair."

"Lovely," I said. "Could you go see if there's a nurse available now? I need to piss." She went off in search of a nurse, and I turned to Luke. "Is there anything you can do? Any kind of helpful magic properties in your bite or something?"

"There are quite a few side effects of being bitten by a vampire, Quincy, but I do not believe that making your bones knit more quickly is one of them. Should you desire to never again walk in the sun, I may be of some assistance. But I feel this is an area in which I will be of no use."

"What's the use of having a magical uncle if he can't magic you all better when you break your leg?" I asked.

"How did you come to be walking in the path of that truck?" Luke asked.

"I was reading."

"This?" He held up the Christie book, covered in muck from the street and scuffed from its encounter with the cobbles.

"It's very enthralling," I said, as if that were some defense.

"I'm sure. Well, now you will have ample time to catch up on your reading. Here comes the nurse. I believe it best if Madeline and I retire to give you some privacy." He did, and the nurse helped me relieve myself into one of the small urinals they kept for just that purpose.

Later, as I lay on my back staring at the ceiling, I couldn't help but think about how my inattention had changed my life forever. I was to be trapped in a bed and a chair for months and walk ever after with a limp and a cane. I was partially correct. My life had certainly changed in the instant the truck slammed into me, but not at all in any way I could have anticipated.

6

A month later, Maddy came into the den one morning to find me sitting in an armchair by the fire, reading. Renfield had kindly gone out the day before to pick up a new Agatha Christie novel for me, and I was buried in the story when my sister arrived.

"Quincy! You're awake. How lovely. Did Renfield help you into the chair? Have you had breakfast? Can I get you the chamber pot?" My baby sister had quite enjoyed my convalescence, having a life-sized doll to play with, but I was significantly less enamored with the arrangement. I loved Maddy and was perfectly content to be waited on hand and foot, but having a girl barely out of school bringing me the pot to piss in got old quickly. I'm not terribly modest, but having my sister tend to my lavatory was a little much.

I picked up the cane leaning on the arm of the chair and levered myself to an upright position. "No, dear sister, I am perfectly capable of attending to my own needs in the washroom, thank you." Then I stood there grinning like an idiot at the dumbfounded expression on her face.

"How? The doctors said that it would take three months at least for you to be able to stand."

"Either I heal faster than anyone they've ever encountered, or their X-Ray machine was malfunctioning," I replied. "Because I can stand with almost no pain and walk with only the slightest limp." I demonstrated by walking over to her and giving her an awkward one-armed hug. "Thank you for all you've done for me these past few weeks." I stepped back, still a little wobbly on my weakened limb.

Maddy was still staring at me, wide-eyed. "This is a miracle, Brother. A miracle from Heaven itself! Come, kneel down with me. We must give thanks." She dropped to her knees, right there in the living room. I stared down at her, taken aback. We were a family of skeptics, to put it mildly, even before I had encounters of a personal nature with actual denizens of Heaven and Hell, so dropping to my knees in religious fervor was not something I would have done before I'd broken my leg. I sure as hell wasn't going to do it now, when I wasn't completely sure how I'd get back up.

"I think I'll pass on the glory be, Sister. And since when did you become so devout?" I limped back to my chair, having exhausted my puny reserves of strength just standing up for a couple of minutes.

"I've been praying for your recovery every day, Quincy. There is a lovely church a few streets over, and I go there every morning. I go to confession, and I pray for you to get better. And here you are, the answer to my prayers!"

The irony of her thinking my leg healed faster because of her prayers is not lost on me, given the actual source of my accelerated recuperation. I didn't say that to Maddy, of course. "I appreciate the prayers, Sister. I'm not entirely convinced that my leg feels better because God wants it to, as opposed to the doctor misjudging the severity of the injury, but either way I'll take it. And another thing I'll take, if you'll assist me upstairs, is a bath. A real one, in the tub, not a sponge bath." It had been five weeks of cleaning myself with a damp cloth, and I wanted a good soak.

"What about your cast?" Maddy asked.

"This cast?" I replied, slamming my fist into the plaster sheath around my thigh, shattering it. I winced as the folly of hitting my still-broken leg became apparent to me but remained standing. Barely. The cast fell to white chunks and puffs of dust, and I grinned at Maddy. "What cast?"

"You are incorrigible, Quincy," she said.

"You are absolutely correct," I agreed. "Now would you be a dear and draw me a bath? I think it may take me a little longer than normal to make it upstairs." Maddy, still looking extremely confused by seeing me upright after weeks of bed rest, turned and walked up the stairs.

"You can come out now," I said once I was fairly certain she was out of earshot.

"I am fairly certain you did not hear me breathing," Luke said from the doorway, stepping into the light.

"You developing a sense of humor is far more traumatic than me breaking my leg, Uncle," I said. "But no, I was working an assumption that you would be eavesdropping, and if you weren't there, I would only look foolish in front of an empty room."

He looked me up and down. "It has been a very long time since I have seen a normal person recover from an injury such as yours, but this seems…extraordinary."

"Did you actually ever see anyone recover from a broken femur on the battlefield?"

"No, I did not. But there was a man in a village nearby who fell from a cart and broke his leg in almost the same spot. He did not walk for almost half a year, and never without a limp. Now here you stand, barely four weeks after your accident, and you are moving better than he did for years."

"I suppose I should attribute it to clean living," I said with a smirk.

"You can attribute it to many things, Quincy, but I do not believe that anyone in their right mind would refer to anything about your life as 'clean.' No, I fear that your rapid healing may be a side effect of my influence, or…contact, rather, with your parents."

"What do you mean?" I asked, knowing exactly what he meant.

"You are aware of the circumstances through which I met your mother and father, I assume?"

"I've read the book, but neither of them were very keen on

discussing it with their children. They always classified the entire thing as fiction. I know better, at least in part, but I don't know how much of Stoker's tale was true and how much was invention."

"It was in large part accurate," Luke replied.

"So my father…and *three* of your…'wives?'" My eyes widened.

"I was impressed with his stamina myself," Luke agreed, taking the conversation even further down a road I ever wished to travel.

"And you…bit my mother?"

"I did in fact drink from Mina. And I shared my blood with her. I also killed her friend Lucy and turned her. It was not something I was proud of, but I was smitten with the young Miss Westenra, as was nearly every man who met her."

"So I've heard. Apparently I'm named after several of her suitors."

"You are indeed. What Stoker was not accurate about was whether I turned your mother. Obviously, I did not, since she did not return to life as a vampire upon her passing."

"But you think your biting Mother, and Father's…dalliance with your wives—"

Luke held up a hand, a pained look upon his face. "Please. Let's not refer to them as such. I had a wife, Justina, who I loved greatly. The vampires that fed upon your father were many things to me: companions, concubines, perhaps even friends. But none of them was ever my wife."

I nodded. "I understand. But you believe that Father trading blood with them, and you drinking from Mother, along with her drinking from you in turn…did something to *me*?"

"I have always suspected that such may be the case. And now it seems that I was correct." He seemed inordinately pleased with himself for someone who was telling me that I was some sort of human-vampire hybrid.

"But I can go out in the sun. And I've never felt a need to drink blood," I protested.

"You also have no sense of decorum, cannot wield a broadsword, and share none of my striking good looks," Luke agreed. "But you are especially healthy for someone who drinks as much as you do, you remain fit no matter how lazy and gluttonous you become, and now you seem to heal rapidly to boot."

I wasn't sure how I felt about my uncle's assassination of my character, but I felt that wasn't the time to address it. Also, my leg was beginning to throb. I'd been standing for a very long time for someone who spent the last month either flat on his back or sitting in a cushioned chair. "As much as I would love to continue this exploration of my physical gifts and my moral shortcomings, I believe I hear a tub of scalding water calling my name," I said, turning and reaching out to the arm of the couch for balance. I looked back at Luke. "Could you…walk behind me up the stairs? Just in case my balance is not what I hope it is." The prospect of falling and breaking my leg all over again was enough to make me shove my pride to the rear and let good sense take the lead for once.

A few minutes later, Luke and Maddy had me safely ensconced in a steaming tub of water, and I spent several minutes rubbing myself pink and raw, then draining and refilling the bath for a long soak. I leaned back, thinking about what Luke proposed. Was I part vampire? Why had this never manifested itself before now? Was it only passed to me? If his gifts came to all of us, why didn't it save Orly and James from the flu? The questions swirled around me, a whirlpool in placid water, and no matter how long I sat there and steamed myself, no answers boiled to the surface. Eventually, the warmth and relaxation took hold, and I fell asleep in the tub, safe and secure in my thoughts that despite this new development physically, everything would soon be back to normal.

7

I was right, at least for a little while. I healed much more rapidly, and much more completely, than anyone expected, and within a few months was back to my normal activities, albeit somewhat more attentive when crossing the street. I began to develop other abilities, noting that my strength and agility had grown past the norm, and I began going to various gyms around the city to test myself in different types of exercise. I had to switch facilities constantly, as if I overstayed my anonymity, it could raise questions about my last name, and about Luke.

Not that Luke wasn't starting to raise questions himself. I was sitting in the den one evening reading when he came down the stairs with a face like a thundercloud. He came to me and stood, glaring down at me. I set my book aside and asked, "Can I help you, Uncle?"

"We have to leave," he replied. "There are people in the neighborhood who are beginning to remark on my unchanging appearance. Too many people. I can handle a paperboy making a remark about the fact that I don't seem to age, because no one listens to them. But the butcher made a remark to Renfield today that something in the meat must be keeping me young, because I never grow a day older."

"Well, you don't," I pointed out. "But you've been here a long time, so we should probably find a new place soon. What do you think of Mayfair? Word around the pub is that some of the old lords can't afford to keep their big houses, so there could be some nice places available there."

"You mistake my meaning, Quincy," Luke said. "I do not mean we must leave this house, or this neighborhood. We must leave London, and likely England altogether. I have been here for nearly three decades, and there are simply too many people who have met Lucas Card, or variations of that name, for this place to be safe for us any longer. It is time to return to America."

Well, that would certainly put some distance between us and anyone who had seen Luke. Even without a name change, he would be able to start his life anew. Again.

"Is there anywhere in particular you would like to go?" I asked. I knew there was no point in arguing with Luke. There never has been. Once his mind is made up, there's no dissuading him. The same qualities that made him a fearsome general make him a stubborn bastard when off the battlefield.

"I think Chicago," Luke said. "I was there briefly for the World's Fair and met some of the most charming people. One young doctor in particular was quite charming and sold me completely on the city. He invited me to stay at his hotel, which he told me was built atop his pharmacy, but I had already secured lodgings before my arrival. I wonder what became of him?"

"There's no telling, Uncle. Chicago sounds fine. I've never been there, obviously, but I've read a bit about it." I had never been to America at the time, and little did I know that I would spend a great deal of the next century in this strange, noisy place. "Have you told Maddy?"

"Not yet," Luke replied. "I shall tell her over dinner tonight. Will you be joining us, or are you going out?"

For a notorious blood-sucking monster, Luke had some prudish tendencies. One of them was his stark disapproval of the amount of time I spent in pubs. His condemnation of my drinking may also have been caused by the fact that I was spending his money on said drinking, but for whatever reason, Luke thought I drank too much. Probably still does. "I'll stay here and have dinner with you two. It might be received better if Maddy sees that we are both in agreement on the move. What story have you concocted to explain the trip to her?"

Luke's eyes widened, ever so slightly, and I smiled. It wasn't often that I caught him off guard, but the level of deception required to keep my sister unaware of his true nature was significantly higher than he was accustomed to. "I...I will think of something by dinner, I'm sure," Luke stammered, then turned to leave. "Enjoy your book, Quincy." And he was gone, off somewhere to fabricate a tale to explain our sudden transatlantic relocation. I couldn't wait to see what he came up with.

I SHOULDN'T HAVE DOUBTED HIM. BY THE TIME RENFIELD SET THE table, Luke had spun some yarn about business dealings with a shop in Chicago specializing in ancient Eastern European artifacts that had Maddy completely snowed about our trip. That was Luke's "profession" at the time—antiquities collector and dealer. In theory, he brokered private sales of artifacts thought to be lost to the ravages of history. This gave him leave to be in and out of the house at odd hours, as the people who wanted to sell such artifacts didn't keep regular office hours. Or regular offices. Or inventory. Or exist, really, but Maddy was still a young teenaged girl at the time, so she never thought to question Luke's story. He was her uncle; of course he was completely truthful. I love the naïveté of youth. Too bad it never lasts.

Chicago in the 1920s was an...interesting place, to be sure, and if Luke had mentioned the existence of Prohibition, I'm sure I would have argued strenuously for Paris, Madrid, Rome, or basically any civilized place where a man could buy a damn drink. But there was a speakeasy on every block, if you knew how to find them, and I have always been quite resourceful when it comes to my drinking. And that eventually became the undoing of our happiness in Chicago, and the reason I never saw my sister again.

It was a cold night in February, and I had taken refuge in a private club in the basement of a barber shop not far from the apartment building where we lived. We'd moved around Chicago for several years until we finally settled into a building with enough exits to make Luke happy, and enough vacancies for him to just acquire the entire ground floor and basement for our living quarters and escape routes. I had one apartment to myself, as did Maddy, having turned nineteen back in the summer. Luke and Renfield shared an apartment, and Luke had workmen cut a staircase directly from the master bedroom down into the basement so that he could rest in a light-tight and secure place.

I found a little speakeasy within a week of our moving to the neighborhood, by my usual method of overpaying the shoeshine guy and pumping him for information about the area. If you ever want to know what's going on somewhere, ask the invisible people. The stuffed shirts and moneyed assholes who think they're so discreet are remarkably loose lipped around waiters, newsstand owners, and cleaning ladies, to say nothing of the guy who shines their shoes or cuts their hair. I've always found those people to be at least as good a source of information as bartenders, and better in a time when you had to know somebody to find out where the bartenders were.

So, I was sitting at the bar minding the business of the pretty brunette singer on stage, and ignoring the daggers being stared at me by her boyfriend across the room, when there was a commotion by the door. I turned, making eye contact with the boyfriend and giving him a friendly nod as I spun around, and saw my sister proceeding through the room like a queen, hanging on the arm of "Smiling" Al Kachellek, right-hand man of the North Side Gang, run by Bugs Moran. Al got the name "Smiling" the same way the seven-footer gets nicknamed "Tiny." According to the word on the street, the only time a smile crossed Al's face was when someone was about to die. It bode well for the evening that he looked like someone had just shit in his oatmeal, even with my sister on his arm.

I didn't approve of my sister dating a mobster, but I also didn't protest much. For one part, she was an adult and able to make her own decisions, a fact that she made very clear to me the one and only time I made any objections to her dalliance with Kachellek. For another, it felt hypocritical in the extreme to forbid her to associate with this guy just because he was a known killer, when we lived under the roof of a man responsible for more deaths than some plague outbreaks. And for a third, I really enjoyed drinking in Kachellek's bar, so if she liked spending time with him, and it meant I could find good bourbon close to home, who was I to judge?

I gave Maddy a nod and stood, making my way through the tables to Kachellek's table. He looked up at me and gave me a nod, waving off the two goons who stepped forward as if they wanted to either stop me or frisk me. I'm not sure what would have happened if they actually put their hands on me. I was in a pretty mellow mood that night. I might even have let them do their job.

"Quincy," Al said, giving me a nod. "Good to see you again. Sit?"

"No, I'm good," I replied. "Just wanted to come over and say hello. You doing well?"

"As good as can be expected. You still fleecing the boys in my poker game?" The little smirk he gave me was as close to a grin as I ever wanted to see on Al's face. He knew I played in his poker game a couple times a week, and he knew full well how much money I took off the rubes at the table. They were, to be brutally honest, godawful card players, and I was already developing my sharper senses, so reading their bluffs was child's play. Al didn't care who won or lost, as long as the table was full and he got his rake. He just found it funny that this skinny Brit could come in and take money off all those tough guys and make it out with his skin. I didn't find it necessary to tell him about the pile of broken noses, jaws, and arms I left in the alley behind the card room whenever someone objected too vigorously to my "luck."

"They are very generous," I replied with a smirk of my own.

Al actually laughed, as much a bark as anything, but a laugh none-theless. "You're funny, Quincy. Isn't he funny, doll?" He squeezed Maddy's side, and she laughed, giving me "go away" eyes the whole time.

"Hilarious, Al," Maddy replied. "But he's loud, too, and this singer's good. I wish I could hear her."

I tipped an imaginary hat to my sister. "Then I'll leave you two to the music. Good to see you again, Al. I'll see you later at home, Sis?" I didn't often play the brother card in public, but sometimes it was good to remind men, especially men who considered themselves dangerous, that everyone has a family, especially the woman on his arm.

"Don't wait up," she replied, waving me off. I wasn't sure who was giving me dirtier looks, the singer's boyfriend or my sister, but I headed up the stairs regardless. It was getting late, and I had a new Poirot novel calling my name. Unfortunately, it was going to be a longer walk home than I expected, and a bloodier one.

8

I made it almost halfway home before I heard the scuff of shoes on pavement closer behind me than I liked. I spun around and caught the thick wrist of the man about to bash in my skull with a beer bottle. I found myself staring into the wide eyes of the lounge singer's boyfriend, a low-ranking member of Moran's North Side Gang named Tad or Todd or something like that. Even back then I didn't pay too much attention to the names of the thugs who hung around the powerful. I just put them on the list of "People I Might Have to Beat Up" and went on with my life. Looked like Todd's name had just moved to the top of the list.

"If you walk away now, we can pretend like this didn't happen," I said. I was wearing my favorite overcoat, and I'd already learned that getting blood out of wool was hell on my dry-cleaning bills.

"When I'm done with you, I'll be the only one walking away," Todd growled, yanking his hand free and throwing a wild punch with his other fist. He swung somewhere in the same zip code as my face, but not close enough to worry me, and I just slapped his hand away.

"I'm warning you, Todd, if you don't lay off, somebody's going to get hurt."

"My name's Jerry, asshole. And somebody's for sure gettin' hurt.

You." He swung the bottle at my face again, and I just took one step back as the improvised club swooshed harmlessly by my nose. Jerry, huh. I was way off on the name thing. Oh well. His name might as well have been Unconscious Idiot, since that's what he was about to be.

I stepped in as he tried to recover from his wild strike at my face and slammed my elbow into his nose. I felt the cartilage crunch as his nose fountained blood down the front of his shirt, and I could just tell that I was going to end up covered in the red stuff before this little scrap was through. All I could do at that point was try to end it quick, so my coat was the only thing that got wrecked.

Jerry staggered back, dropping the bottle as both hands flew to his face. I kicked him in the balls, then punched him in the side of the head as he bent over clutching his nuts. He went down in a heap, landing in a pile of snow up against the curb. I rolled him over so he could breathe and turned to head home again.

I hadn't made it ten steps before he came to his senses and started screaming after me. "You bastard, I'll get you for screwing my girl. And if I can't get you, I'll take it out on that pretty little sister of yours!"

I stopped dead in my tracks. "Well, that was a mistake, Jerry," I said, my voice colder than the snow I was walking through. I turned around and walked back to the goon struggling to his feet holding his bloody nose. "You shouldn't threaten a man's family." I punched Jerry in the jaw, straightening him up onto his tiptoes. Then I slammed my left fist into his gut, dropping him back down. I clubbed him on the back of the head with both hands, then kicked him in the ribs a few times, getting a satisfying *crack* for my efforts.

I knelt down and took Jerry's head in my hands, grabbing his hair just above the ears. "Jerry, I care a lot about my little sister, and it makes me very upset when someone threatens her. You don't want to upset me, do you, Jerry?"

"Screw you," he said, bloody bubbles popping in each nostril.

I slammed his head into the sidewalk, scrubbing his face from side to side across the concrete, peeling his skin like I was grating cheese. I picked him up by his hair, dragged him all the way to his feet, and slammed him face-first into the brick wall of the women's dress shop beside us. Jerry's eyes rolled back in his head, and I slapped him on each cheek to keep him awake.

"Stay with me, pal. We're not finished yet. Not by a long shot." I punched him in the gut a few more times, then laid a few solid cracks on his face, breaking a lot of the little bones that held everything in place and kept Jerry looking like Jerry, then I let him go to flop on his back, spread out like he was making snow angels.

"Sorry about that, Jerry," I said, kicking him in the balls one more time. "Not the kicking your ass part. I was going to do that the first time you took a swing at me. But I didn't want to have to kick your ass quite this bad. But you went and threatened my sister, and I can't let that stand. You understand, right? Good."

Then I turned around to head home, only to find myself staring right into the chest of Bert and Sal O'Halloran, two of Kachellek's main enforcers. I knew them from working security at the club and had never had a problem with them. They generally stayed out of any beef between the players, so while they'd seen me beat up guys before, they'd never gotten quite so close while I did it.

"Hello, fellas," I said. "You boys doing okay tonight?"

"You gotta come with us, Harker," Bert said. He looked like he wasn't happy about what was about to happen, which probably meant I was going to be very unhappy about what was about to happen.

"What's wrong, Bert?" I asked. "Jerry and I just had a little disagreement is all. I'm pretty sure we've got everything straightened out now. I'll just head on home and we can all forget this ever happened." I was pretty sure Jerry was going to remember the beating I just laid on him for the rest of his life, but I was willing to forget the whole mess if it meant I didn't have to take on both O'Halloran boys at once. They were big, rangy Irishmen, and I'd seen both of them in some of the city's underground fights before. They'd won me money, which meant they put their opponents face down in the dirt. I didn't relish the idea of being one of those opponents.

"You gotta come with us, Harker," Sal said. "Al told us if you beat

Jerry up, we hadda make an example outta you. He says we can't have nobody beating up our guys. Makes us look weak."

"That's crazy talk, Sal-pal," I said, holding up my hands. "Me kicking this mook's ass makes him look weak, but it doesn't reflect on you guys."

"We just do what we're told, Harker," Bert said. "Now you gonna come easy, or we gonna have to rough you up?" He cracked his knuckles, and just as I was about to choose doing it the hard way, I caught a flash of a dark coat moving into the shadows behind Sal.

I recognized the pale face of my uncle and decided that this conversation would best be concluded somewhere more private. "I'll come quiet. This gonna be a private party, or will the whole gang be there?"

"Boss said he was bringing an audience. Said there's no point in making a point if there's nobody to make a point to, ya know?" Bert replied, gesturing to a car parked across the street.

Strangely enough, Bert's odd explanation did make sense, if the word choices gave me pause. But I followed the big guy across the street and got in the back seat of the car with him. Sal slid in behind the wheel, and we were off to see a man about a beating.

We drove for about thirty minutes before pulling into a garage a few blocks off the water. The wind coming in off the lake was bitter cold and cut right through my thick coat. I shivered getting out and looked around like I was trying to duck the wind. Actually, I was looking for Luke, and saw him a few buildings over, leaning by a lamppost. Bert led me into the building, where a dozen of Moran's boys were standing around a couple of fire barrels passing bottles back and forth. I almost asked for a drink but decided to pretend like I was taking the situation seriously.

Al stepped out of a small office on one side of the garage, my sister and the lounge singer close behind him. "Quincy Harker, I hate that it had to turn out this way."

"Not too late, Al," I replied. "I'll make you the same offer I made your boy Jerry. We can both walk away now and pretend this never happened."

Al shook his head with something like real regret. "Nah, we can't. You see, you beat up one of my guys right outside one of my establishments. That's like walking right up and slapping me in the face. I let somebody disrespect me like that, much less a skinny kid like you, I might as well cut my own throat right here in the garage."

"To be fair, I didn't start anything. Jerry came after me."

"You started it when you screwed Jerry's girl." He gestured to Maria, the singer, who blushed and looked down at her feet.

"I didn't see his name written anywhere on her, Al. And believe me, I looked." That got a laugh from some of the guys, but judging by the stormy expression on Al's face, he didn't find it nearly as funny.

"I'm sorry, Harker. I like you. I really do. But I can't let this stand. If you'd taken your beating like a man, or even just slugged Jerry a little bit, we could do something different. But you went too far, and now I gotta take matters into my own hands."

I had one last card to play before things got ugly, so I went for it. "He threatened Maddy," I said. "Jerry said he was going to hurt Maddy, so I had to defend my sister. You wouldn't want anybody hurting your girl, would ya, Al?" I gave him a smile, like we were best buds and I had his best interests at heart.

"Who, this dame?" He reached behind him and dragged Maddy forward. She looked scared out of her wits. Poor girl. She was barely nineteen and running around with mobsters like she was grown. She didn't know what kind of trouble these guys really were. Hell, I barely knew, and I was a lot older than her. "You think I care about her more than I care about my rep? Not likely." He shoved Maddy, and she fell to the ground with a yelp. She wasn't badly hurt, but the look on her face told me her pride had taken a mortal wound.

"I wish you hadn't done that Al," I said. I rolled my head from side to side, loosening up.

"Why?" Al laughed, and I knew by the grin on his face that things were about to get bloody. "What are you going to do about it?" He had a dozen men, all armed with pistols and half of them holding Tommy guns. All I had was Luke.

It wasn't even close. They were outnumbered and they never even knew it. The first one to raise his gun was the first one to fall in a fountain of blood as Luke sprinted in and opened his throat with one swift slash of his fingernails. I dove toward Maddy, covering her with my body as guns started spitting bullets in every direction. The *rat-a-tat-tat* of a Tommy gun deafened me, but only for a second. The whole thing lasted less than half a minute, from the first moment a finger grazed a trigger to the dual *thump-thump* of Al's body landing, followed by his head.

Silence fell over the building and I got off of my sister, looking around at the carnage. I'd been spared the battlefields of Europe in The Great War, but the garage on Clark Street must have been a reasonable facsimile, because there were veritable rivers of blood running along the floor. All twelve of Moran's men, including Al, were dead, many in states of dismemberment, and Luke stood in the center of the bloodstorm, holding Bert O'Halloran to his neck as he drained the last drops of the big gangster's blood, then snapped the corpse's neck and tossed it aside like a piece of chicken he was finished gnawing on.

"I apologize for the delay, Quincy," Luke said. "I needed to ensure Madeline was out of the field of fire before I stepped in."

"I think you were right on time, Uncle. Come on, Maddy, let's go. Uncle Luke has someone who cleans up messes like this, and I'm sure they would rather we not be here when they arrive."

"I do have someone, but I believe this will require a rather different narrative. I do not believe we can simply make this many people disappear."

"Gang war?" I asked.

"It seems the most likely scenario. I will of course consult with my cleaner when he arrives. I will see you back at our flat." Luke began moving through the dead bodies, snapping necks and taking other measures to insure none of the mobsters woke up thirsty in a few nights.

I turned to Maddy and held out a hand. "Here, let me help you up."

She didn't respond, just sat on the floor staring at Luke and me. Every once in a while, she would pace away, but her eyes would alight on some other bit of gore and her gaze would return to us. "What... what *are* you?" she asked, her voice barely more than a breath.

I knelt by her side. "Mads, remember that silly book that Stoker wrote? The one that talked about Mother and Father and their adventures before we were born? Remember how Stoker paid Mother and Father a sum of money for the use of their names?" She nodded, silent.

"That wasn't for their names, Maddy. That was payment for their story. All of that really happened. Mother and Father met a man named Count Dracula and traveled with a man named Van Helsing to try and kill him."

"Fortunately for everyone involved, they failed," Luke said, earning a glare from me.

"He's right," I said. "Luke is the Mr. Alucard from the book. He is Dracula."

Maddy looked at me, and I saw a tiny speck of blood on her cheek. I wondered how it got there, and then wondered how much was spattered all across my back. "But he's a..."

"Vampire," I said. "Yes. Vampires are real, and magic, and monsters. Uncle Luke hunts them and works to keep people safe."

"Mostly," he added.

"Not helpful, Uncle," I hissed.

"But that means...he...drinks blood? He...kills people?"

"My dear girl, until mere moments ago, you were dating a mobster. What do you think he did, shook people's hands vigorously?" Luke asked, in his strange attempt at humor. "Yes, I kill people. But I generally only kill criminals, and only when it cannot be avoided. Unfortunately, tonight it could not be avoided. Now you really must go."

I pulled Maddy to her feet and walked her out to the O'Halloran's car. She slid into the passenger seat wordlessly, and I drove her home. She never spoke, just stared out the front window. I hoped she was processing things, working through this revelation in her mind, but when I tried to talk to her, all she said was, "You lied to me."

"I did," I replied. "But only to protect you. You didn't need to know about who…what Luke really is, and it was safer for you to not know."

She laughed, and it was shrill, the laugh of someone holding on to sanity by her fingernails. "Safer? I've lived my life under the roof of a monster, a monster that tried to kill our mother and make her into a monster just like him, and *you brought me to him!*" Not for the first time, I regretted allowing her to read Stoker's book. Nothing good ever came from that blasted thing.

We got home, and Renfield was waiting at the bottom of the stairs leading to what I thought of as "our" floor. He took one look at me and sent me into the mud room to strip off everything I was wearing. Bloodstains were an occupational hazard of being Dracula's manservant, so he kept a robe hanging on a hook on the back of the door for moments just like this. When I came out, he was standing at the door to Luke's apartment, looking concerned.

"Did she go to bed?" I asked.

"She did, but I do not think she is sleeping."

I walked down the hall and knocked on Maddy's door. There was no response. I knocked again, louder. Still nothing. I raised my hand to knock again, and the door jerked open.

Maddy stood glaring up at me in a fresh dress with a suitcase in her hand. "Give me all your money," she said.

"Where do you think you're going? It's the middle of the night."

"There's a car parked in front of the house and I'm not spending another night under the roof of a monster and a liar. Now give me all your money."

"Maddy, this is in—" My words cut off when I felt something press into my belly. I looked down to see a snub-nosed revolver pressed up against my gut.

"I believe I asked you for your money." This time when I looked in her eyes, there was rage joining the betrayal. I had no doubt at that moment that she would shoot me if I tried to stop her from leaving. I pulled out my wallet and handed her all the money I had, several hundred dollars from poker winnings. She fanned through it and tucked it into her purse.

"You can find the car at the train station in Milwaukee. Don't try to find me. You betrayed me, Quincy. You brought me into the home of a monster and lied to me about it. You were all I had left, and you betrayed me. I can't stand to look at you right now, but I promise you one thing—this isn't over, Brother." Then she shoved past me and down the stairs. A few seconds later, I heard a car start up outside, and then she was gone.

I suppose she never wanted to find me, because I never saw my sister again. I assume she lived a normal life and died a normal woman, but if she did, it wasn't as Madeline Justina Harker, because despite looking for her for years after she left, I've never found any records of anyone by that name after the night before Valentine's Day, 1929.

9

When I finished my tale, the sun was coming up after another sleepless night. This time it was different. I hadn't been fighting for my life, or trying to drink my life away. This felt good, somehow, like I'd lifted a burden off my soul. I never realized how much I held in about Maddy, and those first few years after the boys died. It felt good to talk about to Becks, to get the reactions of someone who hadn't been there beside me through the whole thing, who hadn't even been alive when it all happened.

"That's really sad, Harker," she said, getting out of bed and stretching. God, she was a beautiful woman. Tall and brown, with muscles and curves all stacked up on a long, lean frame that made me think all kinds of naughty and acrobatic thoughts. She blushed and smiled at me. "Stop that. I'm going to take a shower. Alone. You get your mind out of the gutter and get some coffee started."

I watched her until she closed the bathroom door, then did as I was told. I did stop to slip on a pair of jeans, though. Our friends have developed a habit of coming into our apartment unannounced since it became our de facto headquarters, and that's led to more than one embarrassing incident of me walking around starkers when someone unaccustomed to my bare ass wandered in. Embarrassing for them, that is. I've never given a shit who saw me naked. I figure if they see anything they've never seen before, we've got real problems.

I opened the patio door to let some mostly fresh air in and put a couple of bagels in the toaster to go with the coffee. I had just put some different types of shmear out, including my favorite jalapeño cream cheese, and was heading back from the kitchen with a knife when the front door opened.

"I would ask if you actually owned a shirt, but I've seen them, so I just assume you choose to parade around half-naked whenever possible," Pravesh said, walking in looking ready to go conquer the corporate world in a nice pantsuit with chunky black heels and an expensive-looking briefcase. She grabbed the knife from my hand and walked to the table, looking around for the bagels.

"You're early," I said. "They're still in the toaster." As if to prove my point, I heard the bagels pop up, and turned to get them.

"I'll get them," Pravesh said. "You go get a shower. I hear the water running, and you smell like sex and sweat." I sometimes forget that being a snake, her sense of smell is ridiculously strong. I was pretty sure I didn't smell *that* much like sex, but you can never tell with non-humans. "I have a meeting this morning with the Secretary about DEMON and the Shaw situation, so we need to go over our stories and you need to know my plans moving forward."

I walked into the bathroom and stripped down as Becks stood at the counter toweling off. "Pravesh is in the den. I closed the bedroom door." Then I cranked the shower as hot as I could stand, which is pretty hot given some of the places I've visited, and stepped into the frosted glass stall.

"Thanks, babe," Becks said. "I don't think I'm quite comfortable enough in this new job to have my boss seeing all my birthmarks just yet." She walked out of the bathroom, and I made it a point to watch her birthmarks rock from side to side as she did.

Ten minutes later, I stepped out of the bedroom pulling a vintage Four Horsemen t-shirt over my head, and said, "Okay, Pravesh. What's going on that couldn't wait until Becks made it into the office?"

"First, you do understand that it is customary to finish dressing before coming out into public, don't you?"

I shrugged. "I'm dressed now." I looked down at the boots and socks in my hand. "Mostly."

"We have a lead on the remaining DEMON forces in the city," Pravesh said.

"Now is that DEMON like the agency, or demon like just general assholes that come from Hell?" I asked. I wasn't very interested in hunting normal demons at the moment, but if it was DEMON remnants, I was all about it.

"The government agency called DEMON, not demonic entities," Pravesh replied with a roll of her eyes.

"Okay, then. Where do we go and who do I shoot?" I asked.

"Slow down there, sport," Becks said, holding up a hand. "Let's maybe ask a few questions before we shoot."

"I asked questions," I protested. "I asked who to shoot."

Pravesh and Becks both sighed, and there was a brief knock at the door before it opened almost immediately.

Faustus came in wearing his human suit and dressed similar to me, except he was sporting a Led Zeppelin tour shirt from the 70s. I believed that Faustus saw Zeppelin in their prime. Hell, he may have had something to do with them *having* a prime. "Is the coffee ready?" he asked, heading for the kitchen. "And have you restocked the bar yet?"

"Yes," Becks said. "And no. Also, it's seven in the morning."

"That means it's five o'clock in Mongolia," Faustus shot back. "But that's irrelevant if there's no booze. At least tell me you didn't let Harker make the coffee again."

"You're batting a thousand this morning, Faustus," I said.

"Ugh. Oh well, beggars can't be choosers," he replied, taking a mug down from my cabinet and pouring himself a cup.

"But they can be whiners," I replied.

"And interrupters," Pravesh said, trying to restore some semblance of order to the room. We let her, mostly because Faustus was absorbed in his coffee and I really wanted to know what she'd found out about DEMON. "Our intel reports that there is a small DEMON strike team holed up in an abandoned store in the University area."

"Can you narrow that down a little?" I asked. "There are whole strip malls that have gone out of business up there."

"I have an address. Shall we pay them a visit?"

"Get a to go cup, Faust," I said. "We got assholes to shoot."

"Question," Becks said.

"Question, then shoot," I corrected.

Faustus hurriedly dumped his coffee in a cup with a lid and I locked the door behind everyone. We piled into Pravesh's black SUV —I swear the federal government must buy entire production runs of those things—and tore out onto South Boulevard. It was too early for traffic to be truly stupid, so we were able to get from my building to the shopping center at the intersection of Harris and North Tryon in about twenty minutes. We parked the Suburban in front of a Game-Stop and gathered at the rear cargo compartment to gear up. Flynn and I slipped on Kevlar vests with DHS on Velcro chest panels. Pravesh and Faustus didn't worry so much about body armor, since gunshots wouldn't kill them anyway. Neither of them wanted their human suits ruined by bullet holes, but it wasn't quite the shitty ending to their day that it could be for me or Becks.

I grabbed an H&K MP-7 to go along with the Glock on my hip. Becks took a sweet Benelli shotgun that I was pretty sure I'd never seen in Pravesh's toybox before, and added a pair of flash bangs to her belt. Faustus grabbed an M4 with an underslung grenade launcher, because if there's anything that demon loves, it's blowing shit up. Pravesh just had her sidearm, but if the boss lady had to draw her weapon, it was because the career law enforcement officer, the world's most legendary deal-making demon, and a wizard literally called The Reaper had all gone down, so it didn't really matter what kind of hardware she carried.

"Flynn, you breach and toss in a flash bang. Faustus, you're first through the door and clear right. Harker, you go left. Flynn, follow them in. I'll bring up the rear."

"Copy that," Becks said.

"Yes, ma'am," I agreed. Pravesh gave me an odd look. "What?" I asked. "I've lived in the South a long time now. That shit rubs off."

"Don't get too respectful, Harker," she replied. "I won't recognize you."

"Don't worry," I assured her. "I'm sure I'll color outside the lines plenty before the week is out."

"Oh, I have no doubt." She opened up a building map on her tablet and zoomed in. "This is the building where the DEMON team is supposedly staying. They have no real line of sight to this side of the parking lot, so we should be concealed as we approach."

"Unless they have cameras, or aren't complete idiots," Faustus said.

"Well, if people start shooting at us before we get inside, we'll know they posted a lookout," I said. "Second floor? Let's go." I readied my submachine gun and headed for the building.

"Harker, wait," Pravesh called, but I was already a third of the way to the front door. "Goddammit." That's the response I want to evoke from my boss at least once per day. At least.

Nobody opened fire by the time I got to the door, so I waited until the others joined me before yanking the heavy glass door open and slipping inside. We kept a tight line, moving fast with our weapons up —through the lobby, up the big central staircase, and down the right-hand hallway. The last shop on the left was where we were headed, a travel agency that closed down a few months earlier.

Faustus and I flanked the door as Becks aimed her shotgun at the doorknob. It didn't look like much of a door, just a brown office door I probably could have taken down with a kick, but she put a breaching round just to the side of the doorknob, and the whole thing swung open just like we had a key. She followed that with a flash bang, and we all covered our ears to minimize the effect.

Now let's be clear, minimizing the effect is not the same as eliminating the effect. My ears still rang like a son of a bitch, and there was no way I was going to hear anything for at least half an hour. But I wasn't blinded and dizzy, so Faustus and I went through the door, swinging our guns up to train them on four DEMON agents in folding chairs around a card table.

Or what was left of four DEMON agents, at any rate. Their bodies were sitting upright in their chairs, but their heads were all lined up on the table, facing the door with their eyes pinned open. I walked over to the table and found a message for me written in the agents' blood. In big, messy letters, the unmistakable dried brown that you only get from human blood, were the words "Coming for you, Reaper."

"Huh," Faustus said, looking at the writing. "I don't think they like you very much, Harker."

"Doesn't seem like it," I agreed.

"You gonna do anything about that?" the demon asked.

Sometimes hanging around Faustus and Glory, I really did feel like I had an angel on one shoulder and a demon on the other. It only got scary when they both agreed on a course of action. I was pretty sure Glory wouldn't approve of this one. "Well, if they're looking for me, I guess there's only one thing to do," I said.

"And what's that?" Becks asked.

"Find them first," I said. "Find them and kill the shit out of them."

10

There are a lot of people who want me dead. Between living for over a century, and killing a lot of demons in that time, I've pissed off a lot of bad people, and a lot of bad things that look like people. So it wasn't that I knew where to find whoever murdered the DEMON agents. It was more like I knew where to find the person most likely to know who murdered the DEMON agents. And in Charlotte, that means one place—Mort's Bar.

"I told you not to come back here, Harker!" Mort stepped out from behind the bar and held up a hand. The bartender tossed a sawed-off shotgun toward it, but I swatted it out of the air with a blast of magic.

"No," I said. I didn't feel like explaining myself, so I didn't. I just walked across the tiled floor and slapped the taste out of the demon's mouth. He fell to the floor, and before he could scramble to his feet, I planted one foot in the center of his chest and glared down at him. "Stay."

I turned to the bartender, who was frantically reaching around under the bar. "Whatever you're looking for, I can absolutely promise you that it's better if you don't find it. I'm in a shit mood and looking for someone to break. If you don't want to be that someone, you should fuck off into the back and polish the silverware or something."

After a quick glance down at Mort to make sure he wasn't harboring any ambitions on moving, I spared a glance around the rest of the bar. Demon bars don't see a ton of lunch traffic, so it wasn't terribly surprising that only three tables had anyone sitting at them. There was a pair of witches who were studying their menus so hard I thought they might burn holes in the plastic if they weren't careful, a foursome of giggling college kids taking a Wednesday midday stroll on the wild side, and one giant in a hoodie that hadn't turned to look at the ruckus. If trouble was going to come from anywhere, that was the direction.

I've got you, Becks said in my head. I glanced up to see the back door cracked, and knew my backup was in place. Telepathy is very underrated as a tool for urban assault, I've found.

"Who's the Master, Mort?" I asked, making sure my voice was loud enough for everyone in the room to hear me.

"Fuck if I know, Harker," Mort replied, his words a little distorted by the gold grill this body wore. Mort's a hitchhiker demon, who does favors for mortals in exchange for a piggyback ride in their bodies. This was a new one, a young Black man with short dreads and gold teeth. He was in good shape, and if I was to judge by his watch, had plenty of money, so I wondered idly what he wanted from Mort that got the proprietor of the biggest demon hangout in Charlotte a ride in his skin.

"Why don't I believe you, Mort?" I mused. "Oh yeah, because you're a fucking demon. Now I know killing this meat suit won't really hurt you, so I whipped up this nice little banishing charm that shouldn't harm the body you're inhabiting but oughta send you all the way down to the Ninth Circle. That's where you're from, right?"

It isn't. Mort's strictly a Fourth-Circle demon, way less aggro and bitey than the Ninth-Circle assholes. According to Faustus, Hell has a very strict hierarchy, and if a weaker demon, one from a higher Circle, finds themselves in a lower Circle, surrounded by more powerful demons...well, let's just say it's usually not a good time for the Fourth-Circle interloper. Demons aren't just assholes to humans, they're assholes to everyone, and will torment the fuck out of another demon just as much as they'll torment a human or any other weaker being they come across. So, threatening to send Mort to the Ninth Circle was kinda like threatening to teleport a fat guy right into a cannibal's stew pot.

"I swear to God, Harker, I don't know shit!" Mort blubbered.

I didn't believe him. There are a few absolutes in this world. You never swing at the first pitch, you never buy a dance from the first stripper to approach you at a topless club, and you never believe anything a demon tells you before you've even started the torture. Unless you barter something they want. Oddly enough, they'll usually bargain pretty fairly. Fair for soulless monsters that live to torment humans, that is. But I wasn't there to make a deal. I was there to gather information, no matter who I had to brutalize to get it.

I bent over and picked Mort up. This body was short and thin, which made things easier. Mort was a lot harder to bully when he was riding around in an NFL quarterback, or whenever a pro wrestler loaned out his body to the scheming demon. This guy was only about a buck sixty, so snatching him up by his collar was easy. "Mort, I'm going to ask you one more time, then I'm going to start breaking things. Not on the body. I know it's a rental. No, I'm going to hit you where it really hurts—your wallet. You tell me what I want to know, or I'm breaking every glass in the joint, then I'll move on to the liquor bottles, then the chairs. If I make it through all the furniture before you crack, *then* we start dialing in on which Circle of Hell I'm throwing you down into."

I tossed him into a chair at one of the nearby tables. "Now talk."

"Fuck you," Mort said, wiping blood off his bottom lip. "Would you quit standing there like a bump on a log and shoot this motherfuck-er?" he called to the bartender. I didn't feel any bullets slam into the back of my body armor, or worse, my head, so I assumed the barkeep could see the same thing I could—Rebecca Gail Flynn standing just inside the back door with an MP-7 pointed toward the bar. Mort could be forgiven for not knowing this fact, since I had him sitting with his face pointed in the opposite direction.

I stepped over and sat in a chair facing Mort. "He's not going to shoot me, Mort. Because my partner's standing behind you with a submachine gun pointed at his face, and she is a very good shot. Now why don't you and I have a pleasant little chat, like the old buddies we are?"

"We aren't buddies, Harker. I fucking hate your guts. You got my daughter killed!"

"And I am truly sorry for that, Mort. But I also helped you get revenge on the asshole who killed her, so that oughta count for something. Now, who wants to kill me?"

Mort laughed so hard I thought he was going to rupture something, then laughed long enough that I contemplated rupturing something. Something non-vital, but that he'd miss nonetheless. "What's so goddamn funny?" I asked.

Mort wiped tears from his eyes and a little more blood from his bottom lip. Then he licked his hand clean, turning my stomach and reminding me that regardless of how human and harmless he might look, Mort was a creature born in the fires of Hell thousands of years ago, and I underestimated him at my peril. After a few seconds of reveling in the taste of human blood and tears, Mort leaned back in his chair and smiled at me. His smile was a cold thing, like a snake made of frost that slithered across his face and threatened, but never quite struck.

"Harker, I could save us both a lot of time if I make a list of who *doesn't* want to kill you. I don't think there's more than ten names on that one. The list of people who want to wear your face as a Halloween mask is a lot longer."

"Let's narrow it down to the people who are powerful enough to take out a four-person strike team that's heavily armed and on high alert," I said.

"Okay, there's still a couple of Faerie Knights who like to talk about how they're going to get revenge on you for your uncouth treatment of their princess."

I thought about this, then shook my head. I hadn't agreed to marry her, and I kinda killed a couple of her guys, but I wasn't all that *rude* when I did it. "Not them," I said. "Killing humans to send a message doesn't fit with their sense of honor. Besides, the Fae don't call me Reaper."

"Ooh, that does narrow it down a little," Mort said. "Oh, wait. No, it doesn't. That still leaves a shitload of cryptids, at least a couple dozen humans, *all* the local demons, and a few beings that I don't know what they are. Shit, there's one dude who's been coming around that I wouldn't be surprised if you told me he was a space werewolf or something. I can't tell if he's a monster, or just a fanboy, but that guy's weird."

"I think we can take humans off the table, unless we're talking about ninjas, and I haven't pissed off any Yakuza recently. Or ninjas, for that matter."

"Why ninjas?" Mort asked. "Tyler, bring me two glasses and a bottle of Maker's," he called to the bartender. "I might have to sit with you, Harker, but I don't have to do it sober. Your lady want a drink?"

Becks shook her head.

"Nah, she's good. On duty," I said.

"I heard she quit the cops."

That was a little surprising. I didn't expect Mort to have his finger on the pulse of the Charlotte-Mecklenburg Police Department grapevine. "She did. New gig working for Homeland Security."

"Sweet. I hear federal benefits are great. If you care about things like health insurance, that is. Thanks, Ty. You go in the back room and work on inventory while I finish my conversation with Mr. Fucking Harker, okay?"

"We just did inventory last month," the bartender grumbled. He was a thickly muscled guy with a shaved head and a t-shirt about two sizes too small. I'm sure he was used to being the baddest man in the room, and working here couldn't be good for his ego.

"Then go out back and get stoned. I don't give a fuck, just piss off for half an hour. I'm fucking tired of training new bartenders every time the goddamn Reaper darkens my door," Mort said. He had a point. I had been directly or indirectly responsible for the death of several of his bartenders. An argument could be made that they weren't all my fault, and the ones that were could be considered self-defense, but the end result was the same: any time I came to the bar, Mort needed new furniture and a new bartender by the time I left. Tyler went away, and a few seconds later I heard the door to Mort's back room open and close.

Wanna come sit? I asked Becks.

Nah, she sent back. *I'm gonna keep an eye on the hoodie. He seems to be paying pretty close attention to your conversation. I want to be able to take the shot if he gets frisky.*

Roger that, I replied. We had Pravesh and Faustus covering the outside of the building, and my guardian angel Glory on the roof to handle any threats from above, so I felt like we were pretty secure.

"Okay, Mort," I said, once we both had glasses of bourbon in front of us. "Let's chat. I brought up ninjas because the DEMON agents were all decapitated, and a message was left for me in their blood. So, whoever killed them was strong enough to take their heads with one stroke, and fast enough to kill all four before any of them could draw a weapon."

"Huh," Mort said, leaning back and sipping his bourbon. "That does narrow it down. Vampires are out, because your uncle would know if another bloodsucker strong enough to do that shit was in town. Lycanthropes don't use weapons. Neither do demons, typically. We kinda are the weapons. I dunno, Harker. You sure you haven't pissed off any ninjas? Because right now, that's the best idea I've heard."

Harker, we've got a problem, Becks said across our mental link.

What's up?

Hoodie Guy just shifted around in his seat, and I got a look at something sticking up by his neck.

Something like a conjoined twin? Like a Master Blaster? Does he have a psychotic little person riding on his shoulders?

No, but he does have a sword shoved down the back of that sweatshirt.

Well then, I replied. *This might be a shorter hunt than I expected. Excuse me, while I kill this guy.*

11

I walked over to stand in front of the giant in the hoodie. There was something familiar about the set of his shoulders, or maybe the way he clenched his fists as I stepped up. I knew this guy but couldn't see his face. I briefly called up my Sight, but while there was a hint of magic around him, it wasn't strong enough to hold my attention. His size, however, was definitely attention-getting. It was hard to tell from across the room, with the way he sat kinda hunched over the table with his hands wrapped around a coffee cup, but this dude was *big*. Taller than me, and I'm a bit over six feet. Way broader than me, but that doesn't say much. I tend toward the scrawny. I wondered briefly if there was any ogre in his bloodline.

"Howdy, stranger," I said, putting a hand on the back of a chair and trying to slide it out and sit. The giant hooked his toes under the crossbar on the chair, and it didn't budge. I leaned on the back instead and said, "Nice sword."

"Get lost." He had a pretty thick Southern accent, and the second he spoke, I knew exactly who it was. I wasn't sure what the magic aura was about, but that was a question for another time. The last time I saw Robert Edward Brabham, aka Bubba the Monster Hunter, he was headed back to Georgia to bury one of his best friends. I promised him I'd call him when it was time to get our own back on the killers, and I sure as hell hadn't called him. The last thing I needed was a giant redneck with an itchy trigger finger running around while I was trying to investigate a vast conspiracy.

"What the hell are you doing here, Brabham?" I asked, and his head snapped up, fixing me in place with a glare.

"Goddammit, Harker. I'm tryin' to be incognito and shit!"

"You're a giant redneck with a sword down your shirt. I think that ship sailed a long time ago," I replied. "Aw, shit."

"They're getting up, aren't they?" Bubba asked. That was exactly what the "aw, shit" referenced—the quartet of college kids were standing up and stripping down, while the two witches were calling magic and beginning to chant. Now, four college kids getting naked in a dorm or frat house in the middle of the night is nothing out of the ordinary. But when it happens in a bar in the middle of the day, it either means someone has put Molly in the coffee or the coeds are lycanthropes and they don't want to shred their clothes. The elongating faces and rapidly sprouting body hair told me these were definitely shifters. Were-rodents of some type, maybe ferrets. Whatever they were, they were tall and skinny with long claws at the ends of their fingers.

One of the witches had sliced her palm and was walking a circle along the floor, dribbling blood and chanting along with her pal, who was doing all the unnecessary hand-waving that inexperienced casters think is critical to the success of a spell. It's not. All you need for a spell is a conduit to power and focus. The words, the rhymes, the crystal balls—all that is just to help the caster focus. Some of the sigils, however, those can be important, and from the look of the stuff Witch #1 was drawing on the floor with her blood, she was trying to cast a protection circle around the two of them so whatever they summoned would be outside with me while they sat nice and safe inside their circle.

I didn't approve of that idea. I felt like if those two wanted to summon something bad enough to be a threat to me, they should have the guts to stand right in front of it with me. So, I called up a little power and flung a sphere of purple energy at Witch #2, slamming it right into her chest. She screamed and staggered backward, stepping right on the line of the circle, slipping in her friend's blood and falling down right on her ass. She finished her spell right as she landed, and by the look of sheer terror on her face, whatever she had called up was not something she wanted to be in the same room with.

"Becks, get in here and get that door locked tight!" I yelled. I knew Mort had his place warded up tighter than a nun's porn closet, so if we could get all the doors closed, nothing would get out once he engaged the locks. "Mort, lock this place down!"

Mort didn't hesitate. We hadn't been on the same side in a few years, but we'd stood together in more than one scrap, and the shifty little demon knew when I was dicking around and when playtime was over. He yelled to the bartender to get to the panic room, then shouted, "Houdini!" and I felt the warding spell in the bar slam into place. Now nothing bad could get out, but Pravesh and Faustus couldn't get in, either. I wasn't sure about Glory, but I wasn't counting on her being able to help in this scrap.

"Houdini?" I asked.

"It's something you can't get out of," Mort replied.

"So you trigger it with the name of an escape artist?" Bubba asked. "That don't make a lick of sense."

"You got a better idea, hillbilly?" Mort snarled.

Bubba stood up, unzipping the hoodie as he did. "Alcatraz," he said. "You know, the place nobody ever got out of?" He reached over his left shoulder and drew the sword he had strapped to his back. It was a dark blade, like no metal I'd ever seen, and the hilt looked like some kind of bone. The sword was old, but very much not what I was used to seeing Bubba wield.

"Where's your gun?" I asked, drawing my own.

"Got blowed up," he said.

"You didn't want to just go get another one?"

"Gun didn't save Joe. Maybe if I was better at ending fights without one, he'd still be here."

I got it. His friend died, so he needed something to latch on to, some way to explain the stupidity of an unfair death. So, he got a sword. All in all, it was healthier than any of my coping mechanisms, so I let it go. "Can that thing kill a shifter?" I asked.

Bubba just chuckled. "Yeah. It does okay." He swung it through the air once, and I felt a wave of power come from the blade. There was something going on with it, but I couldn't take the time to study it now. We had four were-ferrets coming at us, and a cloud of inky blackness pooling in the middle of the room with a stench of sulfur and bad intentions pouring off it in waves.

"Becks, help Bubba handle the shifters," I called. "Mort, you take care of the witches. I'll deal with whatever comes out of that cloud." I heard Flynn swap magazines in her pistol and assumed she'd switched to silver loads. I didn't get any acknowledgement out of Mort, so I just counted on him not wanting to scrape any little Harker bits off his ceiling and focused on the cloud of blackness, which was coalescing into a more solid form, and not one that I liked seeing.

It was a Reaver, one of the more vicious types of demons. They usually aren't too bad, only about five feet tall, with sharp claws and teeth, but not much else. But every once in a while, you'll find a Reaver that's fought its way out of their normal Pits and into one of the deeper Circles, and you can only do that by killing a lot of other demons. Those Uber-Reavers are bigger, stronger, faster, and worst of all, smarter. This one was pushing eight feet tall, and as I watched, its form solidified and it was a good thing I already didn't sleep for shit, because the thing standing in front of me was nightmare fodder of the highest degree.

Its skin was mottled red and black, with its surface constantly shifting colors like the evil of it was just oozing across its flesh. It has curved blades grafted or grown out of its wrists that arced back to its elbows, making its forearms into razor-sharp swords. It had an elongated snout like a crocodile, with the same teeth pointing up at the end of its jaw, giving it the impression of a vicious grin. It stood on long, skinny legs that hinged backward at the knee, a hallmark of the Reaver that gave it incredible leaping ability and surprising speed. But the real scary bit was its tail, a prehensile thing that waved over its head with a scorpion-like stinger on the end of it. Not all Reavers had tails, and it was even more rare for one to have a venomous spike. It's entirely possible this thing had killed the demon that originally had the tail, ripped it off the corpse, and magically grafted it onto itself. However it got it, I had to make sure that thing stayed the hell away from me.

"Hello, Reaper," the thing hissed, and its voice sounded like a swarm of locusts speaking, all rasps and dissonant scraping sounds. "Lucifer sends his warmest regards and hopes to see you very soon."

Fuck. That was not good. I had no illusions about where I was going to end up when I died. No matter how many people I saved, and completely ignoring the fact that I helped restore the Archangels themselves to their shiny chairs in Heaven, I had kinda spent the last century tapdancing all over at least nine of the Ten Commandments, so whenever I ended up in the ground, I was going on the express elevator to Hell, and Lucifer had made no bones about the fact that he was looking forward to torturing me for eternity, and then some.

"Well, I hope your boss is used to being disappointed, pal. Because I'm not interested in a return trip to his house." I holstered my pistol and called up my soul blade, grinning a little at the widening of the demon's eyes. The gleaming ribbon of magical energy extended from my fist, and the Reaver drew back just a hair. That's all I needed to see. If I could scare it, I could hurt it. And if I could hurt it, I could send it back to Hell.

I charged in, covering the twenty feet between us in a couple of long strides. The demon slashed at my face, but instead of ducking underneath it, I raised my sword in a block and sucked my stomach in to avoid the lateral cut that came at me. His arm-sword slammed into my soul blade and kept right on going, and I leaned in as the gleaming band of energy cut through the knife edge and arm both, severing the hand and showering me in black demon blood.

The Reaver howled and staggered back, clutching at what remained of its arm. I ducked under the tail as it whipped overhead, barely avoiding a stab to my face that probably would have melted my nose or done something equally unpleasant. I swung my blade through the air, flicking drops of blood to sizzle on the floor. I took a step toward the demon, then fell to the floor as something heavy slammed into my back. I rolled over, trying to shove the twitching were-ferret off me, and looked up at the grinning Reaver, who had grown a new knife-arm and now stood over me, blades pointed at my throat. I raised my hand, trying to stab straight up with my soul blade, but the manifested weapon had vanished when I got decked by a flying ferret and lost concentration.

"Well, shit."

12

I rolled to one side as the tail stabbed downward, hoping I could avoid getting skewered and maybe get lucky and it would break the spike off in the floor. I managed to not get perforated, but the Reaver stopped its jab before it hit the tiled floor and slid the spike sideways in my direction. I scrambled to my feet and kicked at the writhing tail, barely managing to duck under the slashing knife-arm that swung at my throat. I couldn't focus enough to reform my soulblade while so much of my attention was dedicated to not dying, but I managed to keep my shit together enough to fling a couple of balls of power at the demon and make it back off a little.

"Harker! Don't you burn my fucking bar down again!" Mort shouted. I thought that was a little unfair. I'd never burned his bar down, so "again" was a little out of line. I was pretty much responsible for his wall getting blown in, all his furniture getting wrecked several times, and a *lot* of bloodstains on his floor, but I had never set fire to the place. Yet. It wasn't off the table, but fire doesn't do a whole lot to Upper-Circle demons. They're kinda born in and on fire, so that doesn't really faze them. Pure magical energy, however, can be way more effective. If you can land a shot. Which is a lot harder to do with a were-ferret climbing on your back trying to bite through your carotid artery.

I decided to focus on the easier problem first—the lycanthrope at my throat. I spread my arms out wide and bent my knees just a little, then flung myself backward at the floor, intending to squash the ferret between my spine and the tiles. Except I underestimated the agility of a six-foot ferret, and when it scampered off to the left, I slammed my back to the floor, barely keeping from cracking my head and probably giving myself one hell of a concussion. I felt the air rush out of me in a loud *OOOF* and turned to see the were-asshole grinning at me with its little ferret teeth bared in a rictus that would have been terrifying if I hadn't been so pissed off. I rolled to my right, avoiding another stab from the Reaver's tail, and thanked my lucky whatevers that Mort hadn't bolted the tables to the floor.

I stood up, grabbing a table as I rose, and flung it at the were-rodent asshole. I don't know if he wasn't expecting me to throw a table, if he wasn't expecting me to throw it quite that damn hard, or if he didn't expect the table to be as heavy as it was, but the fuzzy little shit got a face full of two-inch-thick oak and went down like a sack of potatoes. I turned back to the Reaver and called up power to wrap my left arm in a shield of magical energy. I blocked a slashing strike from the demon's bladed arm, then thrust my right arm forward and focused my will. A beam of purple-white energy streaked forward and slammed into the Reaver's midsection, lifting it off its feet and flinging the creature twenty feet back, bowling over a pair of were-ferrets as it landed.

"Would you two quit screwing around and kill those damn rats?" I called to Bubba and Becks. My fiancée just flipped me off, but Bubba turned to glare at me.

"The little shitballs are fast, Harker. You wanna shout orders, or you wanna do your damn job and hunt a demon?" the big redneck yelled in my direction.

I didn't reply, because just as I opened my mouth to say something that I'm sure would have been cripplingly witty, a hundred-fifty-pound ball of fur and stink tackled me around the waist. Or tried to, anyway. I'm on the skinny side, but still more substantial than a hundred fifty pounds, so while I staggered sideways, I didn't go down. I looked down at the fuzzy half-shifted were-ferret that had its arms wrapped around my waist and shook my head.

"That was a bad move, Mickey," I said, and pressed my fist to the back of the shifter's head. I cut loose with a blast of power that pulped the ferret's skull, and it dropped to the floor, flat on what used to be a face. It shifted back to human form when it died, which was inconvenient for explaining corpses to the authorities, but after a second, I remembered that I kinda *was* the authorities now, so I was probably not getting arrested for killing the little shit.

Then I had to stop worrying about that bullshit, because I saw movement out of the corner of my eye and dodged another tail strike from the Reaver. Well, mostly dodged. I thought I was clear until a half second after the stinger whizzed by my shoulder and I felt a line of fire erupt across my upper arm.

"Fuck!" I yelled as pain radiated out from the scratch. It could have been molten steel rolling down my arm and not felt any hotter. I dropped to a knee and held my energy shield overhead to keep the demon from ripping my head off while I tried to direct enough energy into my shoulder to purge the venom. It wasn't really working, and I could feel the numbness radiating up and down along my right arm, rendering it useless. The Reaver slammed into my shield once, twice, three times, hammering me down to both knees, then into a huddled ball on the floor. I was trapped with a demon beating on my only protection, with poison rushing through my veins, and only a human, a hitchhiker demon, and whatever Bubba was to save me. And he'd decided to go on some kind of lame gun-free penance mission or something, so what would normally have been a dangerous man with a massive pistol was now a redneck with a magic sword.

I had a fleeting thought of, *Huh. So, this is how I die. I somehow always thought it would happen in Arkansas.* Then Becks's voice rang out in my head. *Ovary up, bitch!*

Her quoting *The Magicians* telepathically was just about the motivation I needed, so I shoved myself to my feet, throwing the demon off me and dropping my shield. I redirected that power into a cauterizing blast at my right arm, trying to burn the poison out of my system. It kinda worked, in that the poison didn't get any worse. But it also added my own eldritch fire on top of the poisonous burning in my arm, and my vision started to get all sparkly at the edges.

Don't you dare pass out, asshole, Becks said. *I've still got one of these bitey little furry fuckwits over here, so you need to find your balls and kill that goddamned demon, Harker!*

Her tough love worked, at least in the sense that I got pissed off and stopped being such a mopey whiny assclown. I used the last bits of strength in my beleaguered right arm to draw my pistol, then swapped hands with it and emptied the magazine into the Reaver's torso.

"You can't kill this form with bullets, Harker," the demon said. "You should know that."

"I know," I said. "But I can distract you long enough for that big redneck to cut your fucking head off."

And he did. Bubba stepped up with that giant letter opener and chopped right through the Reaver's neck. The demon's head rolled off to one side, already dissolving into a puddle of steaming black ichor. I dropped my pistol and fired off a blast of energy, blowing a hole right through the torso of a were-ferret about to pounce on Bubba's back. The fuzzy prick flew a good six feet back before dropping to the floor, stone dead.

"Thanks for the assist," I said.

"Likewise," he replied.

I looked around the room for more targets and found nothing. The lycanthropes were now just dead naked people lying all over the floor, there wasn't enough left of either witch to Carbon-14 date, and the demon was just a puddle of stinky goop. I walked over to Bubba and looked up at him. He was wiping down his sword with a shred of fabric that had probably begun the day as a were-ferret's shirt, but now was just another blood-soaked rag.

"What the fuck are you doing here?" I asked the big man. "I thought I sent you back to Georgia."

The massive monster hunter looked down at me, something not many people get to do, and slid his sword back in its sheath with a steely hiss. "I'm pretty sure I don't work for you, and I know for damn sure I ain't sleeping with you, so you don't get to *send* me anywhere, Harker. You wanted me to go back home and bury my friend, and you said you'd call me when you had something. I did my part, and I even waited a little while for you to call, hoping you weren't as much of an asshole as everybody says you are and that you'd bring me in when it was time to get this Master prick."

I opened my mouth to protest, but he just barreled right over me. This was turning into a day of unfamiliar occurrences for me, and I was pretty sure I didn't like it. "I waited a month, Harker. A. Month. I put my friend in the ground. One of my best friends. One of the three people I care most about in this world. Then I sat on my mountain for a goddamn *month* waiting on you to get your thumb out of your ass and call me so we could hunt down the son of a bitch that got Joe killed. And what were you doing all that time? Drinking expensive whiskey and whining about your life?"

I didn't have a whole lot to say to that, because he was pretty damn close to the mark. "I'm sorry," I said. I was spending a lot of time lately apologizing, and I didn't enjoy it. "I haven't made near as much progress as I wanted to, unless we're counting progress through the liquor cabinet. Because you're right, I've pretty much handled every bit of that shit. But I've gotten started now, so if you'll just go home and give me another week or so, I should be able to bring you back up when we're close to the Master."

"No."

"Excuse me?" I looked up at the big man and took a step back at the scowl on his face. I've stared down a lot of monsters, but a mountain of tattooed hillbilly actually got me to back up.

"I ain't going nowhere. You had your shot, now I'm taking mine. I'm going after this Master, and you can lead, follow, or get out of the way. But the days of me sitting on a mountain mourning my friend while you sip Scotch and look at your bellybutton are over."

"And if I tell you that's not an option, and you need to stand the fuck down?" I knew it was probably a mistake as soon as I said it, but I was tired, and my shoulder hurt like a motherfucker, and I really didn't like this big bastard telling me "no" in front of Mort, who I pretty much needed to stay afraid of me if our relationship was going to keep working.

"Well, I reckon I'd slap the taste out of your mouth," Bubba said, clenching and unclenching his fists.

Okay. We were going to do this. I needed to be seen as the baddest motherfucker in the valley, and if it meant I had to beat the shit out of this dude with one arm—well, not tied behind my back, but numb and useless from a poisoned demon stinger—then that's what I'd do.

I took a deep breath and quoted one of the greatest movies in history. "Well, Bubba," I said. "You're a daisy if you do."

Then he backhanded the piss out of me and the fight was on.

13

I didn't go down when he hit me, but it was a near thing. I've been hit harder, but not by a human. My head snapped to the side, and I felt my bottom lip tear a little. "Nice shot," I said, running my tongue across and tasting blood. "Let's see what you can do when I'm expecting it."

Bubba grinned at me. "If you weren't expecting me to knock the piss out of you, then you're a—"

I'm pretty sure my punch to his gut cut off the word "dumbass." Might have been some other insult, but after fighting a demon and then getting slapped by a redneck, I wasn't in the mood for anything that impugned my intellect, parentage, or even my taste in clothing. I slammed a fist into his breadbasket and was impressed to see that he didn't drop, either. I don't even pretend to be human, and while I didn't hit him as hard as I possibly could, I didn't pull much, either.

Bubba doubled over but got a forearm up to knock away my follow-up punch. I expected him to straighten up, but he stayed down and charged forward, wrapping his arms around my waist and picking me up. He picked up speed as he ran, and after about ten yards slammed into the polished brass rail surrounding Mort's bar. With my spine.

I saw stars, my breath rushed out of me, and if I could have made a noise, I probably would have invented new conjugations of the word "fuck." That shit *hurt*. I held myself up on the bar, but barely, as Bubba backed away and watched me try to stand.

"You gonna get your head outta your ass about me working this case, or are we gonna scrap some more?" he asked. I kinda just wanted to let it go, but Mort was still watching the proceedings with way more glee than I liked, so I figured I needed to at least put the big bastard off his feet once before I could stop getting the shit beat out of me.

"Let's go with Option B," I said, firing two blasts of pure force right into his chest. The magical bolts lifted Bubba off his feet and flung him across the room to crash into, and through, one of Mort's tables, sending splinters flying. I sprinted over to where the big man lay in a pile of kindling that used to be furniture and yanked him up by his belt. One, two, three hard shots to the jaw, and I let him go with a shove backward. He staggered a few steps, then put a hand down on the back of a chair to steady himself.

I moved in, ready to lay in a couple more punches and end this, but the redneck was playing possum. He straightened, yanked the heavy wooden chair up, and slammed it into my left shoulder. I went crashing to the floor and curled up to protect my head from the massive boot that slammed into my side. A couple of stiff kicks, and then it was my turn to be picked up off the floor like a sack of potatoes. Bubba snatched me up over his head, let out a roar like how I imagined a Sasquatch would sound, and hurled me back in the direction of the bar. I hit the slick wooden surface and bounced once like skipping a stone before I crashed into the mirror behind the bar, bringing down three or four glass shelves full of liquor bottles on top of me.

"Stop it!" Mort yelled. "How can there be two of you?!?"

Bubba ignored him, and I barely heard him over the tinkling of shattered glass and the *glug-glug* of spilled booze. I rolled onto the floor, wincing as more shards of glass dug into my arms and legs, and managed to struggle to my feet just as Bubba reached the bar. He stretched out to pull me over by my shirt, but I grabbed him by the elbows and yanked, slamming his gut into the bar. He bent over just enough for me to get a grip on his ponytail, and I used that to bounce his face off the bar a few times until I heard a nasty *crack* come from his face. I let go, not wanting to do any permanent damage, and he backed away from the bar, blood pouring from his nose.

I felt a little better. A broken nose sucked, but it was way better than a busted orbital socket, jaw, or skull, which were pretty much my other options for the damage I'd inflicted. I watched as he pressed one side of his nose closed with a finger and blew outward, sending a gobbet of bloody snot to *thwack* on the floor. Making a mental note to try very hard not to get knocked down into the bloody phlegm, I hopped over the bar, instantly reminded exactly how bad my ribs hurt from getting thrown around. I stepped forward and planted my left foot, but froze in mid-punt as Bubba held up one hand, palm out.

"Hold it," he said. Somehow I managed to arrest my kick, and I stepped back to listen. "We can beat the shit out of each other as much as we want, and I ain't even gonna get mad about you flinging your little magic missiles at me. But you kick me in the balls and I'm gonna do my level best to cut that goddamn foot off and stick it up your ass."

I thought about it for a second, then nodded. "Fair enough. No balls." I turned to the left and stepped into a big roundhouse kick that probably *would* have broken his jaw if it had landed.

But it didn't. Not because Bubba blocked the kick. No, I didn't kick his head completely around because suddenly a blast of white light exploded between us and I found myself flat on my back, flash-blinded, and with brand new pain blossoming from pretty much every part of my body. I think there might have been one toe that didn't hurt, but that was about it.

I lay there for a few seconds trying to get myself back together, figuring if anything wanted to kill me at that moment, I was in the hands of Becks, Mort, and maybe God, because Bubba was probably just as flattened as I was. The groans coming from a few feet away confirmed my expectations of his combat readiness, which is to say not at all.

"What the hell was that?" Bubba asked.

Without opening my eyes to see if I was right, because I knew I was, I replied, "Pretty sure that was a pissed off Guardian Angel."

"You're goddamned right it was," Glory's voice said from above me. "You two assholes need to get over yourselves and put away your dicks before somebody gets seriously hurt. There are bad guys to hunt, and you two measuring peckers in a demon bar isn't going to get us any closer to finding out who the Master is."

"Did your angel just say dicks?" Bubba asked. "Or do I have a concussion?"

I pulled myself up to a sitting position and looked at the giant redneck. I extended my middle finger to him. "How many fingers am I holding up?"

"Screw you, Harker."

"Not a concussion," I said. "And Glory developed quite the potty mouth when she got turned into a human for a couple years."

"Pretty sure that's your fault, Harker," Glory said.

"That makes way more sense," Bubba agreed.

I dragged myself to my feet and staggered over to the fallen Hunter. I stretched out a hand to help him up. "We good?"

He grabbed my hand and together we managed to get him upright. "I reckon we're good. But just so you know, I coulda taken you."

"Sure you could," I said. I looked around. There were two tables still intact, and maybe eight chairs. Easily the best shape I'd ever left Mort's in after a brawl. "Let's go home and make a plan. Mort's got a hell of a mess to clean up."

"Fuck you, Harker!" the demon yelled at my back as we walked toward the exit. "I'm sending you a bill for damages."

"Go for it," I said. "I'll put it with the others."

In the garbage? Becks asked.

The recycling bin, I replied. *I'm fucking progressive like that.*

14

I thought you sent him home?" Faustus said when he walked into my apartment and saw Bubba sitting on my couch with an ice pack pressed to his face.

"Kiss my ass, demon," Bubba replied, although his words were muffled from the ice. "Nobody sends me anywhere, least of all not some half-assed vampire who dresses like a 90s goth kid."

I looked down at my black jeans, Doc Martens, black *Sandman* t-shirt, and black overshirt, and shrugged. He had a point about my fashion sense. But at least if I was dressing like the *1990s*, I wasn't dressing like the century I was born in. I call that a win. "I did send him home," I said through my own ice pack. "It didn't take."

"So, he came back, and you two fought to decide who had the biggest dick?" the demon said, making a beeline for my wet bar. "You still haven't restocked?" he asked when he found the bar empty.

"You just cleaned me out this morning, asshole," I said. "I didn't have time to go to the liquor store."

"Not if you were busy measuring wieners with Grizzly Adams," Faustus said.

"Why does everyone keep saying that?" I asked.

"Because it's kinda the truth, Q," Glory said. "You two big morons were trying to find out who was the bigger dog, and instead of just whipping them out and laying them on a table, you wrecked Mort's bar. Again."

"Really?" Faustus asked. "Goddammit, Harker. If you're not going to keep any booze around, could you at least not destroy one of the few places in the city where I can get a drink without putting on my human suit?"

"Do your people always bitch this much?" Bubba asked.

"Yeah, pretty much," Becks said, sitting down beside me and passing beers out to me and Bubba. "So, Mort's is off the table as a source of intel. What's next?"

"Mort didn't know anything anyway." Skeeter's face appeared on the screen over my fireplace. At least it was mostly his face. He'd gotten most of Dennis's code out of my video conferencing software, so we could see who we were talking to, but he hadn't gotten all of it, so there was still a rainbow unicorn horn sticking out of the middle of his forehead. I didn't comment on it. Not out of any sense of discretion, but because there were so many options for smartassed comments, I couldn't pick just one. So, I let it go.

"How do you know that?" I asked.

"Because your boss lady there has had his place bugged for the past three months, and I spent the last eight hours scanning through all the tapes for keywords. Do you have any idea how many times the word 'demon' is uttered in that place? Makes me really wish the bad guys hadn't been so dead set on making their acronym match a real word."

"How exactly did you gain access to those files, Mr. Brown?" Pravesh asked. One of her eyebrows had climbed halfway to her hairline, and she had the arch look of a woman who would happily inject you with lethal venom if she didn't like your answer. Because she could. Inject you with lethal venom, that is. Keya Pravesh is a lamia, a half-snake creature thought to be extinct for at least half a century. Apparently rumors of her extinction had been greatly exaggerated.

"I hacked your cell phone, Director. You shouldn't use your birthday as your passcode, by the way."

"It shouldn't be an issue, since my birthdate is also classified information," Pravesh replied.

"Okay, I'll admit it did take a little work getting that information. But I have it, and I used it, and now we know that no one in Mort's for the past ninety days has had anything substantial to say about DEMON. Even the DEMON agents that were there. And since…since their last place got blown up, there's been no mention of the organization at all."

Skeeter's pause didn't go unnoticed. That explosion killed his uncle, along with Gabriella Van Helsing, one of our Shadow Council Members. Those deaths, following close on the heels of the murder of Cassie Harrison and the summary execution of Jack Watson, had rocked both my team and Bubba's crew to the core. Today was the first action we'd seen since then, and even though it was a small skirmish, relatively speaking, I was happy we all made it out alive.

"So where do we go next?" Bubba asked. I didn't bother trying to correct him. I might as well just assume that he was going to be part of anything we did until we got to whoever was behind DEMON. He'd lost as much in this as I had, if not more, and I wasn't someone to stand in the way of good old-fashioned vengeance.

"Washington," I said. Every eye locked onto me, and I chuckled a little bit. "Come on, where else are we going to go to find out about a secret government agency? We have to go to where all the government secrets are kept. It's Occam's Razor."

"Pretty sure that's not what Occam's Razor says," Becks murmured.

"Close enough," I replied.

"He has a point," Pravesh said. "There are physical files in DEMON headquarters that may shed some light on this 'Master.' And the only way to access them is to—"

"Break into a secure government facility like Tom Cruise in *Mission Impossible?*" Faustus asked.

"I was going to say meet with my superiors face to face and get them to allow us into the DEMON facility," Pravesh replied. "And also, we need to cancel your Netflix subscription. You've obviously watched too many action movies."

"Becks, check Faustus's video history before we leave. If he's been bingeing *The Fast and the Furious*, then he doesn't get to drive anywhere. Ever again," I said.

"So we all just pile into Pravesh's Suburbans and drive to the nation's capitol?" Faustus said. "I'm in."

"No, you're still translating that damn book with Luke," Becks said. "There are only so many Suburbans and I can only keep an eye on so many overgrown toddlers in Washington, D.C."

"Pretty sure she means us," I said to Bubba.

"Safe bet."

"I totally mean you two. Skeeter, you're still in Georgia, right?" Becks asked.

"Yep. Geri and Amy, too. Geri's running Bubba's CrossFit gym and Amy's working on getting the regional office in Atlanta set up."

"You own a CrossFit gym?" I asked Bubba with a smirk.

"You own a pink apartment building that's literally the ugliest thing in five zip codes."

"Touché."

"So, Glory, Harker, me, Bubba, and Director Pravesh will leave tomorrow morning for D.C. Maybe we can find some answers to who was funding DEMON."

"And beat the shit out of them," I said.

"I can get behind that," Bubba agreed.

Glory and Becks exchanged a look. "Yeah," Glory said. "There are two of them."

A COUPLE HOURS LATER, I STEPPED OUT ONTO MY BALCONY WITH A bottle of Johnny Walker Black and two glasses. Bubba was leaning over the railing in what I was coming to think of as the default "thinking pose" for my balcony. "You want a drink to go with those heavy thoughts?"

He took a glass, and I poured it half full of whiskey. "Thanks," he said.

I set the bottle on the patio table and leaned back against the wall, facing him. "Wanna talk about it?"

"Not really."

"Wanna listen to me talk about it?"

"Even less."

"Want to fight some more?"

He thought about that one for a long moment, long enough that I thought I might have to replace my own furniture if things went sideways, then he spoke. "I'm tired, man. How do you keep going, after all the shit you've seen?"

"What do you think I've seen?" I asked. I've seen a *lot*, but most people don't know anywhere near all of it. But his fiancée worked for my fiancée's boss, so he probably had access to more than most people.

"I know you lived through the Nazi occupation of Europe. I know they killed somebody you loved. I know you watched everybody in your family die. I know you've killed more people than Ebola. There's even a rumor you went to Hell. Literally."

"Yeah."

"Yeah, there's a rumor, or yeah, you went to Hell."

"Yeah, I went to Hell."

"So how do you keep at it? With everything you've done, seen, and lost, how do you keep going?"

I thought a long time before I answered. I felt like he deserved the truth, or at least a big chunk of it, but this was also a guy I didn't know before a couple months ago. We might be in the same line of work, and on the same side, even. But we weren't friends. Not yet. If we got there, it would take more than a couple drinks and a couple punches. "Well, for one thing, there are still people I give a shit about. Becks, Luke...shit, even Faustus and Pravesh. They matter. And keeping them safe matters."

"I get that. I feel like if I didn't have Skeeter and Amy, I would have crawled in a case of beer this past few weeks and just stayed there."

"But they're not the only reason. I could stand here and tell you it's some big moral thing, that somebody needs to stand up to the bad people in the world and protect the humans from the nasties that they don't even believe exist, but that would be bullshit. The fact is, I'm only really good at one thing, and that's killing. I'm a decent magician, but I've never had a knack for anything other than combat magic. I'm a decent detective when I need to be, but I've only ever used those skills to hunt down people or things that need killing. It's what I do. I kill things. So, if I can kill bad things, then maybe I can pretend to be a little less of a monster than the things I hunt. That's how I keep going. I either kill things, or I die. And even after all these years, I'm not ready to die."

He stood there for a long moment, not looking at me, just sipping his drink and staring out at the Charlotte skyline. Finally, he knocked back the last of the brown liquid and said, "That's one of the most depressing things I've ever heard, Harker."

I laughed and poured him another drink. "Well, nobody calls me Quincy Harker, Spirit Raiser. I'm the fucking Reaper. It's just what I do." I drained my own glass and turned to go back inside. I put my hand on the door but stopped when Bubba spoke again.

"Do you think we'll find him? The Master, I mean. We've been trying to get to the bottom of this DEMON shit for two years, and a whole lot of people had to die just for us to find out this guy exists. Do you really think we'll be able to find him?"

I moved closer and put a hand on Bubba's shoulder. He turned to look me in the eyes, not always a good idea with a wizard. As he stared into the depths of my soul, I said, "We're going to find him. We're going to find the Master, and we're going to kill him and every son of a bitch stupid enough to stand beside him. I give you my word."

He kept his gaze locked on mine, and I saw a lot of my same pain reflected there. After another moment, he nodded and said, "Alright, then. Let's ride."

15

The building that housed the nation headquarters of DEMON was perfect for a super-secret government agency. At least, perfect in the sense that no one would ever suspect a super-secret government agency was located there. There was a small door on the side wall of a landscaping company, situated across the street from a pawn shop and an adult video store, with a nondescript yellow metal sign with "PEST CONTROL DEPT" in big block letters.

We piled out of Pravesh's SUV, Bubba and I stretching from being cooped up in the back seat for several hours. I wasn't sure how neither of the tallest people got the passenger seat, but since I was sleeping with the woman who rode shotgun, I wasn't stupid enough to ask questions. Not for the first time, I envied Glory's ability to just kinda pop in and out of wherever she wanted to. She'd taken one look at me and Bubba and the back seat of the Suburban and noped right out. I figured she'd meet up with us at some point in D.C., either when we were in dire need of her help or when she saw a golden opportunity to give me a ration of shit. I looked around the area as we got out of the SUV. "This parking lot looks familiar."

"There was a press conference here about a year ago," Pravesh said as she walked toward the door.

"A press conference? In the parking lot of a landscaping company?" Bubba asked. "What dumbass booked that?"

"It's a long story," Pravesh replied. She didn't knock, just slid the metal sign to the right and leaned down to look into the retina scanner. Every once in a while, I wondered why those things were never placed high enough, then I realized that while it's a pain in the ass for me to always bend over to get my eye at the right height, there are people in the world who aren't six feet tall, and they couldn't exactly keep a stepladder beside the hidden retina scanner. I mean, they *could*, but it would be about as smart as betting against Bubba in a wing-eating contest. There was a loud *click* from the wall, and a section of brick slid aside to reveal a palm scanner. Pravesh put her hand on it, and after a few seconds, it flashed green and the door popped open.

Does it not notice that she's cold-blooded? I thought to Becks.

I don't know that she is. Lamiae are part snake, but I don't know which part controls their circulatory system.

Good point. Either way, we're in, so I guess don't look a gift horse in the mouth.

Right. Becks followed close on Pravesh's heels, her badge wallet out to show her credentials. Bubba and I bumped shoulders trying to get through the door at the same time, but after a couple seconds of jostling, I slipped in just ahead of him.

I wore my usual uniform of a black long-sleeved shirt over a t-shirt and had my overshirt flipped back to give me free access to my pistol. Bubba had his sword slung over his back and some kind of oversized brass knuckles on his hands. I wasn't sure how he'd be able to swing the sword and use the knuckle dusters, but figured his weapons weren't my problem, as long as nobody looked at the giant with the sword and just started shooting.

"Have you ever considered wearing something a little more subtle than a longsword over your shoulder?" I asked.

"Harker, I'm six and a half feet tall, three hundred fifty pounds, with a beard like ZZ Top and more tattoos than your average Hell's

Angel. I'm pretty sure I left subtle in the dust before I got out of college. Besides, you walk into every room like a John Constantine cosplayer, complete with glowing eyes and potty mouth. Long as you're around, I *am* the subtle one."

He had a point. I wasn't sure I liked it, but it was valid. Rather than admit he was right, I took stock of the room. It looked like your basic exterminator's front office. Or at least what I thought an exterminator's front office looks like. I've never actually been in one, but there were a couple chairs, a table with magazines about bugs, and an ant farm. There was one door leading into the rest of the building, and a sliding window in one wall that opened into what looked like a generic receptionist's office. A generic-looking receptionist smiled out at us from behind the glass but made no moves to open the window.

The only thing that didn't look perfectly Middle American Office Park was the high-tech camera in a corner of the ceiling, its red light steady as it panned across the room. Pravesh pressed a button on the intercom box by the window and said, "Director Keya Pravesh, Homeland Security, Paranormal Division. I'm here to see Director Shaw."

We all knew full well that the real Director Shaw, or at least the woman we *believed* was the real Director Shaw, was in a maximum-security cell courtesy of Homeland Security, not that anyone with Homeland, including Pravesh, would even admit that they *had* maximum-security cells. But we didn't know if the receptionist knew that, and we weren't one hundred percent sure that there wasn't another Director Shaw running around. That had been a favorite tactic of the one we captured—creating a bunch of subordinates with the same name to keep us from finding her.

"I'm sorry, ma'am, we don't have anyone here by that name. But if you would like to take a number, I can have one of our pest specialists come out and meet with you as soon as one becomes available." The receptionist's smile never wavered, as though government agents wandered in every day and wanted consultations on how to deal with their termite problems. Of course, given that we were in the middle of the largest collection of useless government functionaries in the free world, maybe they did.

"I don't know if you missed my name, my badge, or my title, but I want to speak with your boss right now," Pravesh said, ice dripping off her words. "Now get them out here before my oversized friend here loses patience and just pulls the door off the hinges." She jerked a thumb back over one shoulder at Bubba, who gave a little wave.

"Go ahead. Not my budget," the receptionist replied. Somewhere in the conversation she'd switched from "happy receptionist working hard at her cover story" to "bored government functionary with no interest in helping anyone with anything, ever." While I found the bored functionary more relatable, I kinda missed the cheerful role-player. But I was definitely looking forward to watching the mayhem that was about to ensue. Especially since it seemed like I wasn't going to be part of it for once. I stepped over to the wall farthest away from the interior door and leaned against it, folding my arms across my chest.

"Okay, then," Pravesh said. "Bubba, do what you do."

"You mean break shit, right? We haven't worked together much, and I wanna make sure there's no confusion."

"Yes, I mean break shit."

"On it." Bubba walked over to the door and grabbed the knob. I was impressed. I figured he'd be more of a "kick the door in and check to see if it was locked later" type. His body went rigid and started to twitch a little, then it started to twitch *a lot*.

"Don't touch him!" I barked at Pravesh, who had instinctively moved toward the now-vibrating giant. I called up power and flung a bolt of force at the back of his knees. He toppled over backward, and while his hand couldn't unclench from the doorknob, his weight did pull the knob out of the door, breaking the circuit. Bubba slammed to the floor and lay there, undoubtedly wishing that his jaw wasn't clenched shut so he could unleash some of the stream of profanity he was trying to utter.

"Are you dead?" I asked.

"NNNNNNNN," he replied. I've been around enough people who

are temporarily paralyzed to know what "no" sounds like in electrocuted, plus his ability to respond meant he had probably suffered less brain damage from getting fried than from his college football career.

"Good," I replied. I stepped over to the window and smiled at the receptionist. She smiled back, a look of complete and utter innocence on her face.

"May I help you?" she asked, in a "butter won't melt in my pure, innocent mouth" tone.

"You may," I replied. "You have my full authorization and permission to help me."

"That's not what I—"

I cut her off, channeling just enough power into my eyes to make them glow purple. I've found this to be a very effective negotiating technique over the years. It says, "I can bring the ceiling down on you if I want to" rather than the glowing fists, which kinda says, "I'm about to bring the ceiling down on you." A narrow, but important distinction. "That was cute, the whole letting my large friend electrocute himself on the door. But the time for cute is over, and I need you to open the fucking door before I melt that window you're sitting behind, drag you out of that office by your hair, and use your face as a master key. Do you understand me?"

She looked remarkably unshaken for someone being threatened with dramatic levels of violence by a man with glowing eyes. Either she was made of sterner stuff than I expected, or DEMON hired its receptionists from a talent pool that stretched all the way down to the Fifth Circle. "I understand perfectly." The receptionist smiled at me, reached over, and pressed a button on the counter. Then continued to smile as a steel plate slammed down in front of the window. A similar plate slammed down in front of both interior and exterior doors, and a hissing sound began to emanate from the vents. We were being gassed. Great.

"I understand that you and your rude bitch of a boss can go fuck yourselves. I don't work for Homeland Security, I work for the Master, and he shall reward me greatly when I bring him the desiccated corpse of Quincy Harker."

I turned to Becks and Pravesh, who had both pulled shirts up over their noses to try and keep some of whatever kind of gas was rushing in from affecting them. "Okay, so it seems my reputation, and mugshot, have preceded me. Let me deal with this gas bullshit first."

I called up power until my hair tingled, then shoved both hands out from my chest at the exterior wall. *"Forzare!"* I shouted, releasing all of the energy in a huge burst. The wall blew outward in a shower of brick and drywall, giving the gas plenty of space to dissipate. Also giving Pravesh a chance to go grab some gas masks out of the back of her Suburban.

"Subtle," Bubba said from the floor. He had managed to drag himself up into a sitting position, but his hands were still clenched into claws and he hadn't quite managed to fully extend his arms yet, giving him the look of a hairy T-Rex.

"I've always thought it dumb that people will spend all that money reinforcing a door and its frame, but nothing on strengthening the wall three feet away from it," I said.

"Yeah, I've said the same thing when I blew big holes in buildings, too," Bubba replied.

Pravesh came back with four gas masks, and after we all masked up and Bubba managed to get to his feet, I turned my attention to the inner door. It was my favorite time of day—time to blow shit up.

16

I looked at the inner door, then at Bubba, who was flexing his arms and hands as the feeling and mobility returned. "I think that maybe just knocking is probably off the table," I said. We knew there was at least one mundane trap on the door, but I dropped my Sight down over my normal vision to take a peek at things in the magical spectrum. The whole place lit up like a Christmas tree. There was magical energy *everywhere*. For an organization that worked hard at getting rid of cryptids and magical beings, they certainly slung plenty of magic around their office.

The front door was warded to protect from basically any kind of extradimensional entity, the lobby floor was warded to dampen magical powers, and the ceiling was covered in sigils and glyphs designed to make the whole place uncomfortable to any non-humans. The only problem was, none of them seemed to actually work. Three of the four of us were at least partially non-human, and no one seemed to be suffering any ill effects, and I definitely didn't have any trouble calling up my mojo to blast the wall out of existence.

I looked more closely at the symbols on the door, and after a minute or two of searching, I found the flaw in the design. One of the letters was touching the outer circle, reducing the effectiveness of the ward. I kept looking and found a few other spots where that happened. These wards had been drawn by someone who knew what they were doing, but they had also been intentionally sabotaged, probably by the same person, and done so in such a way that only a master magician would be able to tell what was happening. To anyone with only a little training or not much magical ability, it would look like the caster just wasn't very powerful. The same thing went for the wards on the ceiling, and the floor as well. Someone had sabotaged the wards at DEMON headquarters, and whoever it was had enough skill and power to hide it from almost anyone who looked at the casting. This place just got curiouser and curiouser the more I looked around.

Then I focused my attention on the interior door, and things got even weirder. Every surface in the front office was warded, even if the wards were half-assed and nearly useless. But they were there. The front door, the floor, the ceiling, even the Ficus tree in the corner had a spell on it to make it return to that spot if it was moved. But there was nothing on the door leading into the rest of the building.

"Huh," I said. "That's kinda fucked up."

"What is it?" Pravesh asked.

I dropped my Sight and blinked a few times as my eyes adjusted back to the normal spectrum. It was extra difficult because there was so much magic thrown around the room. It took several seconds for the hyper-saturated colors of the magical spectrum to fade and me to look at people without them having Day-Glo skin. "There's nothing on the door."

"I beg to damn differ," Bubba grumbled.

"There's nothing *magical* on the door," I said by way of clarification. "I can't just look at the thing and see through it. I'm not Superman."

"Boy, I wish I'd had a recorder going to catch that last sentence," Becks said.

"Love you too, babe," I replied. "But seriously, this is weird. There's magic on every surface of this room. Shit, even the *plant* is warded.

But not the door. The thing with the mundane boobytrap doesn't warrant a magical one? I don't get it."

"I don't know, bud, but does that mean you can just whammy the door out of the way so I can go find whoever rigged it to zap my ass and slap the piss out of them?" Bubba asked. I had to give the big lummox credit, he had a brand and he stuck to it.

"Sounds like a plan." I called up power and raised my fists to blast through the wall, then stopped as Becks held up a hand.

"Wait a second, Harker."

I lowered my hands but didn't let the power flow back out of me. For one thing, it's easier to hold power than to draw it from the surrounding environment. For another, it made my fists glow, which looked cool as hell. "What's up?" I asked.

"Just hold that thought for a second." Becks stepped through the gaping hole I'd made in the wall, then walked backward about ten feet, turned to the right, and disappeared from view. A few seconds later, she reappeared through the hole and walked off to the left. She came back into the lobby and said, "That wall? The one you're about to reduce to concrete dust? It's the side of the landscape company's warehouse."

"Wait, what?" I asked.

"Look for yourself. We came into this building on the side. We're facing the landscape company's wall. If you blow that door out, it'll make a hole right into a bunch of shovels, pavers, and bags of cement."

We all walked outside and looked around, and sure enough, she was right. There was no way the interior door of that office led anywhere but into the landscape company's warehouse. Unless there was a Gate framed in the doorway, and that would definitely have shown up in my Sight.

"So, where's the headquarters?" I asked.

"And where did the receptionist go?" Bubba added.

"Why don't we go in there and find out?" Pravesh asked, pointing at the steel panel that dropped in over the sliding window to the reception area. If there wasn't any kind of dimensional monkey business going on with the building, I figured I should be able to blast my way through the steel without wrecking the adjoining business. But I decided to try a more subtle approach regardless.

I walked over and placed the palms of both hands on the steel, realizing about half a second too late that if it was electrified my day was about to take a turn for the truly shitty, but nothing zapped me. I drew energy from the air around me, concentrating on the water vapor in the air, then slowly pushed that power into the steel, whispering, *"Transvorto,"* as I did. I felt the power flow out of me, a rippling wave instead of the blasts I typically use, and as it slid through the metal, I felt the surface shift, buckle, and begin to ripple outward from my palms.

I poured power into the steel for almost a solid minute, keeping the word *"transvorto"* in the front of my mind all the while, and finally, when I felt like there was no more space in the steel panel for more power, I stepped back and released the spell, repeating my trigger word as I did. *"Transvorto!"*

The massive sheet of steel turned to liquid and flowed down and across the floor, causing all of us to jump back and to the side to keep from ruining our shoes. And from possibly being fused to the floor when the steel re-solidified. I kinda didn't think about how long it was going to stay liquid when I transformed it. After a few seconds of liquid steel flowing across the floor, we were all perched on various pieces of office furniture and the outer office had been redecorated in Silver Surfer.

"Cool," I said. "That worked."

"You didn't know if it would work?" Bubba asked.

"There's always the potential for a new spell to go horribly wrong."

"What would have happened if this went horribly wrong?" he asked.

"No idea," I replied. "I always assume things are going to work out perfectly."

"Which is why he has the most exhausted Guardian Angel in history," Becks said.

I ignored her and hopped down off the chair I was standing on, then walked across the sliding window and knocked on it. Nobody answered, and the office beyond looked empty, so I put my hand on the glass.

"You gonna melt this, too?" Bubba asked.

"Nah," I said, sending a pulse of magical force through my palm, shattering the glass. "I blow out a window, there's a bunch of glass to sift through when I'm done. I blow out a massive metal blast door, who knows what kind of mess I'm going to have to deal with. Plus, this time I could see that I wasn't going to squish anybody on the other side."

I took off my overshirt, wrapped it around my right hand, and used that to clear the glass from the window frame. Then I hauled myself through the opening and looked around the office. "Hey gang?" I called over my shoulder.

"What is it, babe?" Becks replied.

"There's no door in here."

"Yeah, we were wondering how we get from out here to in there, too."

"You're missing part of my meaning," I said. "There's *no* door. Like, nothing."

"Seriously?" Becks asked, then hopped through the window herself. I'm constantly amazed at how nimble she is, especially for someone without any kind of enhanced abilities.

"If y'all think I'm getting through that hole, you got another think comin'," Bubba said. "I could probably do it, but I don't know who you think is gonna catch me on the other side."

I looked back at the behemoth and shook my head. I could certainly handle his weight, but let's be real: I didn't want to. I just stepped sideways, put my hands on the wall, and blew out the plaster-board, a motivational poster, and about three wall studs. "That should do you," I said, dusting off my hands. I was starting to hope that we didn't run into too much opposition that required magic, because I'd expended a lot of my reserves melting steel and blowing up parts of the building.

I don't have to use my own power for magic. I can draw it in from living things around me, and from the internal energy of the world.

There are leylines running everywhere, carrying magical power from place to place like a network of rivers. Sometimes they're closer to the surface than others, and occasionally they intersect, forming nodes of power, collection points that people like me can draw upon for powerful workings.

Unfortunately, that also means that a lot of other people can draw on those nodes, too. So they're often not the fantastic sources of energy they seem to be, because somebody else has drained a node temporarily, or polluted one with a bad casting, or just corrupted one completely with evil magic. I haven't seen any of those in the U.S., though. It's generally too young a country to have nodes gone really foul.

But even with nodes and leylines, and there are plenty of lines running under Washington D.C., it takes personal energy to direct the flow of power, and it takes willpower to make sure the magic does what you want it to do, or at least a reasonable approximation. So, after blowing up a lot of shit, my reserves were low, the leylines around D.C. were crowded and sucked pretty thin, and *now* we were about to start exploring the headquarters of the government agency that had been trying to kill me and everyone I loved for at least the past two years.

One of these days, I'll have an easy gig. Of course, this was not going to be that day.

17

I'll look through the desk, you two see if you can find the exit," Becks said.

"You don't just want your boyfriend to make one?" Bubba asked.

"In a pinch, sure, but I'm a little curious as to where the receptionist went, and I don't think blowing the walls out is going to tell us that." Becks sat down at the abandoned desk and jiggled the mouse.

"Hold on," I said. "It's probably got some kind of tamper protection on it."

Becks turned the chair around and looked at me like I was the biggest moron in the room. "And what exactly are you going to do about it? You can't even set the clock on the microwave."

"I know," I replied. "I just wanted to make sure you thought about it."

She shook her head and turned back around to the keyboard. The monitor lit up to a screen asking for a password, so I turned to my assigned task rather than trying to play super-hacker. I'm a lot of things, but tech-savvy isn't really on the list. Comes from being born in a time when trains still ran on coal and the telegraph was considered high-tech communication. Bubba was tapping on the walls opposite the window, and the one to my right was the exterior, so I started running my fingers along the bottom of the counter, then to the sides of the window frame, and finally followed the big guy's lead and started tapping on the walls. Nothing seemed out of the ordinary, until I shifted into my Sight and looked around the room magically.

The same wards and protections were drawn on the floor and ceiling here, and the remaining pane of glass was heavily enchanted, too. I assumed the one I blew out was similarly protected, which explained why I was tired. Blowing up a window is pretty easy. Blowing up a magically protected window takes a lot more oomph. Something odd caught my eye, and I stuck my head through the hole into the lobby to confirm my suspicion. The same "snap-back" charm was on both the Ficus tree in the lobby and the coat rack in the small office. Not a huge deal, but potentially significant, since nothing else was enchanted to return to its proper place if moved.

"Hey Pravesh," I called to the lobby.

"Yes, Quincy?"

"Can you pick up the Ficus tree and move it to the middle of the floor?"

"Why?"

"Testing a theory. Also, maybe kick it first to make sure it's not trapped. I don't see anything, but if it's not magical, I wouldn't."

I watched as she prodded the plant with her foot, and when nothing happened, grabbed the trunk of the fake tree and lifted it. Or tried to, at any rate. The plant seemed to be firmly affixed to the floor.

Pravesh turned to glare at me. "Very funny, Quincy."

I held up both hands. "Not me, boss lady. I just saw it's been enchanted to return to its position if moved, there's nothing magical holding it where it is."

Pravesh looked more closely at the plant, then knelt by the woven basket that served as a pot. From a distance, it looked like the fake Ficus tree you see in every cheaply decorated office and public access TV studio in the nation. But as she fiddled with it, the whole assemblage slid out from the corner at a forty-five-degree angle, and the floor of the lobby dropped away.

"Holy shit," I said. I reached over and grabbed the coat rack, jerking it all around until I found the track where it slid, and a narrow section of the office floor fell away, leaving a trapdoor open right behind Bubba's feet.

"Careful with that shit, Harker," Bubba said, shooting me a dirty look. Becks drew her sidearm and aimed it straight down into the darkness. We had found where the receptionist went, at least.

"Well," I said. "Let's go down into the secret lair underneath the secret headquarters of the secret government agency that wants to murder us all, shall we?"

I led the way, since I have better night vision than Bubba, Becks, and pretty much everybody. We left Pravesh in the lobby to keep the outside door covered and to handle anyone who tried to run out through that hole in the floor. We had no idea how big the underground lair was, but I assumed that the two entrances connected somehow. I was right, as there was a set of stairs leading up to the light as soon as we got down into the...office? It felt like "lair" should be the right word, but lairs don't usually have cheap motivational posters on the wall and crappy indoor/outdoor carpet. I flipped a switch on the wall, and cold LED lights illuminated everything in their stark glare.

"I don't know what I was expecting," I said. "But this isn't it."

"Looks about like every other secret DEMON facility I've been in," Bubba said.

"He's not wrong, Harker," Becks agreed. And he wasn't. It had the same feel as the place in Memphis where I first learned DEMON even *had* secret facilities, and it was a lot like the place in Charlotte where I fought a were-bear and freed a faerie princess. That went well, said literally no one involved.

"Which way?" Becks asked. "Do you see anything magical?"

I looked around with my Sight, but the hall we were in was completely devoid of magic. It was just a long corridor with two sets of stairs and a nondescript door at each end. No wards, no magic boobytraps, nothing like the protections I'd seen upstairs. "Nothing at all," I said. "Which is almost stranger than finding something, given the levels of protection in the front offices."

"Maybe they figure if anything bad gets down here, they're already so screwed it don't matter," Bubba said.

"Could be," I agreed, drawing my pistol. "But that doesn't mean there's not bad shit down here."

"Copy that," the big guy said, drawing his sword.

"You sure you don't want a gun?" I asked. "I can throw fireballs and you can use mine."

He locked eyes with me and shook his head. "Nah. If I need to kill something, I'll get up close and personal with 'em."

The look in his eyes worried me more than if he was still toting around that ridiculous handgun he'd carried when we first met. He felt like he had nothing left to lose, so he didn't care if he lived or died. Might even have preferred Option B. I knew that look. I'd seen it in my own eyes enough, and I knew there wasn't fuckall I could do to help him feel better about Father Joe's death. That was a weight he'd have to carry for the rest of his days. Or he'd decide he couldn't, and he wouldn't have very many more days. That was just how our business worked. It sucked, but that was the deal.

"Go left," Becks said. "Everybody always goes right, so let's screw with that. If there's anybody down here, they won't be expecting us to go left."

"Unless they know we know that everyone goes right, so they expect us to go left," I said.

"Are you gonna do the whole poison scene from *The Princess Bride*, or are we gonna go down the frickin' hallway?" Bubba asked, starting off toward the left-hand door.

He opened it, and I'll admit to being a little disappointed he didn't get electrocuted again, but that's just because I'm a jerk. Bubba moved right as he went through the door, and I came through behind him sweeping left. Becks followed me and slapped a panel on the wall, bringing more LED tubes to life. The reveal was anti-climactic, just what looked like it used to be a cube farm, but everything was gone. And I mean everything was gone. Desks, chairs, computers, even the cubicle walls were gone. Some network cables hung from the ceiling in a few spots, and there was one lonely clear plastic chair mat on the floor, but otherwise it was deserted.

"Well, that certainly speaks to there being a larger entrance some-where," Becks said. "Because no way did anyone cart all this stuff out of here up those narrow stairs."

She was right. There had to be some kind of loading dock or something, and that meant that there was more facility on the other side of the wooden door at the far end of the empty room. We walked through the deserted room, sticking to the aisles marked out by depressions in the carpet. It's funny how that works. No matter if all the furnishings and equipment is gone from a place, if you can see where the traffic patterns used to be, you instinctively follow them.

I gave the door a glance, then turned to Bubba. "You're our designated lock pick, big guy. Go for it."

He gave me a tight grin and planted his foot right next to the door-knob. The frame splintered and the door swung inward. I gave him a questioning look and he shrugged. "Maybe the last one wasn't trapped to give us a false sense of security."

"You just wanted to break something," Becks accused.

"It's been a few minutes, and Harker got to blow up the last thing."

My fiancée shook her head, muttering something about "two of them," and stepped through the door. She flipped on the lights and let out a low whistle. I followed her into the space beyond the door and stopped cold, stunned by the size of the room before me.

"Holy shit," I said in a low voice.

"What?" Bubba asked, pushing past me. "Holy shit is right."

We were standing in what looked like an aircraft hangar, but not one of the little hangars like at a private airfield. No, this space was big enough to park a pair of jumbo jets in side by side and not have their wings overlap. It was at least a hundred yards long, and twice that wide, with a ceiling arching at least fifty feet above us. The space was huge, and brightly lit with hundreds of LED fixtures mounted in the ceiling, and completely, utterly empty.

I stepped forward and clapped my hands, listening as the *crack* echoed through the massive room. It was a spartan space, with bare concrete floors, sheetrock on the walls only up to about ten feet, then bare joists and insulation above that, and open roof joists overhead. Power drops came down about every ten feet, and I walked over to take a look at the nearest one. A blue ethernet cable twined around a pair of heavy black electrical cords, one ending in a regular three-pronged plug and the other with a five-slotted round connector that didn't look like anything I was familiar with. I held it up to the others, and Bubba nodded.

"That's a 208V connector. Whatever they were running in here used some serious power."

"And there are data drops everywhere. What the hell was this place?"

"Well, they were experimenting on all kinds of cryptids in Florida," Bubba said. "Could be this place was more of the same."

"There was a facility in Charlotte doing the same thing, but it was nothing like this," I said.

"You think maybe this is where they sent the biggest and baddest critters?" the big Hunter asked.

"I don't think I want to know what they needed a room this big to study," I replied. My mind flashed back to the dragon I'd met in Memphis a couple years ago, and I wondered if she, or one of her people, had been trapped in a facility like this.

"Let's fan out and give this place a quick once-over," Becks said. "Doesn't look like there's much to see, but maybe something important got dropped when they were packing up."

I walked off to the right to begin my search for anything useful but froze when I heard something coming from the far end of the hangar. "On me," I called to the others. "Pretty sure I just heard somebody start an engine."

We started sprinting toward the far end of the hangar just as a chunk of wall exploded and a black Suburban roared into the hangar with the receptionist from upstairs behind the wheel. She roared across the concrete, and I shifted course to intercept. Guess we should have picked the right-hand door after all.

18

I hauled ass across the warehouse after the fleeing SUV. *Can we just go one fucking month without someone driving a black Suburban through a wall and trying to murder me?*

Apparently not, Becks thought back to me. *Maybe you should stop pissing off people with access to the government's motor pool.* A trio of flat *crack*s came from behind and to the right of me, and three bullet marks appeared on the side of the Suburban. Becks's bullets didn't penetrate the SUV's armor plating, and a segment of the far wall started to slide down into the floor, revealing a ramp and daylight above.

I stopped running, realizing that my hundred eighty pounds of wizard was not going to be able to stop a bulletproof three-ton Suburban hauling ass across a football field-sized warehouse floor. Not by jumping on it, anyway. I could stop it, but this was not a time for brute force. I reached down to the nearly depleted leyline and drew up power, feeling the line go completely dry as energy flowed into me, making my hair stand on end and magic crackle all over my skin in purple sparks.

I thrust my hands forward, aiming at a wide section of floor about twenty yards in front of the exit, and shouted, *"CALOR!"* A ball of shimmering power flew from my palms, and I dropped to one knee, exhausted. The magic struck the concrete, and where once a smooth floor had been, a second later a span of bubbling melted goo several yards across and thirty feet long remained. The Suburban couldn't avoid the molten concrete, and all four tires exploded when they made contact. The run-flat wheels couldn't do anything buried to the axle in thousand-degree glowing red stone, and the vehicle stopped short.

The nose of the SUV dipped from the momentum, and steam shot out of the radiator as every drop of water instantly boiled away to nothing. Flames billowed from under the hood, which buckled and bowed in the extreme heat. The driver's door flew open, and the terrified receptionist looked out at the lake of melted slab under her feet. She ducked back into the SUV, and a few seconds later, the back glass of the Suburban exploded outward and she clambered through, landing on an unmelted section of floor. The heat must have still been incredible, and she threw a hand up to cover her face. She looked right, then left, and sprinted around the melted section of floor toward the ramp.

A bullet ricocheted off the ground in front of her and she froze, whirling around. Becks stood about twenty yards away from her, pistol in hand, waving merrily. Bubba was still closing in on her, sword drawn. I had managed to struggle back to my feet, but I was not going to be relevant to any fight for the near future. I was completely out of juice, and the nearest leyline was drained down to a dry streamed of magical energy. It would replenish eventually, and so would I, but neither of us were good for any workings, major or minor, for a while. But magic isn't the only weapon at my disposal, so I drew my Glock and held it down by my side as I staggered toward our quarry.

"Just stop," I called to her. "Stop running. It's getting embarrassing. You disappear, and we find you. You bolt in a car, and we stop you. If you turn around and run now, we're just going to catch you again, so why not just save us the trouble and hold still until we ask you a few questions?"

"Yeah, like who's the Master and where can we find his ass?" Bubba said, approaching from the left. Becks had the receptionist covered from the right, and I was walking straight toward her, with just enough magic left to give my eyes a purple flicker.

She looked from Bubba to me, to Becks, back to me, then smiled and raised her right arm straight out, palm down, in a chilling salute that took me back to Europe in the 40s. "You will never defeat the Master. The Reich shall rule for a thousand years. *Heil Führer!*" Then she bit down hard and fell to the ground. We all sprinted to her, but by the time anyone reached her, she was dead, her lips flecked with foam and a vicious grin on her face. She might have died, but she kept us from learning anything from her in the process.

My guts roiled, as much from emotion as from the outlay of power. Nazis? Again? Real life, no shit Nazis in Washington, D.C.? Working for the U.S. government? What the fuck? I'd fought those bastards the first time around and paid a heavy price for it. Exacted a heavy toll, too. I didn't have any idea how many Nazis I killed through Germany, France, and Austria during the War, and didn't want to know. That was during a dark time for me, after one of them murdered Anna right in front of my face and I went berserk for a little while. When I came back to myself, I was in America, and Luke has steadfastly refused to give me details on the things I did while in my murderous fugue state, only saying that it was bloody, it was far-reaching, and I never killed anyone that didn't deserve it. I promise, it's a cold comfort indeed having Vlad the Impaler give you his stamp of approval on your murderous rampage.

And now there were Nazis working for the U.S. government. I mean, I kinda knew it, but I thought they were watered-down, white shirt and khakis kind of mama's boys chickenshit incel Nazis that march around chanting and are only brave when they're standing behind a bunch of cops or driving cars into unarmed civilians. The kind of half-assed Nazis that listen to the music but don't get the tattoos. But these were real, Hitler-saluting Nazis, embedded deep into federal law enforcement, with poison teeth and everything. They weren't carrying tiki torches looking like the opening act at a Grindr convention. The fuckers were carrying badges, just like me. Indistinguishable from the good guys. This woman looked like a soccer mom, or that bitchy neighbor. But she threw up the Nazi salute like she'd been Heiling Hitler her whole life. Fuck.

"Well, shit," Bubba said. "That's going to make her harder to interrogate."

"True, but it doesn't mean no forensics. And it certainly doesn't mean we don't search the vehicle for anything she was trying to escape with," Becks said.

"Nazis," I muttered, looking down at the receptionist's corpse. "Fucking Nazis."

"Reckon you've got some experience with the O.G. version," Bubba said.

"Yeah," I replied. "Too much."

"So what do we do about 'em?" he asked.

"Kill them. Kill every fucking one of them, burn the bodies, salt the earth, and piss on their graves." I looked up at the big man, expecting some comment on how I was going too far.

He just nodded. "Sounds about right."

SIX HOURS LATER, I WAS COMPLETELY EXHAUSTED. NOT JUST MY MAGIC reserves, but physically and mentally, too. I was up to my eyeballs in folders, receipts, calendars, planners, and boxes upon boxes of boring-ass paperwork. I sat on the floor of a ten-by-twenty file room filled to the ceiling with banker's boxes trying to decide exactly how likely it was that setting fire to the entire goddamn mess would kill me. I finally settled on the fact that it might not kill me but would probably do some grievous harm to Becks, so I just flung a folder across the room and let out a yell of frustration.

"You alright in there, little buddy?" Bubba called from across the hall. I'm not sure when in our quest through the magical jungles of Paperworklandia that he decided to start calling me "little buddy," but apparently I hadn't been quick enough to put the kibosh on it, and now it was stuck.

"Fine," I replied. "Just hating all this paperwork bullshit. Couldn't these assholes put their information on a network like civilized Nazi fuckwads?"

"They probably could," Pravesh called from another file room further down the hall. "But then we'd have to hack it, and search it, and that would take at least as long."

And that's assuming they're stupid enough to leave important information on the server. The smartest way to hide data these days is on paper in the middle of a bunch of other paper. The proverbial needle in the haystack, Becks said through our mental link.

I stood up, hearing popping sounds in my knees, my back, and a couple of random pops that I don't know where they came from. "Let's regroup," I called. "Everybody meet up in the break room."

I had to hand it to DEMON: they had the whole hiding in plain sight thing down cold. Nothing in the break room looked like it was a place run by Nazis. It was your basic tiny corporate break room, the kind of place where you walk in and wonder why a room that size even existed. It was too small for all the shit crammed into it and too big to serve as a broom closet.

There were four lights sunk into the drop ceiling, and three of them even worked. There was a small counter with a sink, a microwave, a toaster, one of those little one-cup coffee makers, a real coffeepot, an electric kettle for tea, a bagel toaster, and a toaster oven. Then there was about six inches of clear countertop for people to actually prepare food. The fridge was a massive double-door model with tape over the place in the door where ice came out. "Broken" was written on the tape in big black Sharpie. There was a round table dominating the center of the room, its surface covered in takeout menus, soy sauce packets, packs of plastic silverware from restaurants, and stacks of napkins with various logos of fast-food places on them. There was also a coffee cup full of salt and pepper packets and a jar of non-dairy powdered creamer that had turned into a solid block of whatever chemicals go into non-dairy creamer. It looked like the kind of place where mid-level government functionaries gather to spread gossip and rumors about other mid-level government functionaries.

I sat down at the table and grabbed a napkin, folding it into a small square and wedging it under one leg to stop the wobble. "This is getting us nowhere," I said as the others walked in.

"And I'm gettin' hungry," Bubba said as he walked to the fridge and pulled open the door. "I'm about ready to eat whatever the hell is in Carol's Tupperware here, just because it's got less shit growing on it than anything else."

"I don't know if that's a mark of safety or an indicator that it can murder mold," I replied.

"Shit. Good point." He reached into the fridge and grabbed a can of soda. I held up a hand and he passed me one, then cracked his own.

"Unfortunately, I agree with you," Pravesh said as she sat down, having abandoned her post in the lobby once it became apparent that no one was going to try to escape that way, because there was no one here besides us. "Our searching has been fruitless, and there is still a mountain of paper to sort through. Our time is better spent elsewhere. I will assign some of our newer agents to come over here and look for clues. But where should we direct our efforts? This trip has been somewhat less than productive."

"I'm not quite sure about that, Director," Becks said. She stood in the doorway with a thick ledger in one hand and her phone in the other. "I think I've got something."

She sat down and opened the ledger on the table. Bubba came over and took the last chair, much to the protest of its thin metal legs. "After the first couple of hours of turning up a big bag of fuck-all, I asked myself the question every investigator must ask—"

"Where's the nearest doughnut shop?" I cut in, earning myself a nasty look.

"What would Batman do?" Becks replied. "I thought back to all the mysteries I've read, and all the cases I've worked, and the first question we always asked, unless the murderer was standing at the crime scene covered in blood with a weapon in their hand, which happens more often than you'd think, was 'who benefits?' In this case, the Master ultimately benefits, but to make that happen, he's going to have to benefit a lot of unsavory assholes along the way. We just need to find out which unsavory asshole not only benefits but can give us information as well."

"And you figured this out how?" I asked.

"This ledger seems to have been our receptionist's insurance policy. It was hidden in a box labeled 'Christmas Decorations,' which seemed pretty out of place on a shelf full of purchase requisitions. There were Christmas ornaments in there, but also a record of every lobbyist DEMON has paid off in the last three years."

"Three years? Is that how long DEMON has been dirty?" Bubba asked.

"At least. That seems to be when Alicia, the receptionist, started working here. There are a lot of lobbyists on this list, most of them with ties to the NRA, various right-wing media outlets, and Big Pharma. But one name came up more often than any other and has an entry from just a few days ago."

"You wanna share that name with us, or just sit there looking smug?" I asked.

"I want to sit here and look smug for just a little longer as you bask in my brilliance." She sat still for a long ten-count, then leaned forward. "Okay, that's good. I think we should concentrate our efforts on one James Liang, owner of JCI Consulting, a lobbying firm with an office in Alexandria."

"Well, let's go pay Mister Liang a visit," I said. "I have about a hundred paper cuts he needs to answer for."

19

The lobbyist's office was empty, but the sign on the door said, "Back in 15 minutes," so we waited in the Suburban until a neatly dressed woman in her forties with her hair in a bun and glasses on a chain walked up carrying a bag of what looked like anonymous takeout food and unlocked the door. I reached for the door handle, but Becks clicked the lock button.

"I'll handle this one, babe," she said.

"Why? You don't think I can interrogate a receptionist?"

"Probably not. And if this one is deep into anything dark, she probably has a cyanide tooth like the woman at DEMON HQ. Best case, she's been warned not to talk to you and given your description, so we get the cops called on us first thing."

"Worst case?" I asked.

"You've met you, right?" Becks asked. "I don't even want to think about what the worst case could be because anything I can think of will pale in comparison to whatever actually happens. Your worst cases are so much worse than any normal person's, it makes me wish there was another word for them because 'worst' seems inadequate."

I opened my mouth to protest, then closed it. She was right. For most people, the worst-case scenario for interrogating someone suspected of helping a bad guy was the police getting called and being thrown out or arrested for trespassing. That was my best case. My worst case was probably something on the level of the receptionist actually being Lucifer himself in disguise, ripping my heart out of my chest and eating it in front of me before dragging my soul to Hell to roast in the fires of torment for all eternity. And that's just the worst case I could think of on the fly. There were probably half a dozen even worse scenarios that would all be perfectly reasonable if I considered them.

So I sat in the back seat of the SUV and watched between Bubba and Pravesh's shoulders as my fiancée went into the office of someone we knew to be at the very least a Nazi sympathizer. With no backup. We were close, as close as possible without being stapled to her, but I'm enough of a chauvinist to still want to protect the woman I love. I'm also acutely aware of how quickly a situation can go pear-shaped, even without me present to stir the pot.

"Lean back a little, buddy," Bubba growled.

"Would you?" I shot back.

"No, but I can't literally read Amy's mind."

He had a point. I do have some advantages over normal people, aside from my sparkling wit and dashing good looks. I closed my eyes and opened the channel from my mind to Becks's as wide as I could, allowing me to see what she was seeing. It was a little disconcerting, riding along in someone's head like that, but it was better than not having any idea what was happening.

You know this makes you like the world's biggest voyeur, right? Becks asked across our mental link.

I know it makes me a little seasick watching the world through your eyes. Did you know you're a touch nearsighted?

Full human, Harker. We actually age. And yes, I know I'm a little near-sighted. I can still see well enough to shoot the wings off a fly at a hundred yards, so don't worry about that.

Yeah, what kind of scope you using to shoot that fly? I teased. *But seriously, this is like a first-person shooter video game, only in VR.*

Well, let's hope you don't have to see any heads explode in this one. Now be quiet and let me get to work.

Becks walked in the office, a digital tone announcing her arrival. The receptionist stood, smiling. "May I help you?" A nameplate on her desk announced her as Marcia Waller.

"Yes, ma'am," Becks replied, holding up her credentials. "I'm Deputy Director Rebecca Flynn, with Homeland Security. I need to speak with Mr. Liang."

The other woman's face fell, and she took a step back from her desk. This was obviously not someone accustomed to having badges in her face. "I'm terribly sorry, but Mr. Liang is not in the office this afternoon. He's on the Hill in meetings."

Becks smiled at her and put her badge wallet away. "That's fine. I'm sure I can catch up to him over there. Who is he meeting with?"

The receptionist kept her smiled glued on, but it slipped a little at the corner as she shook her head. "I'm sorry, I can't divulge that information. Mr. Liang has business dealings with some very important people, and—"

"More important than the agency that renditions people to Gitmo on the regular?" Becks asked, her words coated with threat.

Damn, went from zero to sixty in one sentence. You might have been spending a little too much time with me, I said.

My therapist agrees with you, Harker, but I'm not in the mood to screw around with a functionary. We need to find this Liang so we can hunt down the asshole who's dropped a lot of bodies in my city this summer. So if she wants to play roadblock, I'll just run her ass right over.

Becks took a step forward and put a hand on the reception desk. "Ms. Waller, I don't want to play hardball, but Mr. Liang has gotten mixed up with some very dangerous individuals, and we need his help eliminating a major threat to our national security. It is imperative that I speak with him this afternoon, so if you'll just sit back down at your computer, open up his calendar program, and tell me where he is and who he's meeting, I'll get out of your hair and you can get back to whatever it is you do when you're left to your own devices."

Waller gulped once, almost dramatically, then did exactly what

Becks asked her to do. She sat down, moved her mouse to wake up her computer, clicked her mouse a few times, then tore a sheet of paper off a legal pad and wrote a name and address on it. Between Becks's nearsightedness, the wobbliness of being in someone else's head, and the words being upside down, I couldn't read what she wrote, but Becks seemed satisfied.

"Thank you," Becks said, and turned to go. She put her hand on the doorknob, then stopped and looked back at Waller. "I'm sure it goes without saying that calling Mr. Liang to alert him of our interest in him would be considered at best a very bad idea, and at worst obstruction of a federal investigation. You understand that, don't you?"

"Y-y-yes."

"Excellent. Your country thanks you." Becks walked out the door and back to the SUV, grinning like the cat that ate the canary.

"Nice work, love," I said.

"Thanks. It felt good to be the heavy for a change. Usually my badge and threats of arrest aren't nearly as intimidating as anything you or Luke might do to someone if they don't do what we ask, so it felt good to be able to throw my weight around."

"I can relate," Bubba said. "I throw my weight around all the time. I love it."

No one spoke for a long moment, then he continued. "What? The fat guy doesn't get to make fat jokes? Come on, y'all. Lighten up. Now let's go find this little peckerwood and whoop his ass 'til he tells us everything we want to know."

Pravesh apparently agreed with that plan of action because she backed the Suburban out of its parking space and we headed downtown to do exactly that.

"ACCORDING TO THE SECRETARY, LIANG IS MEETING THE JUNIOR Senator from Alabama for lunch at the Washington Monument. Apparently, there's a burrito truck there that he's a big fan of. If we find Scalzi's Burritos, we're guaranteed to find Liang," Becks said as Pravesh pulled the SUV into a parking garage.

"I could go for a burrito," Bubba said, sliding out of the passenger seat and walking around to the back of the Suburban.

"You know we aren't going there to get lunch, right?" I asked, opening one of the weapons cases Pravesh had bolted to the floor of her vehicle. I didn't know if all the DHS Paranormal Division SUVs came with arsenals, but I was happy to pick up a few extra magazines for my Glock and strap a backup .380 to my ankle.

"I know," Bubba replied. "But after we beat the shit out of this guy, we might have worked up an appetite, and it's good to know there are affordable food options nearby. I don't know if you noticed, but this place is expensive as shit."

"I didn't, actually," I said. "My uncle's rich and my fiancée has an expense account. I kinda don't pay attention to money much."

"Must be nice. I've been broke as a damn convict ever since we got back from Fairyland."

"I thought you owned a gym?" Becks asked, tightening the Velcro straps on a bulletproof vest. I thought that was a little overkill to take down a lobbyist, but I was a lot harder to kill, so I didn't really have a normal person's perspective.

"I do, but it don't generate a whole lot of profit. It basically covers expenses, with a few bucks a month left over to replace antiquated equipment. Titanium weights are great for weres and other cryptids, but they're spendy. It was a good thing Amy got this gig working for Homeland Security. Don't tell her I said so, but she really sucked as a waitress."

"She worked in a restaurant?" I asked.

"We both worked at a local bar until it got burned down by zombies. I was a whole lot better bouncer than she was a waitress. Makes sense, since hitting things is kinda my entire work experience. And lemme tell you, when you switch from punching monsters to humans, it's like you just flipped the whole game to easy mode."

I wasn't exactly sure what he was talking about, but Becks laughed, so I assumed it was some kind of twentieth century thing that I didn't understand. That happens a lot. I lived through the entire century, but since I grew up between the turn of the century and World War I, my formative years were very different from someone who grew up with things like video games. Or television, for that matter. And God forbid I have to talk to someone who has never known life without the internet. It's almost like we don't even speak the same language.

I looked around at the team I was taking into what I really hoped wouldn't be a battle. But I've met me, so I knew the odds of us just strolling up to James Liang and asking him a few questions, then going on our merry way were pretty slim. Pravesh was in a casual pantsuit with her jacket cut to hide her pistol. I knew she carried at least three extra magazines, and that all her rounds were silver-jacketed. Becks was loaded for bear with an MP-7 on a sling, a Kevlar vest, a Glock on her hip, and at least one silver-tipped stake tucked up a sleeve. I had a shirt open and untucked to hide my own Glock, and the Ruger on my right leg, but I hoped I wouldn't have to draw either of them.

Bubba was the anomaly. Everything I'd ever read about him said he was more attached to his firepower than most men are to their dicks, but all he had on him was that weird old sword. I dropped into my Sight for a second to try and figure out what enchantments were on it, but it was something I'd never seen before. There was old magic there, and something else, something that I didn't recognize. And for a guy who's literally fought alongside Archangels and stood toe-to-toe with Lucifer himself, I've seen some shit.

But this wasn't the time to investigate Bubba's magic sword. This was time to go see a man about some money, and about the assholes he'd been taking that money from. I reached down into the earth, feeling the thrumming energy that ran under the Washington Mall. Yeah, casting wouldn't be any problem. I was rested enough to recharge my own batteries, at least partially, and there was more than enough juice flowing through the lines beneath our feet to power anything I wanted to cast.

I clapped my hands and closed the tailgate of the Suburban. "Okay, gang. Let's do this."

20

Pravesh led the way, since me, Becks, and Bubba looked like a trio of bad video game characters ready to storm the boss's citadel. Liang was pretty distinctive, as he was a six-foot tall Asian dude with salt-and-pepper hair and an overpriced suit. And he happened to be sitting on a bench next to a U.S. Senator with a pair of Secret Service agents standing around being not the least bit discreet. We hung back as Pravesh went over to one of the agents and discreetly flashed her badge. The agent said something into his sleeve, then walked away with his buddy in tow.

"Not bad," Bubba murmured. "That's two we don't need to beat the crap out of."

"More like that's two who won't be shooting at us," Becks said.

"Oh, ye of little faith."

The senator noticed his security detail vanishing about the same time Pravesh stepped up to their bench and showed her credentials. A flash of indignation crossed the older man's face, but he buried it with the kind of speed that only comes from a career politician. He gave a curt nod to Liang, then stood up and scurried off, looking around the whole time like he expected a paparazzo to jump out from behind a bush and start taking pictures. I bet he was disappointed when that didn't happen.

Liang leaned back and smiled at Pravesh, stretching his arms out over the back of the park bench like he was just taking in the afternoon sun. I had yet to hear a word the man said, but I hated him. I hated his expensive suit, his expensive haircut, his expensive watch. I hated him for getting in bed with Nazis, for bringing the worst scum humanity had to offer into my adopted home, for whatever part he played in getting Gabby killed.

"You wanna dial it back about twenty percent there, big shooter?" Bubba asked.

I turned to him, and he shrugged. "Something I heard on *Letterkenny*. Doesn't really work for me, either. But you do need to take a deep breath, or let a big fart, or something to chill your ass out a hair."

"Why?"

"Because your eyes are glowing and the tourists are starting to get nervous."

"Oh." I closed my eyes and took several deep breaths. "Better?"

"Yeah. Now you just look like you want to murder someone, not like you are going to murder someone in the next ten seconds."

I could live with that. I did want to murder the little cocksucker, but I wouldn't. Unless Becks told me it was okay. There's a lot of benefit to keeping someone around to be your dedicated conscience. It means I don't have to always deal with the moral complexities of when it's okay to kill a motherfucker. I just decide I want to kill said motherfucker, and if Becks approves, I know it's probably the right thing to do. It feels a little weird asking a human for moral guidance when I have a literal Guardian Angel hanging around, but Glory can get pretty Old Testament sometimes, so while she and I have the same views on when it's appropriate to kill a motherfucker, it might not be the completely proper choice. Becks's moral compass always points true north, so if she approves a murder, it's gonna be justified.

The conversation between Liang and Pravesh wasn't going well.

He'd gotten to his feet, which indicated that she was probably going to have to arrest him to get the information we wanted. I have no problem with torture, personally. It's a shit method of information gathering, but it's a damned fine stress reliever. So, while I liked the idea of clamping jumper cables to Mr. James Liang's nipples and plugging the other end into a wall socket, I knew that would just make me feel better and not necessarily get us any closer to finding the Master.

I saw Pravesh reach behind her back for the cuffs she carried at the small of her back, and I gave Becks a nod. She moved wide left to cover that angle to retreat, while I went right. Bubba did a pretty good job of clogging up the middle egress routes just by existing, but since he used to be a football player, I knew he understood what we were doing—going after the quarterback. But when Liang held up both hands in a faux-surrender, I saw something peeking out from under the sleeves of his no doubt ridiculously expensive dress shirt that chilled me to the bone.

I used to have tattoos running from my wrists to my shoulders. Nothing like the biker-style ink that Bubba's got, all skulls and flames and pinup models. No, mine looked more like vines and geometric shapes, kinda like the cheesy tribal tattoos everybody was sporting back in the 90s except somehow different. The difference, the thing that made my tats hard to look at for normal people, was that they weren't just ink. My tattoos were magic seared into my arms, writhing there under the first few layers of skin, basically a battery where I could dump extra mojo in a lengthy and extremely painful ritual involving needles, ink, blood, some Enochian chanting, and a fuckton of pain. There was one guy I knew of on the East Coast who did that kind of work, and while he generally walked on the side of the angels, he didn't exactly have the ability to vet all his clients when people asked for needlework.

That meant that every once in a while, through no fault of his own, Tuck ended up putting magical tattoos on a dark wizard, someone more concerned with power for personal gain than with doing right by the universe. Someone, if the glimpse of ink peeking out from under his cuffs were any indication, like James Liang, who was apparently a *lot* more than just an asshole Nazi-loving lobbyist. I slipped into my Sight to confirm, and the black roiling mass of power coalescing around Liang told me that I was seeing exactly what I thought I was seeing. Fuck.

"Pravesh!" I yelled. "He's a fucking wizard!" Okay, I've perhaps been more subtle from time to time. Not much, but a little. But it got the point across. *Get the civilians out of here. If he's got enough knowledge to store energy in his tattoos, then he's dangerous as fuck.*

Becks shifted course away from Liang and pointed her submachine gun straight up in the air. She fired off two three-shot bursts, then started yelling for people to clear the area. Folks are pretty willing to ignore the shouting of someone with a badge, especially if they're in the middle of the perfect selfie, but they usually pay attention to gunshots. This time was no exception, and the couple hundred people around the Washington Monument started to scatter like cockroaches in a frat house when the lights come on. Or maybe that's frat boys when someone flashes a badge. Same thing.

Liang didn't miss a beat. As Pravesh dropped her handcuffs and went for her sidearm, he blasted her right in the chest with a beam of pure force. She flew back a good six feet before she crashed to the turf, unconscious with a smoking crater in her chest.

"I'm on the boss lady," Bubba called to me. "You deal with the magic-slinging shithead."

Exactly my plan, big guy. Exactly my plan. I stopped about twenty yards away from Liang and reached out to the leylines I'd found earlier. And felt nothing. Not even a trickle of power flowing through the earth beneath my feet. I couldn't even sense the pathways the lines would have carved in the earth. It was like...son of a bitch. He was *shielding* me. I flickered in my Sight and saw energy streaming out of Liang straight down into the ground, expanding out from him a growing circle. He had a spell set that would reach down into the earth, draw out power from the nearby leylines and nodes, channel that power back into the spell to grow and sustain it, and create a shield that blocked anyone else from touching the lines. It was a genius piece of spellwork, the kind of shit I'd love to take apart over a few hours and more than a few drinks, but right now it was fucking me like I was the last sheep in Scotland.

So now I was stuck dealing with a skilled and powerful mage with only what power I'd managed to regenerate since we left the DEMON headquarters. Which wasn't much. I was starting to really regret not getting my own magical tattoos redone at any point since coming back from Hell. I could use the extra boost right about now. Oh well, no point whining about what I didn't have. Time to use the few advantages I did have. Like strength, speed, and the fact that Liang didn't know who I was.

"Ready to play, Reaper? I've been waiting for a crack at you," he yelled as he turned to me with a canary-eating grin.

So much for him not knowing who I was. "Sure, shithead," I called out. "Let's dance." Then I drew my pistol and fired six rounds right at his chest.

See, there's one thing wizards and other magic-slinging assholes never account for—bullets. Magic is great. It's powerful as hell and can do things almost undreamt of by most people. But it's really hard to cast when you're full of bullet holes. Trust me, I've tried. I was banking on Liang being a lot like most of the asshole wizards I've dealt with over the years: great with spells, not so great with facing real world problems.

When my bullets bounced off a smoky-gray shield of energy, I was disappointed yet again. Apparently, Liang didn't just know my name, he knew my penchant for shooting first and bullshitting later. "Wanna drop the shield and just punch each other in the face like real men?" I called to him as I stalked toward the well-dressed wizard douchebag.

"I don't think so, Harker," Liang replied. "As a matter of fact, I don't think I want to let you punch me at all. Why don't you see how you like punching tourists instead?"

My face probably reflected my confusion, because just before his eyes went completely black and he threw his head back as power from the leylines coursed through him, Liang did the scariest thing anyone can ever do in a fight—he looked me in the eyes and laughed. His voice sounded like it came from somewhere down around his knees, a deep, growling thing that made the Enochian he chanted in sound even worse, and that's a chore. I recognized the words, but not the order. Liang was using a spell I'd never seen or heard before, which wasn't all that unusual, but was pretty concerning. I knew most of the rituals for summoning and banishing demons, but there were a lot I wasn't familiar with that could do all sorts of nasty things.

I found out exactly what kind of nasty things this spell was doing when every civilian within a hundred yards of the wizard froze in their tracks. Every man, woman, and teen stopped their flight from the mayhem we were causing and turned back to face us, eyes blank and faces slack. Then, as one unit, they all charged us. Liang had somehow managed to ensorcell every single person visiting the Washington Monument, from tourists to park cops to office drones on their lunch break. And now they were all coming for me, Becks, Bubba, and the unconscious Pravesh.

Fuck. Well, good thing for me that I don't have any problem with punching tourists. Or anyone else, for that matter. But there were a *lot* of people. A couple hundred, at least. And the odds of Liang getting away while I beat the shit out of a buttload of innocent tourist zombies was pretty high.

Until a white streak of light blazed down from the heavens in front of me and my one-woman cavalry arrived. Glory did a perfect superhero landing, one knee and one fist down, then stood up, her brilliant white wings stretching nearly eight feet out from her sides. She wore her battle angel armor, which wasn't the chain mail bikini *Heavy Metal* cover bullshit, but greaves and vambraces and gauntlets, with a breastplate that looked like it had taken more than one shot in its lifetime. In short, she didn't just look hot, she looked hot and dangerous as hell.

"I'll help with the civilians," she said. "You take care of the wizard." Good call. She was way less likely to get frustrated and shoot somebody in the face than me, and if I focused on Liang, I could pretty much do anything I wanted to him. I didn't want to hurt any innocents, but this Nazi-loving shitbag was as far from that as anything I could imagine.

I smiled at the suddenly less confident magic-user. "Like I said, fuckwit," I said with a grin that had set better men than him to pissing themselves. "Let's dance."

21

There I was, standing on the National Mall in Washington D.C. at the height of lunch hour, with hundreds of office drones, tourists, and schoolchildren hypnotized into murderous meat puppets, a Nazi-fellating wizard prick grinning like a scabrous hyena, practically no magical gas in my tanks, and a really nifty if inconvenient piece of spellwork cockblocking me from reloading my mojo from the leylines nearby. In short, it was turning out to be a really shit Tuesday.

I had just about enough juice for one good spell, but I had one thing in abundance—bullets. I drew my Glock and fired four quick shots at Liang's kneecaps. Energy flared into a dome encasing the dirty little prick in a half-sphere of safety, and my shots ricocheted off harmlessly. Actually harmlessly, because I aimed low. There wasn't a lot of geometry in my education, mostly on account of my education taking place during the reign of King Edward VII, more popularly known before taking the throne as Prince Albert, or "Bertie." Yep, I was educated during the relatively short reign of a cock piercing. But I have bounced enough bullets off enough things to understand angles of reflection, so my ricochets buried themselves harmlessly in the dirt at Liang's feet. I stalked forward, continuing to shoot at the barrier every couple of steps, Liang laughing at me the whole way.

"You can't shoot through my wards, Harker!" he yelled from behind his shield. "And as tapped into the web of power under the city as I am, I'll be able to hold you back forever!"

"Kinda what I'm counting on, you arrogant little prick," I said, leaping high into the air. I used a little bit of my remaining power to put some more *oomph* into my jump, then at the top of my arc, shouted *"Accelero!"* with all my considerable volume behind it. I hurtled down at the very top of Liang's spherical shield, which was glowing yellow in the midday sun, and I slammed into it feet-first, using the last shreds of magic within me to form my own shield of energy *around* the one Liang was hiding within. I watched his brow knit in confusion, then his eyes widened as he realized what I was doing. But by then, it was too late.

I drove the bubble of wizard prick into the ground with all the force of a Mack truck hitting a hard-boiled egg. The shield didn't break, but the ground certainly opened up beneath it, enough to swallow Liang and his entire orb of assholery in a ten-foot pit. I bounced off the shield and fell to the lawn, breath rushing out of my lungs as I landed. Then I rolled to my feet and watched the lip of the crater to see what emerged.

Liang now had a problem on his hands. He was stuck underground in an orb of energy, but he no longer had line of sight on his brainwashed minions. That didn't make them un-brainwashed, but it did leave them with no direction, so instead of continuing to attack my friends, they now started attacking *everyone*—police, civilians, each other—anyone who crossed the line of sight of one of Liang's living zombies was fair game. He also couldn't go anywhere without dropping his orb, because he built his shield to deflect energy. That's why I bounced so high when I dropped on his head, but magic can bend Newton's laws, not break them. All the energy of my fall had to go somewhere, and enough of it transferred to the shield to bury the arrogant wizard up to his hairline.

"You think this will stop me, Harker?" Liang screamed from the bottom of the pit. I felt a slight rush of energy as his shield dispersed, but before I could jump down into the hole and beat him to a bloody pulp, I felt a disturbance in the force.

Yeah, I know. That's not really what it is, but it's as accurate as anything else. Something in the air just felt suddenly *wrong*, and I knew Liang had called in reinforcements. I spun around to see a Gate opening on the Mall ten yards away. This wasn't a summoning circle, where a specific demon is called and bound to one place or the will of its summoner. No, this was a Gate, basically just a door between two dimensions that anything or anyone who feels like it can just waltz through. And this Gate opened into the Fifth Circle of Hell.

Now knowing that there are Nine Circles of Hell, and knowing that the Ninth is the worst of them all, you'd think the Fifth Circle isn't so bad, right? Wrong. Even the First Circle is still in Hell, so it makes literally every place on Earth look like paradise. Even Jersey, and I spent some time in Jersey after World War II. The Fifth Circle of Hell is Rage, ruled by a prick named Asmodeus, who I've had unpleasant dealings with in the past. As a general rule, if you have any pleasant dealings with a demon, there's probably some serious back-lash coming your way, so...maybe don't do that.

So the Gate opening into the Fifth Circle was pretty much bad for anyone and anything living within about a thousand miles of D.C. And of course, I wasn't just within a thousand miles, I was within fifty feet. So I got to stand on the front lines as a horde of demons barreled through and lay waste to everything around. Until they didn't.

"What the fuck?" I asked, staring through an interdimensional circle floating in midair in the middle of the National Mall. Not the Mall of America, although there's probably a Gate to Hell there, too. I saw the sandblasted desolation of Hell, the red-tinged rocks, the red sky on fire with the burning agony of millions of damned souls, the crimson dust that made everything look like an outtake from a horror movie version of *The Martian*.

What I didn't see, not that I was complaining, was any demons. Not even an imp poked its little horns through the Gate to sink its teeth into the succulent flesh of terrified humans. I looked down into the hole where the dapper wizard grinned up at me like the cat that swallowed the canary. "You...got anybody coming through that hole in the sky you opened up?" I asked.

"What do you mean? I opened a Gate to Hell!"

"Yeah, I got that. And you did. Looks like the Fifth Circle. So good on you there. I don't know quite how to tell you this, but it looks more like you opened a Gate to the Circle of Ennui than the Circle of Rage." Just as I said this, a Rage demon walked in front of the Gate. Not through the Gate, by the Gate. It just...ignored it. Looked over, saw a clear pathway out of Hell, and just...walked on by. I'd never seen anything like that. The only other time I'd seen a Gate opened, demons were practically falling all over themselves trying to get through. Then it all made sense.

"Asmodeus!" I called through the portal. "You keeping all your boys at home for this one?"

A voice drifted back to me through the Gate, and it sounded like an avalanche gargling with hot coals. "This human fool has made no bargains with me for my troops. He has made no sacrifices, no offerings, not even a promise of all the blood we can gorge ourselves upon. We are not pets, to be called upon at the whim of some half-trained human whelp. We are the Lords of Rage, the Masters of Mayhem, the Princes of Pain! We do not *serve*, we command, we destroy!"

"Very...alliterative," I said. I looked down into the pit once more. "Looks like your backup plan has backed away, pal. You wanna climb outta that hole and tell me everything you know about DEMON? The secret government agency you've been raising money for, not the real ones. I know plenty about them. Like that they don't like to be summoned, and they sure don't like humans with the audacity to think they can tell them what to do. So...unless you want to see your innards very quickly become your outards, you should probably close that Gate. Because if you just leave it hanging open like that, one of two things is going to happen. Either Asmodeus isn't going to be able to control his entire horde, and a bunch of demons are going to come through and wreak havoc all over Washington—"

"Exactly!" Liang replied, a mad glint in his eye. "I shall unleash a whirlwind of murder and bloodshed the likes of which this town has never—"

I returned the favor and interrupted him. "—Or, and this is the far more likely occurrence, As-man himself, Asmodeus, Ruler of the Fifth Circle and Prince of Hell, is just going to step out for a quick bite to eat, and by that, I mean you, and then pop back home where he can torment your newly dead soul for the rest of eternity. But you do you, boo-boo. If you think the Gate needs to stay open, by all means, let it hang there for a little while longer."

A mad light had been glowing in Liang's eyes since we started our little dance, and now it grew to a truly psychotic level. "Fine," he said, making an odd little finger gesture and closing the Gate. I've never understood the need for hand waving to make magic happen, but some things really do go better with a little panache. "I'll take care of you myself!"

The glowing yellow shield materialized around the wizard again, and with a flourish, he held his hands out to the side of his waist and began to levitate out of the pit, shield and all. He floated up, up, up, until his feet cleared the edge of the hole, and he began to drift backward, putting a little space between us. I approved of this and decided that a little more space would be better, and I should create it. Quickly.

I raised both hands, channeled my will, and shouted, *"Impulsum!"* Power coursed through my arms and slammed into the shield, flinging Liang back a good sixty feet before he slammed into what looked like an old UPS truck painted red with windows cut out of the side and the words "Scalzi's Burritos" in big letters over the red-and-white striped awning. The wizard met the food truck, and both went over in a crash of Mexican food and Asian asshole, the food truck landing on its side and a shortish man with thinning brown hair and a salt-and-pepper beard wearing a red t-shirt scuttled out of the rear door and hauled ass out of there, dragging the weirdest damned guitar case I'd ever seen behind him.

I sprinted over and leapt up onto the side of the truck, caved in from the impact of flying wizardly asshole. Liang lay in the crumpled metal, his shield gone and a baffled look on his face.

"How? Your power...leylines blocked..."

"The leylines on Earth were blocked, you fucking idiot," I said, calling power to my fists and sheathing them in purple flame. "But when you opened a Gate, I could pull in all the power I wanted from Hell, and lemme tell ya, that Hell-juice really supercharges a guy."

"Won't matter," he grunted, dragging himself to his feet. "Still gonna—"

I let him get both feet under himself before I reached down, grabbed a fistful of hair, and snatched him up by it. I flung him back onto the grass of the Mall and turned to watch him land thirty feet away. I didn't extinguish the flames on my hand when I grabbed his hair, so I bet that didn't feel good. I hopped down from the truck and advanced on him, feeling a smile stretch across my face as he scrambled to rebuild his shield. He got to his feet, his defenses flickering in front of him. Instead of the smooth sphere he had been hiding in, this was more just a wall of energy. A wall that slammed into Liang's face when I blasted it with raw power.

"You aren't ready for this, pal," I said as I kept stalking him. "You wanted to play with power? Well, how do you like it when power plays with you?" I threw another bolt of purple fire at his feet, grinning as he hopped back a couple steps.

"I won't tell you anything, Harker!" Liang yelled. The madness in his eyes had fully engulfed him, and there was barely a hint of the well-dressed, suave lobbyist that was having lunch with a senator less than fifteen minutes prior. What stood before me was a trembling, twitching mass of anxiety and hatred, all of it focused on me. Which was baffling, since I'd never met this guy before. It usually takes a good four minutes between someone meeting me and wanting me dead.

Liang dropped his shield, and I could tell by the wild look in his eye that he was going to try something stupid and quite possibly suicidal. I just needed to make sure it wasn't homicidal as well. He drew in power from the leylines until his hair stood on end and his body glowed with an intense white light. Human beings aren't supposed to hold that much power; their bodies just can't survive it. I get away with flinging around way more juice than I should be able to because I'm not strictly human, and the sliver of demon in me gives me added capacity and endurance. Liang didn't have that, and I could tell he was about to blow.

"Fucking hell," I grumbled. I gave up on my cool as shit stalking forward shtick and ran over, grabbed the glowing wizard by his bespoke lapels, and hurled him away from the crowd huddled around the base of the monument. I put a little magic into the toss, and he soared across the grass, slamming once more into the beleaguered Scalzi's Burritos truck. The glow surrounding him grew brighter and brighter until just a few seconds after he smacked into the undercarriage of the food truck, James Liang, lobbyist, power broker, wizard, and all-around Nazi-loving thimbledick, blew the fuck up. A nimbus of pure magical energy exploded from within him, vaporizing his body and igniting the gas tank on the burrito truck, flinging it into the sky to turn end over end twice before it slammed to the grass right in front of the Washington Monument.

It rained burrito bits for at least a minute before everything stopped falling from the sky. Becks and Pravesh walked over to me, surveying the damage. "Well, this went about as well as could be expected," Pravesh said.

I reached out and wiped a glob of something green off Becks's cheek. She stared at me as I put my finger in my mouth and licked it clean. "What?" I asked. "It's just guacamole."

22

I picked up on more than a few shocked glances as we walked through the front door of Pravesh's branch office of the Department of Homeland Security, and after a few steps realized that they were all directed at me.

"Do I still have salsa in my hair?" I asked as we waited for the elevator.

"Nah," Bubba replied. "They just ain't seen anybody as famous as you come walking through the front door."

I thought about it for a second, then shrugged. "Yeah, I guess my name kinda gets around in certain circles."

"I meant that whenever somebody with your reputation comes into a DHS building, it's usually through the basement," the big Hunter said.

"In handcuffs," Becks added.

"And with a black bag over their head," Pravesh chimed in.

"Just what I needed," I grumbled as the elevator doors slid open. "Stand-up night at the Monster Factory."

Glory was waiting for us when we stepped off the elevator, her arms folded across a tattered Reckless Kelly t-shirt that I'm pretty sure she manifested right out of my closet. She fell into step behind us as we walked down the hall and turned into Pravesh's conference room. The trim woman flipped a switch by the door, and I felt a slight hum go through the room as her magical wards and mundane anti-surveillance equipment started up.

I never took the time to understand how the Department of Homeland Security had wired their protective magics to a light switch. It bugged me a little, having a mechanical trigger to an obviously complex spell with no visible source of mystical energy. If magic became something you can just stand in your living room and tell your smart home to turn on, a lot of the, well, *magic* of it would be lost. It offended my sensibilities, which were usually far less Victorian than my birth date would have one expect.

I sat at the far end of the table, with Glory on one side and Becks on the other. Bubba sat next to Pravesh, who had pulled a plain black t-shirt on over her ruined shirt at the monument. She'd taken a blast of magic right to the chest, but it hurt her a lot less than it would a human. Which Pravesh wasn't. Not even close. Keya Pravesh was actually a lamia, a magical cryptid reported in various mythologies to be an ancient queen cursed by Hera, a child-eating monster, a dragoness, or just a woman with the lower half of a snake. I didn't ask which, if any, of these tales were true. If they were anything like the origins of vampirism and Dracula, there was a little bit of fact, a little bit of fiction, a healthy dose of fantasy, and liberal sprinkling of utter bullshit. All I knew was that she was magical as fuck, that I thought lamia were extinct a long time ago, and that she was way more resilient than a human of her size would be.

So, I wasn't terribly concerned that Liang's magical blast would kill her, but I also didn't want her showing off her suit of scales to every Tom, Dick, and cell phone wandering by. Probably not a good look to have the divisional director of a federal agency demonstrating their supernatural nature in the middle of the workday. Better to save that shit for the weekend.

"So now what?" I asked. "Liang was our best lead on chasing down the Master's money, and now lab nerds are trying to figure out which parts are wizard and which parts are fried shrimp and bacon. Who puts fried shrimp and bacon on a burrito, anyway?"

"I love shrimp," Becks said.

"Bacon makes everything better," Bubba added.

"Whatever. Doesn't change the fact that our best lead blew himself sky high," I said.

"No, it doesn't," Pravesh agreed. "But while we were engaged with Liang at the Mall, Deputy Director Hall and Agent Jones were here approaching the matter through other means." She gestured at Amy and Skeeter, who were taking their seats at the table.

"Agent Jones?" Bubba asked.

"Apparently I had to be deputized or something to even know the place they had me working from existed," Skeeter said. "But the benefits package is pretty good. It even has a match for the 401K."

"What other means?" I asked.

"I guess this comes as a surprise to you, because it certainly always does to this big goof," Amy said, poking Bubba in the shoulder. "But there are ways to gather information that don't lead to explosions and massive property damage and have very little chance of ending up on the evening news or a conspiracy theory website."

"Both, in a good day," I said. I figured blowing up a burrito truck, unleashing a horde of pseudo-zombies on a national monument, and blasting a crater in the National Mall would qualify me for CNN and *The Weekly World News*.

"So, we were pursuing less destructive, and in the end, more fruitful avenues of investigation," Amy said. "I subpoenaed Liang's cell phone records, his financials, and checked his property tax records in D.C. and any state within a half a day's drive of here."

"I hacked all his social media, the GPS in his phone and car, his email, his browser history, and his Amazon Prime account. That dude has a serious *Man in the High Castle* fetish," Skeeter said.

It made sense. An alternate history TV show where the Nazis and the Japanese won World War II. That would be better than a Pornhub subscription to this asshole. I wondered a little at Skeeter's technical skills. We'd only been gone a few hours, and this was a remarkable amount of information. The last person I knew that could hack like that was doing it from inside the internet.

He must have seen me looking at him sideways because the skinny little Black man smiled and held up both hands. "Okay, when I say 'hacked,' I really mean I sat in a chair tied into some kind of mega-computer with access to pretty much every—"

"Agent Jones." Pravesh's voice stopped Skeeter cold. His dusky skin went a little ashen at the snake-woman's tone. "You do recall the rather extensive, and exceptionally binding, non-disclosure agreement that you signed, don't you? The one you are coming dangerously close to violating?"

"Oh, come on, Pravesh," I said. "We're all on the same side. Shit, except for Glory, we're all on the same payroll. And I think it might be against the twelfth commandment or something for angels to have day jobs."

"It's not," Glory said. "And there were only nine commandments, not twelve."

"I thought there were ten?" Becks asked.

"Moses added the whole thing about honoring thy father and mother," the angel said. "He remembered what an asshole he was as a kid and thought if he could put a little crowd control into the holy writ for his own kids, it might make adolescence suck less. Didn't work. Teenagers are pricks. Nothing carved on a rock in the desert is going to change that."

"Regardless," Pravesh said, heading off another discussion about what was written down about the Biblical times and what really happened in Biblical times. Good move, too. Whenever Glory started telling stories about how it really was back in the Old Testament days, Becks ended up with serious questions about her faith, and I ended up with a serious hangover. "The non-disclosure agreement Agent Jones signed was a binding contract with one of the stricter members of the Department's Upper Management, and we don't break those. Ever. So, let's move on to what he discovered and ignore for the moment how he discovered it."

She gave Skeeter a small smile. "Don't worry, Agent Jones. Within a day or two after leaving this building, you will forget all about what you saw in the sub-basements. It's for your own protection."

"Good," Skeeter said. "Because if I have that shit running around in my head for too long, I'm gonna have serious nightmares."

Now I really wanted to know what was in the sub-basement, and what this mysterious Upper Management was all about. But this was not the time, so I focused my attention on the scrawny nerd at the other end of the table.

"We know that Liang has been taking massive sums of money from DEMON and funneling them into support of legislation that has subtle but consistently shitty effects on the way the U.S. handles its citizens. Blocking gun control legislation, funding groups that support voting rights restrictions, blocking access to abortion, trying to repeal gay marriage, qualified immunity...if it's shitty and harmful to anyone who isn't White, straight, and at least purportedly Christian, he's thrown money at it hand over fist."

"Yeah, like that doucherocket Senator he was having a burrito with when we walked up. That dick screamed about voter fraud all through the last election, when it was one of *his* party's top consultants in *his* home state that was convicted of the only case of widespread voter fraud in the last decade. And that's just the tip of his shitty iceberg," Becks said.

I gave my fiancée an appraising look. I'd never paid much attention to her politics, focusing on the fact that she was legitimately one of the best people I've ever known. But in the past couple of years, as the world spun further and further out of control, she really started to stand up and speak out about what she believed in, to the point where she quit her dream job of being a Charlotte-Mecklenburg Police Department detective when they sparked a riot and then brought the hammer down on largely innocent protestors back in the summer.

Surprised that I pay attention to the world around me, Harker? she asked across our mental link.

Maybe a bit, I admitted.

I might carry a badge, but I'm still a Black woman living in the South. I walk in any room and that's what people see first. Not my badge, not my gun, and sure as hell not my brains. They see my skin and my tits, and for a lot of these pricks, that's all I'll ever be to them. You care about this shit because Nazis hurt you, killed someone you love, and you want revenge. I care about this shit because if I ever have a kid, and God forbid it's a boy, I want him to grow up in a world where he doesn't have to be afraid every time he sees a cop in his rear-view mirror. I want him to grow up in a world where he can run through his own neighborhood without being shot by some redneck who thinks he's fucking Rambo. I want him to grow up in a world where Driving While Black isn't a capital fucking offense. That's why it matters to me. You want to hunt down these assholes because of your past? That's fine. I want to hunt them down so my children can have a future.

Well, that hit me right between the eyes. I stared at Becks, unshed tears of rage pooling in her eyes, and finally understood a little bit of the privilege I carried with me like an invisible shield. I've walked through the worst places this world has to offer, protected not just by my power and the magical heritage I carry, but by the systems built to protect people that look like me. Becks never had that, and if we ever had a kid, they wouldn't have that either. Our mission to stop these pricks was personal before, but now it felt *more* somehow.

Now, I understood that for a lot of people, people who couldn't do a goddamned thing to change the world, our fight was fucking *essential*. I leaned forward and put my elbows on the table. "What have you got, Skeeter? And please tell me it's something that's going to bring these fuckers down."

23

Bubba

I don't know if this is what Harker meant when he was talking
about taking these assholes down," I said into the microphone.

"Pretty sure he said 'fuckers,'" Faustus replied, turning back
to the van and grinning at me.

"Pay attention, demon," I grumbled. "You get my fiancée hurt and
I'm going to spend a long time cutting off some of the less important
parts of you."

"Are you sure you and Harker aren't related?" Faustus replied,
turning back to face the massive glass-fronted office building he was
walking toward. I watched him on a big monitor set into the wall of
the minivan from where Pravesh and I were observing.

Faustus and Amy were going in the front door of the pharmaceu-
tical company we suspected of bankrolling DEMON for the past
several years, and they were going in alone while Harker, Flynn, and
Count friggin' Dracula himself snuck in through the loading dock. I
didn't have eyes on their team, but since none of them were the
woman I wanted to spend the rest of my life with, I only kinda cared.

"I oughta be going in there with them," I said to nobody in particular.

Of course, somebody in particular answered, this somebody being Skeeter. "Bubba, you are three of the most recognizable people I've ever met. If there's going to be a picture at the reception desk saying, 'Do Not Admit,' it'll be of you. We need to *not* start a brawl before we even get to the elevator, and that means sending in people with a little more stealth than you. And by a little, I mean a lot."

"I know. Doesn't mean I have to like it."

"You don't have to like it, but you do have to keep quiet while I'm trying to work my magic. And get that damn soda off the desk."

I picked up my bottle of Pepsi and set it on the floor, double-checking to make sure the cap was on tight. Screwing with Skeeter was one thing, and one of my very favorite things, but I didn't want to chance wrecking the only thing giving me any idea of what Amy and the demon were doing.

Skeeter, Pravesh, and I were on rolling office chairs in the back of a converted cargo van parked across the street from the headquarters of Klavier Pharmaceuticals, staring at an array of video feeds. We had one coming from the dash of the rental car Amy left in the parking lot, one from a button on Faustus's lapel, and one from a pendant hanging around Amy's neck. As the duo entered the lobby, Skeeter switched the main display from the dash cam to Faustus's feed, making me blink at the sudden perspective shift.

Suddenly I was looking at the world from the tie pin of a demon in a cheap suit, and if that isn't a metaphor for life as a Monster Hunter, I don't know what is. Not for the first time since I started this most recent "adventure," I wondered what the hell I was doing. I'm a redneck from North Georgia, built more for drinking beer, operating heavy machinery, and fishing off a pontoon boat than tracking down a secret government agency and the horrible people who fund it. But here I was, watching the woman I love on video with nothing to punch. That is not a good place for an over-the-hill football player. I adjusted the sword across my back and leaned in to get a better view of the action on the screen.

"You'd probably be more comfortable if you took that off," Pravesh said, nodding to the giant toothpick.

"I doubt it," I said. "Only thing gonna make me comfortable is getting the information we need and getting all our people out safe. And let's be real, our track record for that sucks lately."

I caught Skeeter's wince out of the corner of my eye and felt bad for a second but shoved that little twinge of regret down into the box next to my grief and guilt and all other flavors of recrimination about Joe's death, and locked it up good and tight again. Time to wallow in my grief when we got home. Because home is where the beer is, and I don't grieve near as well sober.

"Welcome to Klavier, how may I help you?" the receptionist asked. The audio came through loud and clear, even on the tiny camera Faustus was wearing.

Amy consulted a small notebook in her hand. "We need to speak with Mr. Grube Hanser. I believe he is the CFO?"

The receptionist's smile got several degrees colder, and her voice was clipped when she next spoke. "And who are you, exactly? I don't see any appointments on Mr. Hanser's calendar for today."

The camera shifted as Faustus leaned in, and I heard his voice match the receptionist's temperature. "We're here to discuss a legislative matter Mr. Hanser requested our employer, James Liang, to look into for him." The weight the demon put on Liang's name made it very clear that this woman was supposed to recognize it, and from the look on her face, she did.

She straightened up and plastered a fake smile onto her face as she picked up a phone. "Of course, of course. Just let me show you to a conference room where Mr. Hanser can meet you." She spoke into a handset, then stood up and escorted the pair across the marble-tiled lobby and through a heavy pair of double doors. They went down a long, carpeted hallway, then turned right into a conference room. The receptionist left them alone in the room with a massive oak table and imposing leather swivel chairs. A monitor dominated one wall of the room, and Faustus walked over to the other end and set a small box down next to a water pitcher. Skeeter pressed a couple of buttons, and the main display switched to the tiny camera Faustus just set down.

The door opened, and a chubby little man in khakis, a short-sleeved dress shirt, and a paisley tie walked in. He stopped as he caught sight of the people in the room, and Faustus also started. Apparently the two knew each other.

"What are you doing here?" Chubby asked.

"Working. What are *you* doing here?" Faustus replied.

"Working. Who are you working *for*, Faustus?"

"Nunya Industries. As in Nunya Damn Business. Now clear out of here before you screw up my scam."

"Your scam? Oh, no, Dealmaker. You are not fucking up what we've got going on here. We're working on something big, and I am not letting you screw up *or* jump in and steal the credit. You need to leave, now."

"Come on, Felderon," Faustus said. "What could you *possibly* be working on that's of any size? You're barely a millennium out of The Pits. Nobody trusts you with anything serious."

"Shit," I said. "He's a demon." I started to roll my chair over to the door and haul ass in there, but Pravesh stopped me cold with a hand on my shoulder.

"Wait," she said. "Let them try to talk their way out of it first. Remember, Faustus is one of the best deal brokers in history, and he's fooled his share of demons as well as humans. Let's not go barreling in there unless we have no choice.

"Okay," I replied. "But how about you get behind the wheel and be ready in case you need to barrel us right the hell through the front door?"

She did as I asked, and I turned my attention back to the video feed. Faustus had walked over to the new guy, who was apparently a demon as well, and knew Faustus, blowing our plan of sending less recognizable members of our team straight to shit, and had his arm around the short round man's shoulders and was walking him over to a chair.

"Feldy," the smooth-talking demon said as he moved to stand

between Felderon and the door. "You've known me for a very long time, right?"

"Exactly why I don't trust you, Faustus."

"But in all that time, have you ever known me to betray one of my brothers from below?"

"All the fucking time. You're literally one of the most backstabbing pieces of shit I've ever known. You give demons a bad name as far as trustworthiness goes. If you had a mother, you'd sell her out for an extra slice of bacon at breakfast."

"Seems like you've been selling a lot of mothers, then, Feldy. Your human suit is a little tight around the middle."

"Fuck you, Faustus. I don't know why you're here, but last I heard you were hanging out with the Reaper and the boss had declared you persona non grata downstairs. So you need to take your pet human and get out of here before I call security."

"I guess I was hoping I wouldn't have to do this," Faustus said, pulling a small pistol from beneath his suit jacket and firing twice into the short man's forehead. "Tell Lucifer I said go fuck himself when you get downstairs."

Amy looked at the camera and said, "I think subtle just went out the window. We'll meet you at the front door." Then Faustus flung the door open and ran out of the room, leaving us with a view of a dead demon splattered all over the conference table. They were just gonna have to chuck that thing. The black icky sludge demons turn into when they die play hell with varnish.

I leaned back in my chair and said to Pravesh, "Remember when I mentioned us maybe needing to haul ass to the front of the building?"

She put the van in drive and said, "Way ahead of you. Hold on to something. This might get bumpy." Then she peeled rubber as we sped toward the blown remnants of our attempted stealth operation. I hoped Harker and Luke were having better luck at being sneaky.

24

Harker

S tealthy is not a word that's often used to describe me, so when
Pravesh decided that Me, Becks, Luke, and Glory should
sneak in the back of the Klavier Pharmaceuticals main building, I'll admit to laughing a little. "You really want me to sneak in
somewhere? I've blown up more buildings than TNT. My idea of a
stealthy entrance is not yelling out 'hey motherfuckers, guess who?'
before I blow the door in."

"And the other option is Bubba," Pravesh said, pointing at the
gargantuan redneck taking up most of the space in the back of the
surveillance van.

"Okay," I said. "Team Skulk it is." Me and the rest of my merry
sneakers piled out of the van and ran across the highway into the
woods that surrounded the drug company's main facility.

We didn't look all that stealthy, but we were at least smaller than
Bubba, if not appreciably quieter. I had on my typical long-sleeved
dress shirt open over a black tee, with a pistol strapped to one hip and
a silver-edged dagger on the other. Glory had on a Jane's Addiction
tank top and a pair of torn blue jeans, but I knew that was just what

she was manifesting at the moment. She could look like anything she wanted to, on account of that whole not having a physical form thing. Becks was in jeans, a scoop-necked maroon shirt, and boots that were good for running. All of us wore Kevlar vests, a nod to previous encounters with these assholes where they weren't just armed, they were armed with bullets that could hurt Luke as well as humans.

But it was Luke that tripped all the ridiculous meters, covered head to toe in black, with a nylon jacket zipped all the way up on his neck to keep the sun off his skin. I'd never seen Luke go out in the daylight, not in all the years we'd been together. But this was a special case. We were going to get justice for Cassie, and he wasn't going to sit on the sidelines. I certainly wasn't stupid enough to ask him to, and neither was anyone else who wanted to keep their face.

It was only about a fifteen-minute jog through the woods to come out behind the employee parking lot and loading dock. A tractor trailer truck was just pulling out, and another was backing up to the dock, where three big loading doors stood open. There was a ramp up to the dock, presumably for smaller deliveries, and a set of stairs at each end of the building. A door on the side had a sign marking it as the employee entrance, and it seemed to have the fewest eyes on it. Organic eyes, anyway. I saw a pair of surveillance cameras scanning the side of the building and pointed them out to the others.

"I can blast them, but that's going to tell anybody who isn't a moron that somebody's breaking in," I said.

"I think counting on the stupidity of our enemies may be a poor decision in this instance," Luke said.

"Yeah," I agreed. "These definitely aren't the same flavor of morons that we usually tussle with. So, we can try to time our approach to run to the door when the cameras are pointed away, or we can—"

"The farthest loading dock," Becks said, pointing. "There's no one visible near it, and if we circle around, sticking to the trees, we can come in from the far side of the building and get there without being seen. Hopefully."

I looked at where she was pointing, and we did have cover from the cameras in the form of the truck. I couldn't see any guards, but that didn't mean there weren't any. Still, the cameras seemed to leave too small a gap in their coverage for a human to get through. Luke and I could probably make it, but Becks was just too slow. The dock was our best chance at getting everybody inside without being noticed.

I nodded. "Let's do that, then." I led the way through the woods, hopefully sounding less like a bull elephant to everyone else than I did to myself, and five minutes later we were crouched a hundred yards away from where we had been, looking at the other side of the building. "I really miss the gigs where I just walk in and blow shit up."

"I know, Quincy, but occasionally you have to expand your horizons," Luke said.

"Next time I promise I'll try the new sushi roll at Ru San's," I replied. I looked at the rest of my little team and tried to figure out the best way to keep them all alive for the next hour. If I was lucky, this shit would be over before we left this building. Too bad I hadn't been lucky in the past few years. "Okay, there's only one camera here, so blasting that is fifty percent less likely to get security's attention than blowing out both cameras on the other side of the building. But just in case their guards are actually being paid enough to give a shit, when I knock it out, haul ass to the nearest loading bay and scamper inside. Luke, you go first, because if there's resistance waiting for us, you'll be able to handle it. Glory, you and Becks go after Luke, and I'll bring up the rear. That way if anyone spots us, we'll have a heavy hitter in front and back."

Glory gave me a cocky grin. "You saying I'm not a heavy hitter, Q? Pretty sure I've been in more battles than you have."

"That's why I've got you watching Flynn's back. You're in charge of the person most important to me." I smiled back at her. She knew exactly why I paired her with Becks, and she knew I knew she knew. But that didn't stop us from taking the piss out of each other a little, which helped ease the tension.

You're sweet, but I can take care of myself, Becks's voice echoed in my head.

Usually, but if we really are headed for a boss fight, then I expect tougher henchmen than we've seen the last few encounters.

This is what happens when you play too many video games, Harker. You start to think life is one.

You mean I don't get a badass new weapon if I beat the bad guy? Shit, then what's the point?

You get the girl.

I'll take it.

"If you two are done making googly eyes at each other, can we get this show on the road?" Glory asked. "I like a good kissy scene as much as the next genderless celestial being, but if we stop for a makeout session, we're either going to get busted or Bubba's going to beat the bad guys without us."

"Then let's boogie," I said, motioning for Luke. I guess he was in a mood to impress, because one second he was crouched beside me in the woods, and the next I saw a black-clad shadow flow like night itself up the wall and disappear into the gaping loading dock door. "Showoff. Okay, you two, showtime."

As Becks and Glory stepped into the open, I let loose a marble-sized sphere of energy straight at the video camera. It smacked into the lens, and a small shower of sparks cascaded down to the asphalt. I noticed a guard over by the far bay look up, but apparently he couldn't tell where the noise came from, because after a moment of swiveling his head around, he turned his attention back to the massive pallets being wheeled onto the tractor trailer truck. The two most important women in my life ran hellbent for leather across the parking lot, apparently unnoticed, because no one raised an alarm or shot at them. Good thing, too. People shooting at my fiancée really annoys me.

They hopped up onto the dock and disappeared inside, and I stepped out of the tree line. I took a look over at the first dock, but both guards seemed to be occupied, so I sprinted the fifty yards or so to the dock and leapt from the ground straight up to the loading bay, forgoing the superhero landing this time to just stay on both feet.

I looked left and was relieved to see that the three dock bays were separated on the inside of the warehouse, at least for the first ten feet or so. After that, the warehouse was wide open, and Becks, Glory, and Luke were all tucked tight to the wall between the second and third loading bays to stay out of sight.

I, on the other hand, was standing right out in the open, framed in the open bay door with sunlight cascading in behind me. So, when the fat guy with a folded-up newspaper in one hand and a pen in his mouth stepped out of a small nondescript room set in a back corner of the room, I was pretty impossible to miss. I froze for a second, then decided that my best bet was to bluff my way out of it.

"Hey," I said, waving and walking over to him. "Where's the shipment for DC? My boss sent me out here to make sure it was ready to go before the trucks get here, but I can't find our pallets."

The guy stared blankly at me for a second, then asked, "What shipment for DC? I got no records of a DC shipment."

"Are you sure?" I asked, reaching around like I was digging in my back pocket for paperwork. "My boss was going apeshit about it, saying if we didn't get it out today some big deal would be ruined and it would be all on my ass. I don't know, I only kinda half listened. Chicks, you know? Put 'em in management and all of a sudden they're total ballbusters."

My casual misogyny worked, and my new broad-bashing buddy held out a hand. "Yeah, I feel ya, bro. Lemme have your paperwork and I'll go check with the dock master to see what I can find out for you."

"Not a problem," I said, bringing my empty right hand out from around my back. He looked at me, puzzled, but when my left fist swung around and found the hinge of his jaw, he understood. Well, he probably didn't really understand shit, but at least he was unconscious. I dragged him back into the crapper from whence he came, took off his shoes and socks, stuffed one sock into his mouth, and used the other to tie his hands behind his back. When I was satisfied he was as trussed up as the average Christmas turkey, I closed the bathroom door and stepped out to the disapproving glares of my guardian angel and fiancée.

"Ballbuster, huh?" Becks asked, giving me one of those looks that said my word choice left a lot to be desired.

"I wanted to immediately establish a rapport with the dude, and I guessed that a guy wearing a QAnon t-shirt wasn't winning any intellectual Olympics. And since rampant sexism is a sign of decreased intellect, I figured I could shortcut the friend-building process by pretending to be a sexist douchebag."

Glory and Becks shared a look. "That was pretty good," Glory said. "I know he's completely full of shit, but that was creative enough that I'm almost inclined to let him off the hook."

"And he did subdue the guy without calling attention to himself," Becks agreed.

"For once," Glory added.

"Yeah, for once." Becks looked at me. "Okay, we're gonna let it go. This time. But if I ever hear you call someone, even an imaginary someone, a ballbuster again, it had better be because they literally crushed somebody's testicles. Got it?"

"Got it," I replied. "Now that we've made it inside without raising an alarm, wanna skulk on over to Bay One and see what they're putting on those trucks?" And of course, as soon as I said a goddamned thing about *not* raising an alarm, red lights began to flash over every door and a loud klaxon started to blare.

"I swear to God, it's not my fault," I said as everyone looked at me. Everyone's earwigs crackled to life simultaneously and Skeeter's nasal voice pierced our skulls.

"Faustus and Amy got made," he screeched. "Time for Plan B."

"We have a Plan B?" I asked.

"Yeah," Skeeter replied. "Blow shit up and kill all the bad guys."

"When did that stop being Plan A?" I asked. Then a dozen heavily armed assholes burst through the door at the far end of the loading dock, and it didn't matter what plan we were on, it had gone to shit.

25

Bubba

I have to hand it to Pravesh, she is nothing if not direct. And direct in this instance meant that she jumped the curb, hauled ass across the manicured front lawn, and drove the teched-out Sprinter van right through the glass front wall of the Klavier Pharma HQ. This was a woman after my own heart, even if hers happened to be cold-blooded.

Faustus and Amy busted into the huge lobby with at least a dozen people hot on their heels, then froze as Pravesh spun a van in between a pair of overstuffed couches and slammed on the brakes. I flung open the double rear doors and yelled, "Get in! Let's go!" I held out a hand to Amy, hauling her into the van, then turned back to Faustus.

"Come on, demon, let's move," I said.

He stood there, a conflicted look on his face, then shook his head. "You go. Get your people out of here."

"Get in the van, Faustus," I said, looking over his shoulder at the approaching crowd. They were splitting out of their skin suits and turning into creatures of nightmare, with long arms ending in vicious claws and horns poking through the flesh of their foreheads.

"Sorry, Bubba. I can't," he said. "Harker and Flynn are in there. I can't leave them."

"Harker's a superhero!" I shouted. "He'll be fine."

"He's my friend," the demon said simply. "I'm not leaving him." Then he turned to the onrushing passel of demons with his gun drawn and started shooting monsters in the face.

"Dammit," I muttered. "When the demon is your moral compass, you know it's gonna be a crappy day." I turned back to Pravesh. "Get them somewhere safe." Then I jumped out of the van and drew my sword. Time to see how Great-Grandpappy Beauregard's sword did against demons.

Pretty good, actually. At least against the first one stupid enough to run straight at me. I mean, come on. I might be human, mostly, and I might not fight demons as often as Harker, but this thing thought I was gonna freak out and just die on the spot because a monster with razor-sharp talons and a double row of pointy teeth in a slavering mouth was running straight at me. Hell, I played against Alabama. I know what scary shit looks like.

I stepped a little to the left and swung my sword right through the demon's neck, which in hindsight might not have been my best choice. I mean, it killed the thing, don't get me wrong. I sliced that nasty bastard's head off like I was playing Fruit Ninja. But that did nothing to arrest the momentum of a hundred fifty pounds of oncoming demon, and it was still close enough to clip me as it fell forward. I stumbled sideways, causing one of Faustus's shots to go wide, and we went down in a tangle of demon, redneck, and sword.

I do not recommend getting into a tangle of demon, redneck, and sword, because two of those things have pointy bits, and if you're the one without them, it hurts. Faustus didn't have any horns out, and frankly I don't know if he even *has* horns, but I did manage to give myself a nasty cut along the outside of my right thigh.

"Shit," I said, standing up and looking at the blood oozing through my jeans. "Those were new pants, too."

"You're gonna want to get that looked at if we don't die here," Faustus said. "Demon blood carries all kinds of nasty crap in it."

"Is it harmful to faeries?" I asked. "'Cause I am one. Kinda. Partway, anyhow."

"Oh, you're fine then," he replied. "Faerie blood is what human witches use to cure infection from demon blood. But you might have a—"

I stopped listening when I felt a line of white-hot pain shoot from my knee to my hip. "Mother*fucker*!" I yelled, dropping to one knee.

Faustus calmly blew the head off an onrushing demon and continued his thought. "You might have a bit of a reaction as the demon blood interacts with your own. Looks like I was right."

"Call the goddamn Nobel committee," I growled, standing up with a slash through the middle of another demon. It fell in two halves with a wet *thwap* on the floor, splashing up more black goop. I looked around. All the demons that were chasing Faustus and Amy were dead, either shot or sliced. "That was easy."

"Yeah, except those were just Reavers. Low-level menial labor sent to keep us occupied," Faustus said.

"Occupied until what?"

"That," he said, pointing toward a quartet of giant demons that walked into the lobby and grinned at us.

"What the living hell are those?" I asked. These things were massive, easily eight feet tall and built like Andre the Giant had a baby with Colossus. They had gray skin, wide heads with beady eyes, and jaws with two curved fangs jutting out like wild hogs. Come to think of it, they looked a little bit like wild hogs, except way uglier and meaner looking.

"Those are Torment demons," Faustus said. "You know that whole thing about swimming in a lake of fire with demons sticking you with pitchforks for all eternity? Well, those are the guys who stand on the bottom of the lake holding the pitchforks. They're impervious to most mundane weapons, strong as oxen, meaner than the average snake, and unbelievably stupid."

"How stupid is that?" I asked. "I'm from Georgia. I know stupid."

"They're too stupid for me to even try to bullshit. We're going to have to fight them. And it's not going to go well. I don't have anything that can hurt them."

"Well, it's a good thing I do," Pravesh's voice came from the back of the van. I turned, and just as I was about to bitch at her for not hauling ass to get Amy and Skeeter to safety, I noticed two things. One, heavy-duty metal blast shades had dropped over the entire front of the building, so there was no way she could have gotten away. And two, she was holding a goddamn rocket launcher.

I dove to one side as she pulled the trigger, and a streak of fire blazed over my head. The entire world turned into a massive *BOOM* and I lay on my belly for a second covering my head in case the whole building fell on me. I don't know how that was going to make me any less dead, but at least if I had my face covered when the building fell on me, I wouldn't see it coming. When I was unsquished a couple seconds after the explosion, I pushed myself up to my hands and knees and looked at where the four demons had stood.

Correction. I looked over to where the four demons stood. As in, were still standing. As in, were not bothered by having a small missile detonate either right on top of them or literally *on them*. Like I said, I wasn't watching the impact, I was busy ducking and covering. But it didn't matter, because all four demons still stood there grinning at us.

"Well, fuck," Pravesh said.

"My turn," I said, getting to my feet. "Let's see if I can pull a Sasquatch on these assholes."

"Just don't grab the demon's wiener, Bubba," Skeeter said. "I don't think there's enough soap in Georgia to wash that off."

"Hey asshole!" I yelled, swinging Great-Grandpappy's sword around like I had the damnedest clue what I was doing. About everything I know about sword fighting I learned from *The Witcher*, and I started to think the third time Amy wanted to watch it that it might not really be for the fight scenes. I told her I could do that half-ponytail thing with my hair if she wanted me to, but she said it wasn't the same.

"You want some? Why don't one of you bastards come over here and get some? I'll take on the biggest, baddest one of you, and if I win, the rest of you crawl back in whatever hole you came out of and leave us alone."

They all looked at one another kinda confused-like, then all four of 'em started walking across the lobby in my direction.

"Remember when I said they were too stupid to bluff?" Faustus asked. "Well, they're not so stupid that they'll give up the numbers advantage. This is going to suck." I looked to my right, and his human face was gone, replaced by a smooth jet-black hairless head, pointy chin, and bright yellow eyes. In his hand was a dagger so black it seemed to absorb light, and it pulsed with an unhealthy darkness.

"You really don't want to look at that. Not if you like your soul where it is," Faustus said.

I looked away, and my eyes settled on Amy, who stepped up beside me. She had on a Kevlar plate carrier over her civilian clothes, and in her hands was a walking stick that looked familiar. It was about six feet long, with metal cording around both ends, and strange glowing sigils carved up and down the length of it. "What's that?" I asked.

"Found it in Joe's house," Skeeter said from the door of the van. "He had a whole closet full of weapons I'd never seen. Medieval-looking stuff, like shields and armor, too. I thought Amy might like this staff."

"And since the carvings glow in the presence of demons, I thought it might be able to hurt them," Amy said.

I didn't mention the fact that we'd been riding around in the van with Faustus and that stick for a couple hours and it didn't glow once. Maybe it knew bad demons from…less bad demons? "Okay, so we got a sword, a knife, a stick, a nerd, and a snake lady against four big-ass demons. To quote the great philosopher Han Solo, 'I got a bad feeling about this,'" I said.

"Well, this nerd's about to find out if holy water does any good against these bastards," Skeeter said, and I noticed for the first time he was holding a Remington 700 rifle with a bipod and scope—Joe's rifle. He raised the rifle, sighted on the quartet of demons, squeezed the trigger, and sent a blessed missile of full metal jacketed ass-kicking toward the oncoming bad guys.

And missed by a mile, because Skeeter's got to be the worst shot of anybody to ever grow up in backwoods Georgia. He blew the shit out of a lamp about six feet to the left of one of the demons and did manage to distract them long enough for me to give a holler and draw my sword before I charged the big bastards.

"Come get some, assholes!" I yelled, Great-Grandpappy's sword held high above my head. I ran straight at the lead demon, and just before I got within his arm's reach, I dropped to both knees in a Pete Townsend knee slide and lashed out with my blade, aiming to chop the bastard's leg clean off.

Except there was no leg there, and my sword passed through empty air as the demon hopped right over me, spun around, and grabbed me by the back of my collar. As it flung me through the air, the only thing I could think was *Goddammit, Faustus never said they were fast, too.*

26

Harker

When the men with rifles burst into the loading dock, all the beefy assholes two bays over stopped what they were doing and looked around. I suppose we kinda stood out as not belonging, since we were a guy, two gorgeous women, and somebody cosplaying a ninja in the back of a drug company warehouse. One of the warehouse guys pointed in our direction and let out a yell, then he and four of his buddies headed toward us, snatching up random tools and heavy-looking crap along the way. I don't know what they thought they were going to do that the twelve men with guns and body armor couldn't do, but I did admire their chutzpah.

"Becks and I will take the loaders. You and Luke deal with the real security. And try not to murder everybody," Glory said.

I didn't bother asking why she decided to worry about my body count now, after all these years. I'm pretty sure a dozen more dead assholes won't tip the balance when Ammit puts my heart on her scales. If Ammit is real. I've bumped into one or two gods from other pantheons in my travels, but not her. I've never really given too much thought to the coexistence of multiple deities with angels, Archangels, and Lucifer. I just kinda assumed that since I was raised Christian, the celestial beings I bump into tweak themselves to fit what I expect them to be like. The other gods I've met all seemed to hang out around the same power level as Glory, but they definitely referred to themselves by their godly names once I saw through their human suits. Lemme tell you, very little will give you a magical hangover like staring at a god through your Sight. That is not something I want to experience again.

Neither is getting shot, so I snapped out of my theological navelgazing and focused on the problem at hand. Or problems. The security detail had formed up in two rows, one kneeling in front of the other, and aimed what looked like AR-15s in our direction.

"Don't move!" a guy in the back row shouted. "Put your hands up and get down on the ground!"

I looked at Luke and grinned. "Which do you think he really wants? Should we not move, or should we put our hands up and get down?"

"You choose the oddest times to demonstrate your mediocre sense of humor, Quincy," my uncle replied.

"That stings, Luke. That really stings. You want to handle these assholes, or you want me to?" I had a shield of force stretching from the ground to seven feet high in front of me, so I wasn't terribly worried about getting shot. Luke didn't have any type of cover, but he seldom needed any.

"I'll deal with them," he said, and blurred into motion. And I mean *blurred.* As in, he looked like something out of *The Flash*'s special effects department as he turned and ran for the line of security goons.

And that's when everything went pear-shaped. One of the kneeling assholes fired a shotgun as soon as Luke looked in their direction, and another guard on the other end of the line followed suit. Not usually a big deal, since, well, Dracula. Except they didn't fire buckshot, or even slugs. Nope, their guns were loaded with special rounds—basically shotgun shells full of glitter. Silver glitter. Glitter that saps a vampire's speed and strength on contact. Glitter that made a big cloud of "oh shit" right where Luke ran.

He decelerated instantly, so fast his feet stopped moving but his torso didn't, sending him into an awkward dive that catapulted him right over the first row of guards and into the second. He spread his arms and took down a pair of goons, but with his power mostly nullified, my life had gotten significantly more complicated in half a second.

"Kill the Black chick!" the shouty guy in the back row yelled. "She's his bitch! Kill her and Harker's useless."

Okay, there are a few things wrong with that statement. First, this prick threatened my fiancée. Second, he called Flynn a bitch. And third, he was getting his information from a seriously shitty source, because if anything happened to Becks, I would in fact be incapacitated. Except not in a way that made me easier to take down. I'd been that version of incapacitated before, and it was more "Harker murders everything in a five-mile radius" than "Harker curls up in a ball and cries a lot while listening to 'Everybody Hurts' on repeat."

Even so, I didn't want us to get to that state again, so I did what Captain America would do—I flung my shield at the bad guys. I mean, I kinda did. I let go of that particular strand of magical energy and refocused my power into my hands, thrusting them out in the direction of the guards, palm-first.

"*Potentia!*" I shouted, throwing raw power towards the entire security team. I saw a shimmer of purple light streak from my hands, only to split harmlessly when it reached the guards, like a wave running into a bunch of bridge pilings. My energy just flowed around them, like they weren't even there.

I dropped my Sight into place so I could see them in the magical spectrum and had to blink a couple times to make sure I was seeing what I was seeing. Every one of them was warded to the gills. My magic hadn't just been disrupted by the silver in the air, which was bad enough, but I'd poured enough mojo into my spell to push through that. No, they were all specifically protected against magic. It was like they were armed and armored against me and Luke. This was going to suck.

"Glory! Cover Becks!" I shouted, and glanced over to make sure she heard me. I didn't need to worry. Even before I said anything, Glory had taken up a position behind Flynn with her wings out. As the first rank of guards opened fire on them, my guardian angel wrapped her wings around herself and Flynn, cocooning them in brilliant white feathers. I'd never asked Glory if her wings were bulletproof, but since I still felt Becks in my head, they were doing the trick for now.

The woman I love safe for the next five seconds anyway, I drew my Glock and charged the guards, squeezing off a dozen 9mm rounds as I ran. Only about four of them hit anything, and nobody dropped, but getting shot sucks, even through body armor, so there would certainly be some bruises if these assholes lived long enough. I wasn't counting on any of them living long enough. I hurled my pistol at the face of one of the standing guards, then dropped into a baseball slide to crash into the front row.

They opened fire on me, but I brought my shield back up in time. And while they may have been protected from a magical attack, they weren't warded against two hundred pounds of immortal badass slamming into their face. I took down two in the front row and three in back, managing to grab one of them around the neck as we tumbled over each other in a tangle of legs and profanity. I gave his head a hard jerk straight up, hearing a sickening *crack* as I basically decapitated him. The important part, if not the bloody part. His head dropped to smack into his shoulder as his corpse smacked into the concrete.

My cheek exploded with pain as one of the standing guards leaned down and slammed the butt of his rifle into my face. I returned the favor by slamming the heel of my right palm into his knee, making his leg bend backward like a grasshopper. He fell to the ground, screaming and out of the fight. I got to my feet amidst a flurry of punches and kicks, slamming a fist into a groin or two on my way up.

I looked around for Luke and saw him rolling around on the ground with a pair of goons on top of him.

Can you get a shot on the guys beating Luke's ass? I thought to Becks.

I can't get a shot on anyone. Glory has us wrapped in her wings, which is safe as a bug in a rug, but we're not going to be able to generate much offense. If you can get your friends over there to stop trying to kill me, she might let me come out and play.

You got it. I drew in power, not being at all judicious where it came from. I couldn't get much off the guards due to their wards, but maybe I drained a little life force from them. I channeled that power out of myself through my skin, and I mean through all of it. Pure white light erupted from me, blasting out in a supernova of brightness in all directions. I might not be able to hurt them directly, but I could fuck up their vision pretty hardcore.

The gunfire ceased, and I snatched the shotgun from one of the kneeling assholes near me. I didn't know if they had any silver shells left, but I needed something to cut through these wards, so I pointed the gun at the center of the nearest standing guard's torso and let loose. When he flew backward and slammed to the ground with blood coming out of his mouth, nose, and ears, I figured there weren't any more silver shells. I also learned that a Kevlar vest will, in fact, stop buckshot. But it didn't do shit against the concussive force of the shell, so I racked the slide and dropped another guard before I clicked empty. I crushed the skull of another guard with the shotgun, then wrapped myself in a quick shield as the three remaining guards dropped their rifles and opened up on me with their pistols at point blank range.

My energy shield does a far better job than body armor of diffusing the impact of bullets, but it's not perfect. I still felt like a mule was kicking the fuck out of me every time these assholes fired, so I focused on my palms again. I had to time this right, or it was going to suck *a lot*.

I dropped my shield at the same time I called fire to my hands. *"Ignis!"* I shouted, blasting fire from my hands and spinning around like a lawn sprinkler from Hell. I knew it wouldn't hurt them because of their wards, but I didn't know if they knew. And even if they were warded, there's a reflexive response to a fuckton of fire coming at your face, and it's not to shoot the fire.

The fire licked harmlessly across their shields, but they all threw up their hands and turned away, giving me enough breathing room to snatch the sidearm off one of their dead friends and start shooting bad guys in the face. That's the pesky thing about body armor—it's not *face* armor. And after all this time, I'm a really good shot. I dropped two of them before they realized I was shooting, and just as the last guard turned his pistol back to me, his eyes went wide and a hole appeared in his throat. His hands flew to his neck, and he dropped straight down to his knees, then collapsed on his side as his blood ran out onto the concrete. I looked across the warehouse to see Becks pointing her pistol in my direction.

Thanks.

Not a problem. We've got one survivor. You?

One living plus the two Luke's...never mind. I was going to say something to Flynn about the two Luke was fighting still being alive, then I looked over to where Luke had been fighting. "Had been" was the operative phrase, because he was all finished fighting and was now having a snack on the lifeblood of one guard while the other lay cooling at his feet, head twisted completely around to face his ass. That shit *had* to hurt, albeit probably not for long.

I looked at the one guard whose knee I smashed. "You gonna tell me what I want to know about the Master, or are you a true believer?"

He stuck his right arm toward the sky in a salute I hadn't seen since the 40s, yelled "Deutschland Uber Alles!" then shot himself in the head with his own pistol.

"True believer it is," I said. I looked over to Luke. "I'm gonna go interrogate the last loader. Feel free to join us whenever you finish lunch." He waved at me to go ahead without him, and after finding my Glock among the corpses and reloading, I walked over to interrogate the surviving Klavier employee. This was only going to go one of two ways—bloody and productive, or very bloody and unproductive. Either way, it was a good thing I didn't wear my good shoes.

27

Harker

The last surviving and conscious bad guy was on his knees glaring up at me as I walked over. He was a big guy, but not in a "goes to the gym six days a week" way. He was the kind of thick that comes from lots of carbohydrates and hard work, not lots of moving steel plates up and down in front of a mirror. He had a thick bushy red beard, a flannel shirt, worn Carhartt work pants, and sturdy brown steel-toed boots. In other words, he was the heart and soul of the Carolinas' work force, and he didn't like outsiders coming in and screwing with his paycheck. He probably didn't know fuck-all about what went down in that warehouse, what he was loading onto that truck, or anything that Klavier Pharmaceuticals was up to.

He spat a big glob of bloody phlegm on the toe of my Doc Marten as I stepped in front of him. "I ain't gonna tell you nothing, you Yankee piece of shit. I pick shit up, move it from one place to another, and put it back down. I don't know nothing about what's in the boxes, where it's going, and I don't give a shit, neither."

I didn't say anything, I just reached out and slapped the ever-loving piss out of him. He fell to one side with more blood leaking out of his lips. "You wanna wait til I ask a question before you answer it, or you want to turn the other cheek so I can slap the shit out of that one, too?" I asked.

He grinned up at me and slowly rose to his feet. "You feel like trying, asshole?"

"Oh, for fuck's sake, look around," I said, gesturing to the pile of bodies. "You just watched us go through a dozen security guards like shit through a goose, and now you want to play tough guy? Fuck you, asshole!"

"Fuck you, too, you prick!" he shouted back.

"We don't have time for this," Luke said, and shoved me aside. He put one hand on the man's throat and lifted him off his feet. "You will answer every one of my friend's questions, and you will answer them truthfully and to the best of your knowledge. Then you will go out to your car, drive away from this place, and never return. If you do not do this, I will rip open your throat and lap up the very essence of your being as it pulses from your slowing heart, then I will find everyone you have ever cared about and kill them, slowly, after I tell them whose fault it is that they are experiencing this terrible, terrible torture. Do you understand me?" He dropped the man to his feet and stared deep into his eyes. Luke's face was like something out of a nightmare, half-covered in a black ski mask with nothing exposed but his mouth and jaw, and that painted in the blood of his victims. It was like a shadow came to life and was very, very hungry.

The warehouse guy nodded. I didn't blame him. Luke scared the shit out of me, and I was his family.

Bubba

I PEELED MYSELF OUT OF THE DRYWALL AND SLUMPED TO THE FLOOR, shaking gypsum dust out of my hair and reorienting myself to the battlefield. Which was a bit of an exaggeration, since at best what I saw could be considered a holding action, and they weren't going to be holding on to shit for much longer.

Amy, Faustus, and Pravesh formed a loose triangle at the open rear doors of the van, with Skeeter standing over them firing his rifle wildly at the attacking demons. In his mind he was probably taking careful aim and squeezing the trigger as his breath went out, just like the dude on the *Sniper* TV show. In reality, he might as well be Barney Fife shooting into a tornado with his eyes closed.

I stood up, snatched my sword up off the floor, and ran toward the fight. I didn't holler out this time, which was about as far as I ever go in the efforts of being stealthy, but one of the demons still musta heard me coming, since he turned around just as I got close. I didn't try anything fancy this time, just aimed the pointy end at his belly and kept running. He knocked my blade aside, but since all four of the demons were lined up pretty much perfect, all that did was send me barreling into the asshole next to him, point-first.

The demon's head snapped up as the blade went in, and I caught a glimpse of Faustus burying his dagger into the thing's chest. One quick yank from Faustus, one twist and shove from me, and the bad guys were reduced by a quarter and the carpet in that part of the lobby was damn near ruined. I mean, they had bigger issues than that, since I'd just been thrown most of the way through a wall and we parked a big-ass Sprinter van in front of the reception desk, but the carpet was *also* ruined.

Another demon staggered back as Amy thumped it in the forehead with her glowy stick, and I took advantage of its distraction to remove its head from its shoulders. If I thought they were nasty when they fell down and turned to goop, that didn't have anything on how gross they were when they spewed black gore all over the place standing up. Two down, though. That was a good start.

Until another pair of doors opened and four heavily armed and heavily muscled DEMON agents stepped into the lobby. Two of them carried miniguns like the asshole I fought in the cemetery down in Charlotte, and the other two had gone more old-school on me, one swinging a big Conan-looking axe and the other with a pair of swords straight out of *Game of Thrones* or some damn thing. I shoved a sword through the neck of another demon as Pravesh literally clawed the eyes out of the last one, then she shouted for all of us to get back in the van.

I did as I was told, slamming the doors behind me, just in time for the miniguns to open up on us. The sound was incredible, like being in a house with a tin roof in a hailstorm, but the armor plating on the van held.

"Now what?" I asked. "We're in here, but they're out there and it ain't gonna be long before the one with that axe decides it can do double duty as a can-opener and gets up close and persononal with us."

"Leave that to me," Pravesh said. She reached up to the roof of the van and pulled down a ladder hinged to the ceiling. She climbed up a few steps and slid open a panel, then slid up into a weird seat/step stool contraption and grabbed something I couldn't quite see.

I figured it out when thunder roared above my head and hot brass started falling from the sky. She had a goddamn turret gun mounted to the roof of the van and I hadn't even looked up to see it. "Well, I'll be damned," I said as she poured lead and righteous vengeance out upon our enemies. "She's from the government and she really is here to help."

Harker

I TOOK THE LEAD CREEPING DOWN THE SEEMINGLY DESERTED HALLWAY the warehouse guy told us would lead to the front entrance. There were lots of smaller hallways branching off, befitting the massive building we were in. The warehouse was easily big enough to drop my house inside and still have plenty of room to drive a forklift around. As we threaded past video cameras and open doors, I got the sense of just how massive this place was. And we hadn't even gotten into the lab wing yet.

By my best guess we made it almost halfway to the lobby before our cover was blown. It wasn't getting spotted on video; it wasn't running into a random security patrol. It wasn't anything like that. Nope. I literally bumped into a lone guard coming out of the men's room. He turned back into the room to toss a paper towel and slammed right into my face. I punched him square between the eyes and shoved him back into the crapper as fast as I could, but when his radio went off with a pissed-off voice on the other end asking where he was, I didn't have a good response. I didn't have any response, really, because they were using lots of lingo about zones and ten-somethings and I didn't care enough to try and figure it out.

I just picked up the radio, pushed the button on the side, and said, "He can't take your call right now because I beat the shit out of him. How about you and all your asshole friends meet me in the lobby and we'll sort all this mess out?"

I stepped out into the hallway, and Becks looked at me with some serious side-eye. "Who were you talking to?"

It's hard to lie to somebody who lives in your head, and it's a shitty way to behave in a relationship, so I stuck to my standard rule—be brutally honest. "That was the guard supervisor, looking for the guy I just knocked out. I told him if he wanted to find me, I'd be in the lobby in five minutes."

"The element of surprise really only exists for you in the abstract, doesn't it?" Luke asked.

"Sorry, I was never considered one of the greatest military minds of my time," I snarked back.

"I was never considered one of the most brilliant," Luke replied with a sniff. "Merely the most brutal. In that, I was uncontested."

"That's great and all, and I've heard all those stories. You were a beast," Becks said, pointing down a side hall. "But there's a dozen guys with guns running this way, and we're standing in essentially a shooting lane. So can we please move our asses!" At that, she shoved her way past me and started sprinting toward the lobby.

I couldn't find any real fault with her logic, so I said to Luke and Glory, "I'll take the rear guard. Since I can actually, you know, *guard*

164

us." They nodded and ran ahead, with Luke quickly vanishing out of sight through the door fifty yards in front of us. The sound of gunfire and screaming definitely made me believe the dock guy had been telling the truth about the lobby being in that direction, so I pulled up a shield just a little smaller than the hallway, set it in place between me and the oncoming guards, and hauled ass after my uncle.

You think they're in more or less shit than we are? I asked Becks.

What, do I think your redneck counterpart can get in at least as much trouble as you in under an hour?

Okay, that's a good point. Plus, we haven't heard from Skeeter in a few minutes.

And they're the reason the alarm went off in the first place.

And they have Faustus.

That sealed it for me. Becks was right, they were probably infinitely more fucked than we were. Turns out, I was right. God, sometimes I hate being right.

28

Harker

I stepped into a goddamned war zone. Again. There were four heavily armed assholes shooting the shit out of the Mercedes van we'd left Pravesh and Bubba in, and Pravesh was sitting in a turret in the roof of the van shooting right back at the guards. There was a Torment demon pounding on the closed doors of the van, and three big piles of nastiness that probably used to be other Torment demons. The front of the building was destroyed, the van was parked on the carpet in front of the reception desk, and one wall looked an awful lot like someone had lobbed high explosives at it. Oh yeah, and there were a dozen more security assholes running in our direction and picking up friends along the way.

I slammed the heavy doors shut behind me and yelled for Becks. "Come secure these! I'll take care of the demon while Luke handles whoever these assholes are."

Luke nodded and dashed toward the assholes with guns, forcing Pravesh to hop out of her turret. Hopefully she'd join the scrap when I went hand to hand with a Torment demon. A *blind* Torment demon, as it turned out. When I got close enough to get a good look at the thing, I saw that someone had literally raked the things eyeballs out. "Gotta tell Pravesh her human suit is slipping. Unless Bubba is a kind of eye-munching faerie I've never seen before," I muttered as I called up my soulblade.

My blade manifested blood red, a new color for me. Usually it was white or purple, but this was definitely an angrier, hyped-up soulblade. The demon heard me approaching and lashed out with a massive fist, but I just ducked under and slashed up, slicing through the monstrous torso and dropping the nasty bastard into a puddle of ichor on the floor.

I banged twice on the van's rear doors and yelled, "Cavalry's here, time to get back in the fight!"

I barely got out of the way before Bubba slammed the doors open and headed toward Luke and the four merry assholes. I let him go, thinking that he was expending a lot of energy on trying to help Luke, who was the most powerful person in the room. Then I looked where he was running, and those four goons had beaten the absolute dogshit out of the world's most famous vampire, and some rat bastard with a crew cut and a punchable face was pointing a massive pistol at Luke's face.

I cut loose with a magical blast that knocked Crew Cut into the nearby wall, and Luke yanked himself free of one of the guys trying to hold him down on his knees. And that's where my vision of the world went sideways, as the fourth asshole, the one who had been standing off to one side laughing, drew his sidearm and fired at me four times before I even saw his hand move. Three shots went wide, but one smacked into the center of my chest like I was being kicked by a mule. I flopped onto my back, gasping, and when I caught a good breath, cursing. My Kevlar stopped the bullet, but it didn't stop its momentum. One of these days I'm going to invent some magical gadget that just sucks all the kinetic energy out of projectiles coming your way, and I'll make a billion dollars. Until whoever makes Kevlar puts a hit out on my ass for killing their business. Corporate scheming—safer just to stick with hunting demons.

I struggled to my feet as Bubba got to the guys with guns, slamming into Crew Cut at a dead run and smashing him back into the wall. I was starting to like the way this hillbilly operated. He was about as subtle as a hand grenade, which I could relate to.

"Gonna need a little help over here!" Becks called from the hallway door we'd come through. Faustus and Pravesh headed her way while Amy and Skeeter provided cover fire from the back of the van. At least, Amy provided cover fire. I was as worried about Skeeter shooting me accidentally as I was one of the goons shooting me on purpose. And *that* had already happened.

I waded into the scrum with Luke and Bubba, and I figured out with the first punch I took that these were no ordinary mercenaries or leftover DEMON agents. Crew Cut had just peeled himself off the carpet again when I stepped up and raised a fist to him, but this time he had no intention of going down so easily. He sprang to his feet and laid an uppercut on my jaw that knocked me straight down on my ass in the middle of the fight.

I sat there, flat on my butt with my legs splayed out in front of me, shaking my head to clear the birdies out of the air, and almost didn't see the combat boot coming for my face. I flopped flat onto my back and rolled left, then spun around in a move that would have made any 1983 b-boy proud, sweeping at Crew Cut's legs. I smacked both feet into his shins, but instead of him toppling over like a redwood meeting Paul Bunyan, he just stood there looking down on me with a smirk across his very punchable face.

"What the fuck *are* you?" I asked as I sprang to my feet and attempted to do exactly what his face demanded, namely punch the shit out of it.

"Super-soldiers," Crew Cut replied. "Only not great big liberal cucks like Captain America." He blocked my punch and threw one of his own, a big right cross that would have laid me out again if it landed. So I didn't let it land. He was bigger than me by a couple inches and probably fifty pounds, and at least as strong as me, so I didn't want to let him get his big mitts on me. But I was a little quicker, and more agile, so it was a much more even fight than I liked, but one I could survive if I had enough time.

And that was the big question—did I have enough time? Luke was currently keeping two of the mercs occupied, and Bubba was holding his own with another, but how long could they keep that up? Luke was hurt, and one of the guys he was fighting seemed to be almost as fast as him, so he was taking a lot of punches from the strong one while trying not to get sliced to ribbons by the knife-wielding fast one. I couldn't tell anything about the woman Bubba was fighting, except that she was tall, muscular, and completely capable of going toe to toe with our big redneck without giving an inch.

I focused on the matter at hand, namely the big guy wanting to punch my face in, and started paying attention to his movements, trying to see if I could figure out what he knew and how he wanted to fight. He was strong, but he didn't bull in and try to wrestle me to the ground. He was tall but didn't go with much in the way of kicks or throws. He was more of a brawler than a martial artist, so all I needed to do was watch his footwork and wait for him to make a mistake.

He stepped in, threw a punch, stepped back. Step in, punch, step back. Step in, combination, step back—there! I saw it on the third repetition, the slight grapevine of his feet as he stepped back. Then he stepped in again, swung a big right hand, which I ducked, and as he stepped back, I launched myself at his chest while his feet were crossed over each other. His balance was shit, and he couldn't get his feet back under himself fast enough, and we both went crashing to the floor.

Off his feet, he didn't stand a chance. I'm not much of a wrestler, but I've studied enough of the various flavors of grappling to know how to slip my shoulders past his, wedge myself under one of his arms, and roll him over while holding onto his arm. I put one hand on the back of his elbow, the other on his wrist, and pushed forward while I yanked his arm back. His elbow dislocated with a sickening *crack*, and he let out one of those "I'm out of the fight" screams that are music to my ears.

I dropped his arm and stood up as Crew Cut started writhing on the floor in agony. Bubba was still trading licks with the dark-haired woman in tactical gear, so I focused on Luke. I called up a bolt of magic and shot the bigger of his two opponents right between the shoulder blades. He screamed, but instead of dropping to his knees and collapsing in a quivering pile of suddenly pacified asshole like he was supposed to, he whirled around and came running at me like a bull having a bad day in Pamplona.

I got off one more blast before he was on me, and I didn't even try to brace myself as he slammed into my gut with one shoulder. I actually jumped a little to soften the impact, and as he carried us into a wall, which I met back-first, I snaked my right arm down around his neck and throat. He buried me up to my face in a sheetrock wall, but I just slipped my arm completely into a choke hold and started to squeeze. It doesn't take very long to choke someone out, not if you can consistently control their head to pinch off the carotid arteries. It is considerably harder when that person is pounding you into a wall every three seconds. My grip loosened when he found a building stud with my spine, and he slipped out of my arm, backing up to grin at me.

"Hybrids one, Reaper zero," said as he pulled a big Bowie knife from his belt. "I'm gonna carve your face off and tack it up over my bed, so I can blow you kisses every night before I go to sleep. The big bad Reaper, just another overblown asshole who couldn't live up to his reputation."

"Shut the fuck up," I said, stepping out of the destroyed wall and burying my soulblade in his chest. The light from my blade poured out his back, chest, and eyes, and I yanked it free, decapitating him as his lifeless corpse slumped to the floor. "Only talk when you're actually *winning* the fight, asshole."

In his defense, he probably thought he was winning the fight when he started monologuing. That's the problem with bad guys—poor threat assessment. He was afraid of the chokehold, when he should have been afraid of me realizing I couldn't beat him hand-to-hand. Because as soon as I realized I couldn't choke him out, I decided to cheat. Then I killed him.

I looked around the room and saw that Luke had moved from "legitimate fight with a tough opponent" to "playing with his food" once there was only one of the "super-soldiers" to contend with. I figured the slender Black man he was fighting had about fifteen seconds to live, depending on how fast he bled out into Luke's mouth when my uncle got tired of fucking around and just started draining the dude.

That left Bubba, and as I looked over to where he'd been duking it out with a woman who looked like she bench-pressed Mini Coopers for fun, my eyes widened a little at what I saw. Bubba was on his knees, head bowed, over the corpse of the woman who had been trying to rip him limb from limb. As I watched, he crossed himself, looked up at the sky, said something even I couldn't hear, and stood. He pulled his sword from the dead woman's chest, wiped it clean on the side of his pants, and slid it into the sheath on his back.

He saw me looking. "She mighta tried to kill me, but I don't know if she was really *evil*. I had to kill her. She was a long way from human, and whatever they did to these people messed with their heads as much as it did with their bodies. So I couldn't just knock her out and let her go, if it was even possible *to* knock her out. She had to die, but that don't mean she doesn't deserve a prayer."

"If you're around when I finally bite it, I hope you'll do the same for me," I said, genuinely touched that with everything he'd seen and done, he still had even a shred of faith in higher powers. Speaking of higher powers... "Have you seen Glory?"

"Not since we got in here. Wasn't she with you?"

"Dammit," I muttered. How the hell did I lose a guardian angel in the middle of a fight for my life. Wasn't that kind of *exactly* where she should be?

Then the doors Pravesh and Becks are holding closed blew open, and I really wanted to know where Glory was for a whole different reason—because I thought what was coming through that door might actually be able to kill every damned one of us.

29

It wasn't the dozen security goons I was worried about—we'd taken out plenty of them at the loading dock. It wasn't even the pair of Torment demons pushing their way through the goons to get at us. Nope, my worry was all centered on the big bastard bringing up the rear of the parade—an eight-foot-tall vision of horror that looked like an H.R. Geiger painting came to life and went traipsing through the darker parts of Hieronymus Bosch's psyche before it manifested into a giant pile of walking murder.

"Is that a..." Faustus's voice trailed off.

"Yeah, that's exactly what that is," I confirmed.

"Do you know which one?" the demon at my elbow asked. "Not that they aren't all horrible, but there are a couple that are particularly pissed at me. It's been a few years, but..."

"But what's a millennium or two when you're a Prince of Hell?" I finished.

"Yeah, pretty much."

"I don't know who it is specifically, but if he's here, then whatever they're doing in the other half of this building is important to somebody. Somebody with enough juice downstairs to get one of Lucifer's top henchmen up here to supervise."

"That's one big asshole," Bubba said as he stepped up to my other side. "Kinda makes me wish I still had Bertha."

"That magic sword is gonna be a lot more useful than your hand cannon against most of that crowd," I said.

"I believe you, but something that nasty makes me want to be surrounded by as much firepower as possible."

It was a perfectly reasonable desire. For me, looking at that big bastard made me want to crawl in a hole and pull the hole in after me. It made me want to run west and not stop running until I hit more water than I could drive across. But if I did that, a lot of people would die. Most of the people I actually liked in the world would die, because none of the folks I walked into this mess with had an ounce of run away in them.

You and Amy take out as many of the human security as you can, but work your way back toward cover, I said to Becks. *Huddle up with Skeeter and try not to get dead. Between Luke, Bubba, and Faustus, they can take out the Torment demons.*

Leaving the biggest, baddest bad guy for you? she replied, and I could feel a little humor in her voice. *Quincy Harker, whitest of the white saviors. One of these days we're gonna figure out how to solve that messiah complex you're carrying around. That shit has got to be heavy.*

Yeah, I'll take it up with my therapist.

You have a therapist?

Yeah, a new guy. You'll like him. His name is Johnny. Johnny Walker. Sometimes he consults with his mentor, Pappy Van Winkle.

You're incorrigible. Just get over here and clear me a path.

I relayed the plan, minimal as it was, to the rest of the team, and we split apart to go after our various targets. I didn't move, just stood in the middle of the room and shouted, "Hey! Asshole! You here for me? About time somebody showed up that might make me break a sweat. You wanna get your scaly ass over here so we can get this shit done, or you gonna huddle over their behind the meat shields for a while?"

If there's anything guaranteed to get a demon riled up, it's calling them a coward. That's because they almost always are total cowards, but since so much of their power downstairs relies on people being terrified of them, they can't own their own fear. So calling one a chicken is more effective than "your mama" jokes to middle schoolers.

The demon moved forward with what I assume was a grin stretching its grotesque features, and bellowed at me, "Quincy Harker! I will be feted as a king when I throw your severed head at Lucifer's feet! I will be proclaimed the new Archduke of the Infernos when I wear your skin as a cape! Every demon in the Pits will sing my praises as I—"

I didn't want to know what he was going to do to me next, so I flung a bolt of pure white power into his gaping maw. It didn't do any real damage, but I got the satisfaction of both shutting him up and seeing his yellow alligator eyes bug out even more as I rang his epiglottis like a speed bag. He stopped for a second, shook his head, then let out a roar that actually drove the nearest security goons to their knees. He almost completely unhinged his jaw to scream at me, showing off all three rows of sharklike pointed teeth. He pounded the floor with his enormous fists, cracking the concrete and ripping chunks of the building slab up through the carpet.

"Never learned how to take a punch, huh?" I asked, leaning back against one of the expensive leather lobby sofas. I folded my arms across my chest and gave the ten-foot-tall monstrosity my most condescending look. Which, given the fact that I grew up in Victorian England, can be pretty goddamned condescending. "Maybe if you spent more time battling in the Pits instead of telling everyone how great you are, you would already have been the Archduke of Infernos, instead of just the Marquis of Mediocrity."

That got him. I mean, he was already really pissed, but that put his needle all the way to thermonuclear. He covered the thirty feet between us in a matter of seconds, his talons flashing down to cleave the sofa into shredded chunks. Because I sure as hell wasn't still standing there. I spun away to the right as soon as he raised his hands above his head, manifesting my soulblade and slicing away at his hamstrings. This one was mostly humanoid except for the claws, the massive mouth with all the teeth, and the ram's horns curling out from its forehead.

But it sure as shit didn't cut like a human. Or like a demon, for that matter. My sword smacked into its leg, and instead of cutting right through the leg, bone and all, like it had done with every other demon I'd ever fought, it slammed into the thigh just above the knee and rebounded, leaving my palms stinging with the vibration.

I opened my hands and my soulblade blinked out of existence, then I looked up at the demon's grinning face. "Lycus, duke of Wrath. Pleased to kill you," it said, then it snatched me up by my throat with one hand, grabbed my ankles with the other, and proceeded to try very hard to see how far my guts would stretch.

I've felt a lot of pain in my life. I've been shot, stabbed, blown up, set on fire, and bitten by more different species of things than my parents ever knew existed. But I'd never had anyone literally try to tear me limb from limb before. It was a new, and wholly unpleasant experience, that if I'm given anything resembling a choice, I will never repeat.

Being dropped from a dozen feet onto concrete wasn't a new thing, and it was frankly the most welcome pain I'd felt in a long time, because it meant Lycus wasn't trying to rip my head off anymore. But he was stomping over to the van in search of the source of the thunderous impact that made him drop me on my ass. That source was one Keya Pravesh: government official, understanding boss, badass snake-lady, and wielder of a goddamned rocket launcher in the lobby of a drug company HQ.

Unfortunately, it didn't do what I assume she wanted it to do, namely kill the demon. But it definitely did what I wanted it to do, which was convince the demon to drop me. I rolled over onto my stomach and pushed myself up to my knees, stopping to let the world spin for a second. *Goddammit. Another concussion.* The next few minutes were going to suck, and I once again thanked my lucky stars for the sliver of demon that worked so hard at putting me back together so it would still have a nice, warm body to call home.

Although, if I didn't have the strength, speed, enhanced senses, and longevity that came from possessing a little chunk of demon deep down inside, it's entirely possible I wouldn't have kept finding myself in situations where I *needed* super healing. But I didn't have time for a deep chicken versus egg contemplation. I'd save that for the next time Becks talked me into trying kitten yoga, which was more adorable, and also more bitey, then I expected it to be.

I struggled to my feet and focused what I could of my vision on the massive back of the demonic duke. I called up power and shaped it into a needle of bright blue force, then I shouted, *"Glacio!"* And cut loose with a magical freeze ray intended to chill Lycus right the fuck out.

Spoiler—it didn't work. I mean, my power spike hit him, and it even staggered him a little and jabbed deep into his flesh, causing him to throw his head back and screech like a million bats flew into a classroom and each tried to run their little bat claws down a chalkboard at the same time. But if you, like me, were hoping for a really cool effect shot where the ice spike went in Lycus's back and pierced all the way through to come out its chest, then a heavy glaze of frost formed over the demon's entire body as it slowly turned into the world's ugliest ice sculpture, then you're going to be disappointed. I know I was.

Lycus didn't freeze, didn't even shiver. It just reached over its shoulder, plucked my magical icicle spear out of its back, and flung it at Pravesh. On her, it *did* go all the way through one side and out the other, and since her sides are both squishier and much smaller than the demon's, it had a lot greater effect. She dropped like a stone, basically. A screaming, bloody stone. Lycus turned back to me, took two big strides, and was on me again.

Get Pravesh out of here, I called to Becks. *She's really fucked up.*
On it.

I had to trust that Flynn could get past me and the demon, make it to the van, drive the van (assuming the van was still drivable after running into a building) to a hospital, and then figure out how to explain to the people at the hospital why their trauma patient has scales, cold blood, and fangs. Although, Becks could just flash her federal government ID and everyone would understand the whole snake thing immediately. But I had bigger fish to fry. Or fight, because trying to fry a duke of Hell doesn't usually go well. They kinda dig fire.

Lycus swept a giant hand at my face, but I ducked out of the way. I even managed to avoid the stabbing shot he made at my guts with his claws fully extended. I leapt backward out of range of his snapping teeth but was brought up short when I slammed into a brick wall. That laughed.

Wait, brick walls don't laugh.

Shit.

I looked over my right shoulder just in time to see two massive fists come slamming down on my face as one of the super-soldiers clubbed me to the floor.

Great, now they can fight over who gets to murder me. Yay. The massive mercenary stepped back and gestured to the demon as if to say, "after you," and Lycus grinned. If you've never seen a demon grin, count yourself lucky. They're nasty-looking motherfuckers to start with, which makes sense given the whole born in a lake of fire thing. But when they smile, you can see how they just aren't *right*. Angels are the ideal; they're humanity taken to the nth degree. They're physically perfect, when they choose to manifest. Most of them are assholes, but they're really pretty assholes.

But demons? Nah, they're fucked up. They look like normal, if ugly, monsters until they try to do something that resembles human activity. Then their mouths don't work in sync with their voices, or their heads don't sit quite perfectly atop their necks…it's something. It's like someone took a picture of a person, cut it into a bunch of pieces, then glued it back together, but the pieces weren't lined up just right. It's fucking unnerving, and Lycus smiling was the most terrifying thing I'd seen all day, except maybe Luke. He was pretty scary.

"Prepare to die, Reaper," the demon said, drawing one massive hand back to slice me open from my nuts to my nose.

"Oh, please," came a voice I never thought I'd hear in a fight again. "If Harker was that fucking easy to kill, my life woulda been so much simpler." Then there was a massive *crunch*, and Lycus slammed to the floor on his side. Standing behind him, with her great-grandfather's hammer slung over her shoulder, was Jo Henry. She held out a hand to me and hauled me to my feet.

"Thanks," I said, dodging a punch from the big mercenary and responding with an uppercut that staggered him back a few steps. "Didn't think you were coming back."

"Neither did I," Jo said, taking her hammer into both hands. "Glory got me from the airport. Said you were going to need every friend you've got. So I guess I'm not quite as done with this shit as I thought."

"Glory's here?"

"Healing Pravesh."

"Good deal." I looked at the demon, struggling to its feet with one crushed knee, then looked at the mercenary, who had a long dagger in each hand and a nasty grin on his face. "Which one you want?"

"You take the ugly one," Jo said. "I'll handle the demon." And just like that, she waded back into the fight as if she'd never left. Because no matter how hard we try, we never can.

30

I laid into the big merc while Jo squared off against Lycus. Part of me felt a little concern about her taking on a badass demon with just John Henry's hammer, but since nothing I'd done had even made the motherfucker pause, and she knocked him flat on his ass with one shot, she was in better shape against him than I was. She just needed to make sure not to let him get his hands on her. I could attest to exactly how little fun that was.

The merc was massive, bigger than Bubba, with muscles on top of muscles and the tank top cut to show them off. He looked like he was cosplaying Arnold from *Predator*, only more buff. He was wearing a tactical vest, tactical pants, and a pair of massive pistols on his hips. He reached down to graze the butt of his guns as I turned to face him, then smiled and shook his head.

"I don't need bullets to finish you off, asshole. Looks like your reputation was all bullshit anyway." He pulled a massive survival knife from his right thigh, reversed grip on it, and assumed some kind of crouchy fighty stance that involved him flexing his neck muscles a lot.

I didn't know what style of martial arts he was trained in, because even though I've studied a lot of them over the year, posing like a douche wasn't something any of them covered. Maybe I just kept missing that class. He came at me, dropping his shoulder to catch me in the gut, arms spread wide to keep me from dodging to either side. So I tried something I'd seen on a pro wrestling show recently. I dropped flat on my back in front of him, and when he looked down at me in surprise, I reached up and punched him right in the face.

And son of a bitch, it worked. I slammed my fist into his mouth and felt his lips split wide open. I also cut my knuckle on his front teeth, but that's the price I pay sometimes for being amazing. I didn't try to kip up onto my feet from my back because I'm not a professional athlete and I'm over a hundred fucking years old. I know my limitations, and they are many. One of them includes not doing cool floppy moves in the middle of a fight because I invariably fuck them up and injure myself.

Beefy McMercenary had one hand pressed to his mouth, but the other was slashing wildly in front of his body with that giant toothpick, so I decided to do something about that before he got me with a lucky shot. I focused on the knife and muttered, *"Electricae"* under my breath. Beefy dropped the knife with a curse, and I stepped forward, grabbed his wrist, and pulled his arm straight. Then I brought my knee up and introduced it to his tricep while yanking down on his wrist. The *POP* that came from his shoulder was drowned out by the scream that came from his mouth, but when I pulled on his now-dislocated arm again, his face followed. I cracked a knee across his temple, and he fell to the ground, presumably unconscious. Honestly, I didn't give a shit if I'd just caved in his goddamned skull. He wanted to kill me, so if he didn't walk away from this scrap, it's his own damn fault.

I turned to check in on Jo, and she had things well in hand. And by "well in hand" I mean she was standing on Lycus's chest with her hammer raised over her head, bringing it down again and again into the demon's skull. I watched her bash it three, then four times before she hopped to the ground and turned to look at me. "I think I made a mess."

I stepped over to the pile of steaming black ooze on the carpet as

Lycus rapidly turned into the kind of stain the next owners of this building were going to have to pour new concrete to replace. "Yeah, I'd say so. When did your hammer become a fucking holy weapon?"

"No idea," she replied. "I needed a new handle after Luke shoved the last one through Watson, and Glory hooked me up with the repairs. Guess she did a few upgrades at the same time."

"Guess so," I said, looking across the lobby at Glory, who knelt on the concrete with her hands pressed to Pravesh's chest. "Looks like she's still making sure all Pravesh's innards stay in, so let's finish the cleanup and explore the rest of this place. There's gotta be something here to lead us to the Master."

"I'll help Bubba," Jo said, choking up on her hammer and running to where Brabham had killed one Torment demon but was having trouble finishing off the other while Luke battled another one of the super-soldier assholes back-to-back with him. If we got out of this, I really wanted to hunt down whoever ripped off Captain America's origin story and have a few words with them. Most of those words were going to be some variation on "motherfucker."

My crew had most everything under control, especially once Jo walked over behind the merc Luke was scrapping with and caved his head in with one shot. That let Luke spin around and help Bubba kill the Torment demon, which then freed up all three of them to help Faustus and Amy finish off the last of the security guards.

I focused my attention on Pravesh, who was lying on the floor at the back of the van, Skeeter and Beck providing cover while Glory kept pouring light into the injured woman's body. "Is she going to be okay?" I asked. "The Department of Homeland Security is going to have some real issues with me if I'm responsible for another one of their regional bosses getting killed."

"At least you didn't shoot this one in the face," Glory said. "So you've got that going for you. I think she's going to make it, but if she gets so much as a paper cut in the next few hours, it'll probably kill her. I've done all I can do for her magically. Whatever happens next is on her."

"And your boss," I added, pointing up. "Okay, Skeeter, you and Becks get Pravesh to the nearest hospital. Glory—"

Becks cut me off. "Fuck no. I'm not leaving you, Harker."

"Somebody has to get Pravesh treatment and make sure the authorities aren't called," I said. "That means whoever we send with her has to *be* the authorities. Right now, that's you or Amy, and I need Bubba with me."

"And no way he's letting Amy out of his sight after what happened to Joe," Skeeter added.

"And I'm not letting you out of *my* sight after what happened to everybody the past year or two," Flynn said. "Don't forget, Harker. I'm inside your head. I know better than anybody, maybe better than you, how close you are to breaking." She shot a look to Glory. "And I know what happens if you do."

"I got this," Glory said, standing up and staring intently at Becks for a moment. Then a brilliant white glow originated from somewhere within the angel's form, growing in brightness until it was impossible to look at her. When the supernova faded and I blinked away the spots dancing in front of my eyes, a perfect replica of Rebecca Gail Flynn stood where Glory had been a moment before.

"What the fuck?" I said. Then I felt a corner of my mouth perk up as my mind went places it should really never go when there's an angel involved.

"One, get your mind out of the gutter, Q," Glory/Becks said. "Two, this isn't my real form, remember? I look like what I need to look like, and right now, I need to look like Deputy Director Rebecca Gail Flynn. I'll ride with Skeeter and Pravesh, making sure that she doesn't get jostled around too much in the back of the van. You guys find out everything you can here, and if you need me, I'll find you."

"How will you do that?" Skeeter asked.

Glory/Becks gave him a look that I recognized all too well as Flynn's "are you really fucking asking me that question" face. "I'm his Guardian Angel. He can't hide from me, no matter how hard he tries. Comes with the gig. And speaking of gigs," she said, turning to Flynn. "Give me your badge. I might need something official."

Becks handed it over, looking the angel in her body up and down. "I was right," she said. "That top does look good on me. You make me look good, girl." She held up a hand, and Glory high-fived her.

"Okay, let's get this show on the road," Glory said, picking Pravesh up off the floor and stepping into the back of the van with her cradled in her arms.

Skeeter closed the rear doors and headed for the driver's door. "Tell Bubba what's up, and that I've got an angel looking out for me," he called back.

"From what I hear about your driving, you're gonna need one," I replied. Then I smacked the back of the van twice and went back to the others, looking around the lobby for any survivors to interrogate.

It was a fruitless search. There weren't nearly enough bodies for the number of assholes we'd dispatched, but all the demons turned to sludge when they died, and any of the guards that survived had run for the hills, so we were left with the one comatose mercenary whose shoulder I yanked out of the socket, and one skinny unconscious guard with a leg pointing in the wrong direction for his body.

I knelt down and pressed my palm on his thigh, right about where I guessed the break in his femur was. He came awake with a scream, and I slapped him across the face. His howl of pain cut off short in surprise.

"Shut up," I said. "You speak when I say you speak, but otherwise you shut the fuck up. Got it?"

He nodded. Good. He really did get it. "Is the Master here?" I asked.

He didn't respond.

"You can answer," I said.

"No, I can't."

"Really, you can," I said, pressing down on his leg. Beads of sweat popped out on his forehead, but I couldn't tell if they were from fear or pain.

"No, I really can't," he said, sweat now pouring from his forehead. A little foamy drool escaped from the corner of his mouth, and he wiped it off with the back of his hand. "I'm not telling you anything, no matter how much you torture me!" He looked up. "You hear that? I'm not telling them anything! I don't know anything to tell them! And if I did, I wouldn't tell! I swear it!"

His head shook from side to side, and he began to shake, then convulse wildly under my hands. I stood up and stepped back as he began to thrash like he was being electrocuted, flopping around on the floor like a fish out of water. A few seconds later, he went rigid, his eyes wide, and he let out a scream, then dropped flat on his back, dead.

"What the fuck was that?" I asked.

"We saw something like that in Florida," Amy said from beside me. "When they were questioned about the Master, or Chancellor, it's like there was a self-destruct mechanism in their heads."

I looked at the body with my Sight, and sure enough, there was a tiny sigil behind the left ear that glowed with a sickly green. I didn't recognize it, but that didn't matter. It was more about the intention and the power than about the symbol itself. And the intention of this thing was definitely nothing good.

"Well," I said, reaching down and snatching the ID badge off the dead guard's chest. "If he couldn't give us information, at least he gave us the next best thing."

"What's that?" Bubba asked.

I held up the ID badge, showing the magnetic strip on the back of the card. "Access."

"You saying there's a door around here you don't think we could kick down?"

"Bubba, my boy," I said, reaching up to throw an arm over his beefy shoulders. "This isn't something I get to say often. Hell, this isn't something I get to say ever, but have you ever considered that sometimes a more subtle approach can be effective?"

Bubba looked down at me, his face solemn as a stone. "Nope. Never."

"Well," I said. "We're gonna try it anyway. Now let's go find somebody to beat up for information."

"Now you're speaking my language," he replied, and we headed to the far side of the lobby and the sealed doors leading into the as-yet unexplored half of the headquarters building.

31

We trooped across the lobby to the far side, where a pair of innocuous double doors stood. They were locked, of course, but the dead guard's key card opened it right up. I took the lead, with Bubba right behind me. I didn't love having a giant with a sword just a couple feet to my rear, but since Becks was behind *him*, I knew she had my back just in case Bubba decided it would look better with a few feet of steel sticking out of it. I had no reason to suspect betrayal, other than the fact that suspicion was kinda my default right at that moment.

Amy and Jo anchored the middle, Amy with her DHS-issued pistol, and Jo with an MP-7 she lifted off one of the guards just in case she wasn't within hammer range of the bad guys. Luke brought up the rear, because anything that made it through him to get at us was probably just bad enough to straight murder everyone. The hallway was wide enough for four people to walk abreast, but we kept tight to the right-hand wall regardless. I had my Glock in one hand and a sphere of purple energy in the other, flinging power at surveillance cameras as we went along.

It looked pretty normal. Pictures of people in lab coats doing scientist things lined the wall, along with photos of White people with very large teeth smiling over "Employee of the Month" and "Researcher of the Year" plaques. We went about thirty yards before we came to a heavier door with a sign saying "Authorized Personnel Only." I swiped the key card and waited for the light on the lock pad to go green.

Nothing. I swiped again. More nothing. I swiped a third time, then felt air move to my left as Bubba stepped forward and slammed his massive foot into the door just above the knob. It flung open, slamming into the wall with a thunderous *BOOM*.

"So much for subtle," I said.

"Dude, Pravesh set off a friggin' rocket launcher in the lobby. A rocket launcher! Do you think there's anybody in the damn zip code that don't know we're here?"

"Okay, good point," I said. "Just give me a little warning next time. Okay?"

"I reckon," he grumbled.

I pushed the door open from where it had swung shut and stepped through. At first glance it looked like just more hallway, but then I started to notice some subtle differences. The signs were all in German and English, not just English. And the photos weren't of scientists doing science things anymore. They were of spectacular old buildings in Germany, or huge Nazi rallies from the 30s and 40s, or some more recent photos like one of young White men throwing up Nazi salutes in front of the Capitol building.

"Well, I'm gonna go out on a limb here and say it's probably Nazis," Amy said, looking around.

"I fucking hate Nazis," Jo and I said at the same time.

"Doesn't everybody?" Bubba asked. "I mean, ain't that like the one thing people can agree on? That Nazis suck."

"You'd be surprised," Becks said. "There are a lot more people who think these bastards had the right idea than there should be."

"One is too many," Luke said from the back of the pack. "But yes, as we have seen in recent years, there are many who think that Hitler's ideology did not need to die with him."

We came to a point where the hall kept going, but another hall teed off to the right, and since we hadn't seen any doors so far, we took the right turn and went deeper into the building. Because that never ends badly, right? When the plucky band of misfits goes deeper into the lair of the evil scientists. That's always just fine, right? Thought so.

We'd gone maybe twenty feet when a door opened ahead of us and a pair of men dressed like the mercenaries we'd fought in the library stepped out. One saw us and pulled a pair of long knives from his belt as his face lit up in a grin. The other stuck his head back in the door and yelled, "They're out here!"

I looked over my left shoulder at Bubba, who had already drawn his sword. "Guess we're done with stealth, huh?"

"Were we ever really all that stealthy?" Bubba asked.

I didn't answer, partly because it was a rhetorical question, but mostly because I had a skinny dude about five foot nine standing in front of me twirling a pair of daggers around between his fingers like I was Johnny Ringo to his Doc Holliday. He grinned at me, a maniacal thing that made me seriously question if these guys were too nuts even for Nazis, then he slashed out at my throat with one of his blades.

Nope, not too crazy for Nazis. Too crazy for me, though. I flung the ball of purple energy I had floating above my palm into his eyes, blinding him. Then I grabbed his right arm at the elbow and wrist as he tried to stab me. I bent his arm sharply at the elbow and stepped forward, using my body's mass to push the knife into his belly. I yanked up, leaving a gash from just about his belt to where his ribcage stopped the blade, and then I stepped on his toes and shoved him backward.

He couldn't flop over onto his ass like he usually would, because I was standing on his toes. And he was definitely going *somewhere*, because I gave him a pretty good shove. So, he bent over backward, bending at the knees, but with enough tension on his torso to make his guts erupt out of the zipper I just carved in his abdomen like those joke snakes you get that pop out of a can. Only way messier.

His friend took one look at the carnage and turned to run the other way. Good idea, except that meant he ran right smack dab into the rest of his pals who were coming out of what I assumed was a barracks. Half a dozen mercenary assholes slap-fighting in a hallway trying to get away is usually one of my favorite spectator sports, but I had shit to do today. So, I just cut loose with a massive fireball and scorched them all to briquets. After the sprinklers and fire alarms kicked on, dousing everyone and everything with cold, rusty water, I sagged against the hallway wall.

"You alright, man?" Bubba asked.

"Yeah," I panted. "I will be. That…took a lot of energy."

"I reckon so," the big guy agreed. "I mean you cooked them sumbitches something fierce."

"That was kinda the plan. Just…you take point for a couple minutes until I can recharge, okay?"

"Yeah, no problem. Let's check this room they came out of. Maybe there's more assholes in there, or maybe a clue as to what the Master's plan is. Or who the Master is."

"Where," Becks added. "Where would be good, too."

There were not, in fact, more assholes in the room. At least, no more live assholes. There was one guy just inside the door that must have gotten a face full of superheated magic, because he looked like a piece of beef jerky left out in the desert for about a week. Only stinkier. It was a barracks, with two long rows of bunk beds running the length of the room. Each bunk was pretty squared away, and the footlockers by the beds showed no personal effects. Made sense. If I was somebody who got hired to go exotic places and murder people, I probably wouldn't tote along anything that could link back to the people I cared about, assuming such people existed.

We tossed the room quickly but thoroughly, uncovering just as much useful information as we expected. Which is to say, none at all. There was a small sleeping area at the far end of the room with a bunk in it and a small desk, where I assumed their commander, or whatever you call the chief prick in a bunch of mercenary pricks, answered emails about finding the next bunch of innocent civilians to slaughter in search of the almighty dollar.

I have opinions about mercenaries. I've never had a problem with people who fight for a cause, even if it's misguided. I get that. It's a way to feel like you're part of something larger than yourself. But just fighting for money? That's always felt a bit sociopathic to me.

"There's a door over here," Amy called from the hallway just past the boss's room. "Looks like it leads out into a hall just like the one we —nope, never mind, this is exactly the hall y'all took from the dock to the lobby."

"How can you tell?" Jo asked.

"The doors at each end of the hall are blown to smithereens," Amy replied.

"Yep, might as well spray paint 'Harker was here' on the walls," Jo said.

"No point backtracking. Let's see what's farther down this hall," I said, turning around and heading out.

A little farther down there was a door set into the wall to our left with a biohazard sign next to it and warnings in English, Spanish, French, German, Japanese, Mandarin, and Korean. I don't even read Korean, but I can recognize it when I see it. Whatever was in this joint must be all kinds of dangerous.

"This is it," I said, waving Luke and Bubba forward. I wanted our heaviest hitters to go in first, with Jo guarding the rear with her hammer. I pushed the door open and dashed through, peeling off to the right as Luke and Bubba came in behind. Bubba went right, and Luke covered the middle, as much as an empty room needs to be covered.

We were in a lab, and it was outfitted for people working in some heavy-duty infectious disease prevention gear. There were hoses hanging down at every workstation for people to hook into and get air, and there was a panic button by the door that said "Emergency Quarantine" in big letters.

"What the hell were they making in here?" Bubba asked.

"No idea," I replied. "But it was obviously something heavy."

"This is a DNA sequencer," Jo called from the far side of the room.

"And I think this equipment is designed to extract DNA from a sample."

"How do you recognize all this *Star Trek* shit?" Bubba asked.

"I went out with a biology major in college. Our first date was him showing me all around the lab where he did his work study, telling me how expensive the machines were and how they were working on cutting-edge genetic stuff."

"Sounds positively scintillating," Amy said. "What did you do for a second date? Calculate pi to the hundredth decimal?"

"There wasn't a second date," Jo said. "We went back to my apartment to watch a movie, he tried to feel me up on the couch, I slapped the taste out of his mouth, and he didn't call me again."

"Good for you," Becks said, high-fiving her. "And now we get some benefit of his knowledge."

"And you didn't have to bang him," Bubba said.

"Quiet," I said, waving everyone to silence. "I hear something," I whispered. We all stood frozen, and after a long moment, I heard it again. There was a rattle going from one of the large cabinets marked CHEMICAL STORAGE - EXTREMELY HAZARDOUS. I walked over to the cabinet, Becks and Amy spread out behind me to provide cover, and opened the door.

Out spilled a disheveled middle-aged man with crazy hair, a well-stained necktie, a lab coat, and a look of utter terror on his face. "Please don't kill me! I didn't know we were being evil!"

I looked around at my team, who all looked just as confused as me. I knelt down beside the man and said, "We're not going to kill you."

"Unless we have to," Bubba said.

I glared at him, and he raised his hands in supplication. "What? I thought we were going to do the good cop, bad cop thing."

"Do you really think there's a world in which *I* am going to be the good cop?" I asked.

"Okay, that's fair."

I turned back to the man, who smelled of formaldehyde and grilled onions. "We're not going to kill you. But we do have some questions. What are you doing here that's 'being evil'?"

He looked around at all of us. "You promise you aren't going to kill me?"

"Depends on how long you make me wait for an answer," I replied.

He gulped, then said, "We're building an army to restore the glory of the Third Reich and cleanse the world of all inferior races and species."

"Oh, is that all?" I asked. I stood up, dragging the scientist with me. I plopped him down in a chair so we could have a real conversation. It felt like this was going to take a while. "Okay, pal. Tell me everything you know about what you're doing here, and everything you know about the big boss of this whole operation." I intentionally didn't call him the Master because I hoped that would keep this dickhead's brains from turning to oatmeal.

"Okay, but you probably all want to get chairs. There's a lot, and… well, it's pretty awful."

Awful genetic experiments by Nazis. Must be Tuesday.

32

I suppose the first thing you're going to want to know is how I got mixed up in all this. Well, they recruit the best and brightest—"

"No," I said, cutting off the skinny bastard before he could give me his whole resume. "The first thing I want to know is where to find your boss."

"But even before that, we really want to know what you were doing here," Amy said, walking over to an aluminum table. "This table, for example. It doesn't look like anything you want a test subject to have to lay on."

"Well, not if you care at all about their well-being or comfort, now. That model is usually only used for autopsies. But some of our earlier specimens were less than successful, so we ended up performing plenty of those as well as the infusions we were developing."

"Infusions?" Amy asked, walking over to a big machine with a chair built into the side of it. The thing looked like you would sit in the chair, be strapped down across your thighs, head, and arms, and something would go through a huge opening in the back of the chair to do something nasty to your spine.

"Yes," Evil Bill Nye said, getting up and walking over to the machine. I noticed Becks had already repositioned herself so that she was leaning up against the doorframe, blocking the only exit. "This is the genetic infuser." He gestured to the chair. "The subject would sit here, and we would deposit the new genetic material directly into their spinal fluid and into the amygdala, more efficiently disseminating the enhanced DNA."

"Enhanced with what?" I asked, thinking back to the mercenaries we'd encountered that were faster, stronger, and more durable than they had any right to be.

"Dude, you know what," Bubba said. "These jerks are putting cryptid DNA into humans."

"You just had to say it, didn't you?" I asked, throwing my hands up. "As long as nobody said it, I could hold out the tiniest shred of hope that they were doing something reasonable, like extracting dinosaur DNA from amber and using that to grow velociraptors in a lab!"

"The very fact that you know what a velociraptor is shows exactly how well that idea worked out," Becks said.

"I don't understand," Luke said to Faustus, his voice low. "What are they saying?"

They were behind me, but I could almost see the shrug Faustus gave him. "Dude, you're talking to the one guy in the room who's older than you. There's no chance I know what they're on about."

"So you knew what they were up to? I guess, what you were up to," I corrected.

Science Guy nodded. "It was all theoretical at first. You know, pure science, the kind of stuff us lab junkies dream of. We identified a few sequences in the human genome that seemed to be ripe for modification without too much infringement on other traits. That's one thing you've got to be careful of—the domino effect your change has on the rest of the organism. You don't want to make someone able to lift a Buick without making their bones super-dense to be able to hold it up. They'd be squashed like a bug the first time they tried it."

I looked back over my shoulder at Luke. I'd never seen him lift a Buick, specifically, but there were plenty of times he tossed a *lot* of weight around. He gave me one of Faustus's shrugs. "I don't know,

Quincy. I don't think about how I pick things up, I just pick them up. So far, I have managed to avoid being squashed."

Science Guy looked over my head, an expression of utter glee on his face. You'd think I had just declared it Nerd Christmas. "You have superhuman strength? We must run some tests immediately. The superiors have never given us an opportunity to work with directly with the source material before. This is exciting!" He hopped up, only to run into the palm of my hand, pushing him back down into the chair.

"Slow down there, Demented Bill Nye," I said. "Remember the whole 'evil' thing? That's part of it."

"Oh yeah." He settled himself in the chair and continued his story. "Anyway, I was part of the most recent team to be brought on. There have been some amazing advancements in the field of genetic manipulation, but we are not allowed to publish anything. I couldn't even tell my wife what I was working on because of the NDA I signed. The legal troubles spelled out in the contract were bad enough, but…"

"But what?" Amy asked, leaning in.

"Sometimes you'd hear a rumor that someone was talking too much about work around town or with their family, and then that person wouldn't be back at work again. And their house was suddenly for sale. It was kinda like they'd gotten thrown into witness protection or something."

"More likely they were thrown into a lake," I said.

"Or just a hole with some quicklime. Lots of good soft earth back in some of these woods around here. If you can find a patch of woods big enough to dig a grave in without a condo development sitting on it," Bubba added.

"You two seem to possess an uncomfortable amount of knowledge about body disposal." Science Guy's eyes darted back and forth between me and Bubba, like a rabbit trying to decide which direction leads to freedom and which direction leads to it being lunch.

"You oughta see what we know about body creation. Like the making of dead bodies," Bubba growled.

"He's already scared shitless, man," I said. "Let's dial it back about fifteen percent there, pal."

"See?" Bubba said, slapping his hands together and laughing. "You're totally the good cop."

"Fuck you," I growled. I tried to bring things back to some useful direction. "Okay, so you were splicing cryptid DNA into humans. Why?"

"Money," he said as if it were the most obvious answer in the world. And maybe it was. I motioned for him to go on with his explanation. "Once we were able to associate specific sequences of the cryptid DNA with specific traits, we matched them up with the sequences in human DNA that relates to those same characteristics. Then we unraveled the DNA, snipped out the human part, and dropped in the cryptid's genetic material. In a few days, we started to see changes in the test subjects."

"Where did your test subjects come from, anyway?" Becks asked. Once a cop, always a cop.

"Runaways, homeless, mentally disabled," Science Guy said, and it was the nonchalant way he said it that made my stomach churn. "I don't know where all of them came from. Some were almost certainly prisoners. The state penitentiary isn't far, and we had a lot of subjects with very…interesting tattoos, shall we say. That was in the beginning. Once our processes were more refined, we began to get higher-quality subjects."

"Higher quality?" Jo asked. "You motherfuckers. You mother-fuckers Tuskeegee'in people right here in the twenty-first goddamn century. Nothing changes. Nothing ever fucking changes." She pushed past Bubba to stand right beside me, yanked the pistol from my holster, and pressed it to the center of Science Guy's forehead. "You treat people like they're lab animals because they're broke, or their home life is worse than sleeping on a park bench, or because they need help society won't provide. And for what? So some billionaire prick can buy another island? Take half, hell, take a tenth of the money y'all spent doing experiments on people and you could build houses for every person you murdered."

"Jo," I said. My voice was low, because I could see how much tension she was putting on the trigger. Science Guy was about half a pound away from being splattered all over the monitors behind him.

"What, Harker?" Jo asked, and her finger relaxed just a little. Not enough that I thought I could knock the gun away before she killed our best lead, but enough that she could sneeze and not kill the little prick. "You gonna tell me we need him? You gonna tell me we can't kill him? That it's not what Momma would have wanted?"

"Nope," I said. "Well, we do need him. For a couple more minutes, anyway. But then you can kill him. And I'm not stupid enough to stand right next to you while you've got my gun in one hand and John Henry's hammer in the other and try to tell you a goddamn thing about what your mother would have thought. But I think Cassie probably would have shot the bastard, too."

"No, she wouldn't," Jo said. "But she would definitely beat his ass. So, get everything useful you can out of this asshole, then I'm gonna whip his ass like he owes me money."

"You heard the lady," I said, lightly slapping Science Guy on the cheek to bring his focus back to me. "Talk. You figured out how to splice cryptid DNA into humans to make these super-soldiers that have been running around?"

"Yes, the Chairman calls them his stormtroopers."

"Of course he does," I said.

"I thought it was funny. Like *Star Wars*," Science Guy said.

I looked at him, and suddenly a lot of things made sense to me for the first time. I've wondered for decades how so many Germans didn't see what was going on right under their noses, how they could just miss the fact that millions of people were being murdered just for who they were. But looking at this dipshit sitting there in his willful oblivion, I realized that they didn't know because they didn't *want* to know. They knew every goddamned thing that was happening around them; they just needed to not ever talk about it so they could still think of themselves as good people. This guy was the same way. He knew what he was doing was evil as fuck. He just pretended not to know so he could get away with not giving a shit.

"Yeah, don't think he lifted stormtroopers from a movie, you assclown," I said.

"Okay, but why the whole plan to destroy all the cryptids? And what was all that shit about using Luke's essence to bring Skyffrax back to tear the world apart?" Becks asked. "This plan is nuts. I don't get it."

"Them," Faustus said, and we all turned to look at him. "You don't get them. And that's why you don't understand them. Because there are two plans, and they're so interwoven no one in this plane of existence is evil enough to have thought of it."

"What are you saying, exactly?" I asked, standing up and moving around so I could see Faustus and keep an eye on Science Guy. If he decided to run, I was pretty sure Jo'd shoot him, and that would be the end of the interrogation.

"I'm saying that there's a plan to kill you and destroy everything you've ever loved, and that's what draining Luke's essence, murdering Cassie, and all the personal shit has been about. And that's one person, probably this Chancellor, or Master, or Chairman. Whatever. This prick has more names than a *Game of Thrones* villain. But there's another plan, and it's a lot bigger, a lot nastier, and has the fingerprints of someone who's really, really nasty."

"Lucifer?" I asked. "Because I'd figure him for wanting to kill me, salt the earth of my soul, and *then* move on to something bigger and better."

"I don't know who it is, but I don't think it's Lucifer. This smacks of a takeover bid, and he's already the boss. He doesn't need a big flashy display of power to rally troops to his side. He's already got the troops. No, this is someone trying to *depose* Lucifer."

"Someone actually wants to run Hell?" I asked, incredulous. I mean, I've heard of thankless jobs, but that one would take every slice of cake.

"Haven't you read your Dante?" Luke chided. "Better to rule in Hell than serve in Heaven."

"And sure as shit better to rule in Hell than *serve* in Hell," Faustus agreed.

"Okay," I said, moving back around to sit in front of Science Guy. "So we've got one guy who wants to murder me and everyone I care for, and one guy who wants to take over Hell. How are a bunch of genetically souped-up mercenaries going to be any use in either of those little projects?"

"Oh, they aren't," our prisoner said matter-of-factly. "They're just how the Chairman plans to fund his corporate expansion."

"His own private army?" Becks asked.

"No," the nebbishy little guy replied. "He's selling the process. It took us several years, but we've finally gotten it ninety percent stable, and the bosses seem to think ten percent losses are acceptable. So we figured out how to keep the genetic material viable at a temperature that can be transported, and the first few shipments have already left."

"Wait a minute, are you saying that you can just ship this, for lack of a better term, super-soldier juice anywhere in the world?" Amy asked, pulling out her phone.

"Well, anywhere that someone has several million dollars per dose. It's not cheap."

"Ten percent losses," Jo said. "What does that mean, exactly?"

"It means that in roughly ten percent of the subjects, their bodies proved unable to withstand the rigors of having their genetic code rewritten." Science Guy had the good grace to look a little uncomfortable at that, but not nearly enough for me to think he had a soul.

"So one out of every ten people you shoot this stuff into dies?" Bubba asked.

"Yes."

"Man, that's the kind of thing anti-vaxxer wet dreams are made of," the big man replied. He turned to Amy. "Who're you calling?"

"I'm leaving Pravesh a message. If this stuff is already out in the world, she needs to know about it and start getting people mobilized. Everybody, split up and start yanking out hard drives. I need every piece of information on this genetic stuff. We've got to find out where this stuff has been sent."

"Well, if you're that concerned about it, you should definitely make sure the truck hasn't left on its way to the airport," said Science Guy.

"There's a shipment going out this afternoon, and I believe it's headed to Iran."

"Yeah, let's see about not having werewolf mercenaries running all over the Middle East if we can help it," Becks said. "Harker, you stay with this asshole and see what you can find out about the Chairman or whatever his damned name is. Luke has to stay indoors for a little while longer, so he can help me and Jo strip hard drives. Faustus, you go with Team Bubba and stop that truck. If it's just a human driver, it shouldn't be any trouble. Radio in if you need backup and we'll figure something out."

"Got it," Bubba said, already moving across the lab.

"I have only one question," Luke said as everybody sprang into motion.

"What's that, Uncle?" I asked.

"What is a hard drive?"

33

Bubba

We left Harker and his people in the lab with one really nervous scientist, and me, Faustus, and Amy hauled ass back to the loading dock, but there was no truck in sight. One security guard with a butterfly bandage above one eye and his left arm in a sling got up out of a chair and took one step forward, then held his good arm up in the air as Amy and Faustus aimed pistols at him. Or maybe he froze because I took a giant step forward with a massive sword in my hand. One of those things definitely made him lose interest in stopping us.

"Where is the truck going?" I asked.

"The airport. There's a private runway that they use." The guard's eyes never left Faustus, who was pretty intimidating with his jet-black skin, gleaming bald head, and yellow eyes. I didn't blame him. I mean, I'm a big scary dude with a sword, but "demon" definitely outranks "angry redneck" on the scary shit scale.

"Are we looking for a big damn plane or a little one?" I asked.

"I don't know. I don't make the airport runs. I don't even load the trucks here. I'm just a guard, man. I make twelve dollars an hour, and they don't even let me carry a gun. I've got a radio and a taser, that's all."

"The rest of your buddies had guns," I said, pointing to multiple smears of blood that were the only indicators of the fight we'd had on that loading dock not an hour before.

"I'm new!" he protested. "Come on, man. Don't kill me. I just needed a job. I didn't know they were Nazis when I answered the ad on Craigslist."

Great. Nazis hiring on Craigslist. Gotta love the twenty-first century. I let out an exasperated breath, and Amy holstered her gun and put a hand on my arm. "Let me try," she said, stepping towards the terrified guard. I noticed that she put herself right in between the dude and Faustus, so the demon wasn't the only thing he saw. "How big was the equipment they loaded onto the truck?"

"It was pretty big. The guys loading it were massive, and the pallets had all this stuff on them stacked as tall as me."

"How many pallets like that were there?" Amy asked.

"I didn't count, but the truck was pretty full."

Amy turned back to me. "Even a short trailer is nearly thirty feet long, and the full-sized ones can be over fifty. If they loaded up thirty feet of a trailer with pallets as tall as a man, they're gonna need a pretty big plane."

"Well, that narrows it down. You call Skeeter while we're on our way to the airport and get him to find us a big-ass cargo plane that's set to take off soon," I said.

"There's one problem, Bubba," Faustus said.

"What's that?"

"The van is en route to the hospital with the injured Director Pravesh," he reminded me.

"Oh, that ain't a problem," I replied. I looked at the guard. "Gimme your car keys."

He hesitated, and I leaned forward, dropping my voice so it gave the illusion that only he could hear me. "Give me your goddamned car keys or I'm gonna go talk to Nightcrawler's darker-skinned cousin back there and tell him he can eat your eyeballs. Do you want to have your eyeballs eaten?"

The guard shook his head and crossed his legs. I got the distinct impression that I needed to get out of here before things became damp and smelly. At least he was wearing his brown pants.

"Then give me your keys and tell me which car is yours," I said, holding out my hand.

The guard handed me his keyring and pointed out the loading dock door. "There's a Silverado in the back parking lot. Burgundy, with chrome running boards and amber fog lights."

"It'll be waiting for you at the airport. Assuming I don't crash it into the side of an airplane." I took his keys, sheathed my sword, and hopped down off the dock to the parking lot. Amy and Faustus followed me as we hoofed it over to the guard's truck and got in.

Faustus slid into the back seat behind me and leaned forward, his shiny head between the two front seats. "You know I don't actually eat people, right?"

I looked at him. "You're a demon. You're not just any demon, you're a demon who's friggin' notorious for getting people to sign shit deals and sell their souls. Are you honestly telling me you've never eaten eyeballs?"

He looked almost embarrassed. "Well, not for a long time. But it was the Dark Ages, and protein was hard to come by. It was eat a few people or go back to Hell. And the climate here is so much better for my skin."

"Then sit back and strap in, eyeball-eater," I said. "We got a plane to catch."

AMY GOT ON THE PHONE WITH SKEETER TO LOCATE ANY RUNWAYS, hangars, or dirt roads with a plane departing that was big enough to hold the number of palleted freezers we were looking for, and I hauled ass up I-40 with my blinkers on and my foot mashed to the floor. The guard's big Silverado was almost as nimble as my F-250, which is to say not at all, but I managed to get us the few miles to the airport without running anybody off the road or causing any massive pileups. At least not any massive pileups that I noticed.

I followed Amy's navigation through the cargo terminals, drove straight through a locked chain-link gate, and pulled up right in front of the nose of a big damn airplane with its cargo ramp down. Some dude in gray coveralls got off a forklift and ran over in our direction, while a quartet of big men in tight suits with suspicious bulges under their left arms came down the ramp and looked around for the holdup. Upon seeing me, one of them motioned in our direction and pulled out a cell phone.

"So much for the element of surprise," I said. "Amy, you deal with the forklift driver. He might not be a demon, or super-werewolf, or whatever the hell the next thing we have to fight is gonna be. Faustus, you're with me."

"On it," Amy said, veering off to the left and holding her badge up at the oncoming cargo handler.

I waved a hand at Faustus as he drew his pistol. "Can we maybe try to talk to these guys before we start shooting up the airport? The last thing I need is a TSA agent with an itchy trigger finger thinking I'm a terrorist and shooting me from across the tarmac."

"I would try diplomacy if the people you want to diplomat to didn't already have their guns out," Faustus said.

I turned back to the goons, and sure enough, every damn one of them had his suit coat open and a pistol in his hand. I sprinted under the plane, putting some metal between me and the bullets, and Faustus dropped to one knee and opened fire. I saw one bad guy drop, but at least one more took a round right in the chest and didn't go down. These were obviously more than just big slabs of well-armed muscle; they were cryptid DNA-enhanced slabs of well-armed muscle. I kept the ramp between me and the goons as well as I could until it got too low near the back of the plane and I had to step around it.

I had my sword in my hand, which was probably the only thing that saved me. When I came out from under the ramp, one of the guards was standing there waiting for me, his gun aimed right at my chest. When he saw the sword in my hand, a confused look crossed his face, like he wasn't prepared for anyone to actually bring a knife to a gunfight. Since I knew I was stepping into a shitstorm, I wasn't surprised at all, so when he hesitated, I had enough time to take one giant step forward and slam the pommel of my sword into the side of his head. He went down like a ton of bricks, and I saw a little blood come out of his nose, but he probably had some kind of gecko DNA fused into him to make him regenerate fast, and besides, a traumatic brain injury was a lot easier to recover from than death.

Which is what his buddy tried to deal out to me as soon as he went down. This guy was a little smaller than the others, with a narrow, pinched face that made me think his DNA may have come from a were-ferret, and he carried two guns, probably to compensate for being the runt of the litter. He got off a shot with one pistol, realized he still had the safety on the other, and then was stuck in the unenviable position of having to take the safety off a gun while holding a gun in each hand, so he was downright flummoxed for a few seconds. Then I decked him with the butt of my sword and his situation sorted itself right out.

That left the big guy, the one Faustus had shot in the chest and still hadn't gone down. He turned his attention away from shooting at my demonic sidekick, who was hiding behind the forklift and firing off a round every once in a while, and growled at me. Like, literally. The corner of one lip pulled up like he was a really buff Billy Idol, and he let out a growl like a tiger. Okay, it was more like a real big housecat, but I'm guessing he wanted it to sound like a tiger.

Either way, I wasn't real impressed. Once you've punched Bigfoot in the balls and fought a literal dragon, one asshole with a gun just doesn't light your fire like it used to. "You wanna fight, or you want me to rub your belly?" I asked.

That apparently was every bit as insulting as I'd wanted it to be, because Tony the Two-Legged Tiger pitched his gun to the side and just leapt at me. And it was a good leap, too. He covered nearly ten feet in the air before coming down right in front of me. If I hadn't been prepared for that kind of truly unwelcoming behavior, he might have gotten his paws on me.

As it was, I just held my sword straight out in front of me and let him jump onto it. His eyes went wide just the barest instant before he landed, as it registered that he had made perhaps his very last mistake. Then he landed on two feet, and three more feet of steel went right into his gut. My blade slid in like a hot knife through butter, just under the bottom of his ribcage on the left side, and I heard the *crack* of bone as the sword angled up and came out of the middle of the goon's back.

He opened and closed his mouth like a fish gasping for air, and like the jerk that I am, I leaned in to his head and said, "What was that? I can't quite make it out. Here, let me help you."

Then I took a step back and kicked him in the gut, shoving his body off my sword. He staggered, doubled over, then stood up, still snarling at me. He lunged in my direction, but apparently it's really hard to move after somebody shoves a sword through your belly. I wouldn't know. It only happened to me the once, and all I did afterward was fall down and pass out. So this dude was already way ahead of me.

Well, he was until I swung my sword around and cut his friggin' head off, anyway. I turned to look for Amy, pretty pleased that we managed not to blow anything up, only to see a door slide open in the side of the plane and eight more goons hop out. Apparently, somebody heard the gunshots and got curious. Or they wanted extra peanuts and were looking for the flight attendant. Since they all drew guns the second they saw me, I just kinda assumed it was Option A.

"Well, shit," I said. Then the shooting started.

34

Harker

Evil Bill Nye wasn't much fun to interrogate. I only got to slap him once before he started crying and telling me everything he knew about the Master, which was basically nothing useful. He did know where the big boss lived, though, so I untied him long enough to look up a company-wide email invitation to their last Christmas party, which had been held at the boss's mansion. I almost made some wiseass crack about them being behind the times and not being more inclusive with their holidays, then remembered that I was literally talking about a company run by Nazis. Inclusivity isn't exactly their brand.

So once Becks, Jo, and Luke finished ransacking every computer they could, and I slapped the evil scientist around a little more just for funsies, we headed out to the parking lot and piled into Becks's Suburban. It was still pretty bright, but the sun had dipped below the horizon, so Luke could walk around without getting scorched, as long as he didn't dilly-dally. And believe me, dilly-dallying is not one of my uncle's favorite pastimes.

The Master, who I still hadn't gotten so much as a pseudonym for, lived on a small spit of land outside Cary that jutted out into a lake. You couldn't see any neighbors, that's how much of the surrounding property this creep owned—enough that once you turned into his gated driveway, there might as well not be any other houses within miles, just trees. We left the SUV at the gate and hopped over the eight-foot fence.

Well, Luke and I hopped over. Then we remembered that we had humans with us, and I went back to rip a hole in the fence for Becks and Jo. The look Becks gave me was best described as "withering." We eschewed the driveway in favor of walking through the woods along the gravel road, letting the carpet of pine needles mask our footsteps. There's a lot to be said for skulking around in the South, and not the least of which is the plethora of pine trees. They provide a much better surface for sneaking than just about anything else in nature, with their quiet cushion and resistance to footprints.

The driveway continued for at least half a mile, and as the trees thinned, the driveway curved off to the right, so we didn't come upon the house full front. That's why it took me a moment to recognize the architecture, but when I did, I froze in my tracks.

"Harker, what is it?" Becks asked.

I didn't say anything, just stood there staring at the house. This was no coincidence. None of this had been coincidence. I suddenly felt all the hair on my arms stand up as what I was seeing really came home to me. Everything that had happened from the DEMON takeover, to me and Luke being kidnapped, to Jack's betrayal, to Cassie's murder, to Joe and Gabby's deaths in the explosion, to us coming to Raleigh—it had all been part of a plan. A plan to hurt me, specifically. It wasn't about cleansing the world of cryptids, even though that was part of it. It wasn't about building an army of genetically enhanced super-soldiers, although they were happy to cash those checks.

No, this had been about me the whole time, and as I stood there gaping at a house that would have looked more comfortable in the mountains of France than the middle of North Carolina, I wracked my brain trying to think of who *knew* enough about me to do all this, to hit me where I was truly vulnerable, again and again.

Hey! Becks yelled in my head, and I turned. Not to look at her, but to look past her, to see if Luke was seeing what I was seeing. He was. I could tell from the haunted expression in his eyes that he remembered what happened the last time we saw this house, the last time I was sane for about four years, the last time I held my first true love in my arms.

The Master's home, in an exclusive neighborhood on a lake outside of Raleigh, was an exact replica of the house where I watched Anna Treves die in France seventy years earlier. This was the house where I saw my first love get murdered by a Nazi, where I held her as the light fled her eyes, and where I succumbed to my pain and rage and went berserk for the next several years. All those emotions came rushing back as I looked at the front of the house, all those feelings along with every bit of anger and pain I'd felt for the last two years as some evil motherfucker had used my past as source material for the horror show he'd made out of my life.

Well, it was time to end that shit.

"Spread out," I said, and my voice sounded strange to my ears. Cold, even to me. I felt Becks's consciousness prickling the back of my mind, but I didn't reach out and pick up the thread between us. I didn't cut her out completely, just kinda walled her out of the deepest parts of myself. Those were not good places to be on an average day, and they were getting worse with every step I took toward the house where my world ended once before.

We fanned out as we stepped past the tree line and onto the manicured lawn. I almost felt bad about walking on the guy's grass, then I decided I weigh less than a lawnmower, so it's probably fine. *Then* I remembered it was a Nazi's yard, and I started to twist my heels in a little with every step. "Come out and play, asshole!" I yelled when we were about ten yards from the bottom of the steps. They had everything right, down to the three wide steps leading up to the front door.

A front door that swung open, revealing a thin young man with a wispy goatee who stepped out onto the porch wearing no shit wizard robes and holding a staff. "I'll play, Quincy Harker, but I don't expect you'll enjoy the game."

"Go back to the Ren Faire, Gandalf," I snarled at the guy. "The grownups are talking." Now that his face was revealed in the porch light, I could see that he was seriously young, maybe not even out of college. How the fuck did he know my name? I've pissed off a lot of people, but I usually don't offend them enough to want to kill until they can drink in bars.

He snarled at me, another weird guy making animal noises. If I lived through all this, I should probably have somebody look at what's in the water around Raleigh. Makes everybody think they're Teen Wolf.

"You'll fight me, Harker, or you'll die right here!" Saruman the Barely Out of Puberty said, pointing his staff at me. The tip glowed with a crimson light, and it was all I could do not to laugh at the impressive phallic symbol pointing at my head.

"If that thing spurts out shaving cream, I'll die laughing, kid. Otherwise, I don't think you're putting me down with your glow stick." I stepped up onto the porch, snatched the staff out of his hands, and shattered it over my knee. Right before the walking stick exploded into a shower of splinters, I noticed that Baby Dumbledore was grinning like a cat with a mouthful of canary.

I've seen that look many times, often on the faces of people who want to do me grievous harm. It never happens when I've surprised them, or when I've taken away their greatest weapon. No, I usually get that look when the bad guy is pretty certain that I've just stepped in a huge pile of shit, and that was just what he'd been waiting for. So it was not completely shocking when things took a turn for the worse the second the staff snapped.

But the *way* in which shit went completely sideways was unexpected. I kinda expected the staff to be wired to explode, or maybe have a vial of poison gas hidden inside that would release if anyone other than its wielder tried to use it. I didn't expect a massive magical backlash to flash out of the thing, blinding me and almost flash-frying everyone within twenty feet. I was able to wrap the whole mess in a shield, but holding all that energy took a lot out of me.

When I felt like I could drop my shield without getting the mystical equivalent of a tsunami in my face, I tossed the shattered stick to the ground and looked up at Junior Snape and said, "That was dumb, kid. Anybody with any skill is gonna shield themselves at the drop of a hat. The only people that trap would catch are people you shouldn't need to ruin a weapon to take out."

"How about you come in here and tell me how bad my traps are?" said Little Merlin, as he stepped back through the front door of the house. I didn't follow, just called up an orb of force and flung a sphere of purple fire in after him.

"Well, gang," I said. "I guess we go inside."

"We've got other problems," Luke said, then I heard Becks's pistol bark three times. I turned my attention from the porch and saw four of the same super-soldier types coming at us from each side, weapons out. One went down when Becks shot him, but he had the bad manners not to stay down, and a few seconds later was back on his feet.

"Go after him, Harker," Becks said. "We've got this." Jo nodded her agreement and hefted her hammer.

"There are eight of them," I protested.

"Quincy," Luke said, and his tone brooked no refusal. "Go. And there are six of them."

I opened my mouth to protest that I could count to eight when I heard the *thump-thump* as Luke dropped a pair of severed heads on the ground. Okay, there were six. And I'm pretty sure those six were outnumbered.

I ran up the stairs after the evil wizard *du jour* with an energy shield on my left arm and an orb of pure magical energy glowing in the palm of my right hand. I tried to ignore how even the doorknob was right, how it could have *been* the house that had haunted my memories for decades. I tried not to remember how every detail of that...*this* house was seared in my mind's eye. I tried to do nothing but think about how good it would feel when I chased down this "Master" and ripped him limb from limb.

I ran through the front door, only for it to swing shut behind me, a reinforced vault door dropping from the ceiling behind it. I looked right, then left. I was in a long hallway, but apparently none of the windows on the front of the house were real, because all I saw was concrete stretching out to either side. I was in, but it looked a whole lot like this place was designed to never let anybody *out*.

That was fine by me. I wasn't the one trapped in a building with a spell-slinging toddler with a shitty attitude and worse impulse control. Nope. I wasn't trapped with anything like that kind of a psychopath. But they sure as fuck were.

35

Bubba

I was too far from the forklift to run back and use it for cover, so that left only one place for me to run when the genetically enhanced guards cut loose with their run-of-the-mill bullets, and that was toward the one thing I was pretty sure they wouldn't shoot—the cargo. I hauled ass up the ramp into the back of the plane, which looked like the interior set of every military movie I'd ever seen where the cast had to ride with the cargo all secured to the walls with nets and straps. So, kudos to the production designer. Or was it a chicken-and-egg thing where the production designers made something look right, so design adapted to match the expectations of the audience, and eventually the insides of cargo planes came to look like what people expected them to look like?

Yes, these are the things that run through my head when I'm being shot at. The first few times somebody shoots at you, it's terrifying. It's loud, and if you've lived your life in a better fashion than I have, it's probably the first time anyone has legitimately wanted to kill you. I'm not talking "you put your hand on my daughter's boob and now I'm going to kill you." I'm talking "I have a gun and I am using it to send chunks of lead flying in your direction at a very high rate of speed." And there really is a difference.

Unless you're Gerald Newton, who did open fire on me with his twelve-gauge after he found out I'd taken his daughter to the bonfire underneath Peabody Bridge after one of our high school football games. I never *told* him I touched his daughter's boob, and I sure as hell didn't tell him about anything else of his precious Donna's that I touched, but he definitely opened fire on my retreating tailgate after I dropped her off. Maybe if I'd walked her to the door, he would have had a different opinion of my level of respect for women, or maybe he would have just shot me through the door. We'll never know, but my money then and now was on shooting me through the door. Suffice to say, when the first time you're ever shot at is in high school, and *then* you go into the family monster hunting business, by the time you're pushing forty, you've felt enough bullets whizz by your head that you only worry about the ones you don't hear.

So I kept my wits mostly about me as the new additions to the security team started spraying ammunition around the tarmac like they were on a Mardi Gras float tossing out candy. I ran up the cargo ramp and drew my sword, slicing through some of the load straps as I hurried past. I didn't have a real plan, more just "don't die, then improv." So I got tight to the nose of the plane and settled into a corner formed by pallets, all wired to the roof of the plane with some kind of power umbilical, presumably to keep the serum refrigerated.

I made it so that there was only one direction for the goons to approach from, and stood there waiting, sword out. I didn't have to wait long, as a submachine gun slowly creeped its way around a corner just seconds after I established my hiding place. I waited until the gun's body inched forward, and as soon as both of the goons' wrists were visible, I cut through them.

It's usually a lot harder than you expect, cutting off somebody's hands. There are a lot of bones in the wrist, and if you try to cut too low, your blade can get deflected across one of those, screwing up the cut. I prefer to just slice right through the two main bones of the arm, ignoring the wrist and cutting higher instead. That takes a lot more power in the swing, but power has never been my shortcoming. But even cutting through the main chunk of the forearm is harder when the arm in question has been enhanced with some magical super-juice.

My blade swung down in a huge arc and cleaved the goon's right hand clean off, but either I didn't catch the left square, or he moved at the last instant, or whatever. The long and the short of it was that he still had his left hand. The arm was injured, and quite possibly broken, but I learned the hard way that as long as it's not a compound fracture, you can do a lot with a broken arm. So my sword broke his arm, cut off his other hand, and the goon dropped his gun with a clatter. He fell to his knees, screaming and leaning against a pallet for support, and I took a step back, then kicked him in the face to shut him up. I mean, it's not like it was a big secret where I was hiding, but I didn't need to send up a flare as to *exactly* where in the cargo bay I was.

I heard a gasp from my right and turned to see another guard, his submachine gun pointing to the floor, staring at his friend's hand, which was lying on the floor of the plane, several feet from the rest of his blood-spewing body. I stared at the guard, he stared at me, and I recovered first, throwing my sword at him in a big overhead pitch, sending the massive long sword hurtling end-over-end down the aisle between refrigerated pallets to drive itself hilt-deep in the bad guy's chest, sending him spinning to his death clutching the blade that protruded from his chest.

I mean, that's what happened in the movie in my head, anyway. In real life, the sword thumped him square in the face, right under his left eye, and he stumbled backward and fell flat on his butt. I took four steps in his direction and kicked him in the jaw, snapping his head back and slamming his skull into the unforgiving floor the plane. I didn't bother to check his pupils. When you throw a friggin' sword at somebody, any pretense of giving a shit whether they live or die goes out the window.

I picked up my sword and looked around to see if anyone had heard the commotion. The bullet that ricocheted off the bulkhead near my ear was enough of an answer, and I dove behind another pallet of equipment.

"Don't shoot the cargo, moron! The boss will kill us if it's damaged!" I heard someone say from near the back of the plane.

"What do you think he'll do to us if these assholes wreck it all?" said a gruff voice that sounded a lot like it was right on the other side of the pallet I was hiding behind. I ducked down a little and peered around the side of the crates, and sure enough, I saw a leg in black tactical pants. I knew all my people were outside the plane, and I didn't think either of them were in cargo pants, so I felt pretty secure shoving a sword into the back of the black-clad leg.

The gruff voice went up into a scream, and the guard kinda flopped backward onto the deck of the cargo bay, aiming a submachine gun at me. I moved right to get out of his line of fire, and brought my blade down, severing his head. A short burst of fire from his last nerve twitch, and that was two down. I stripped him out of his tactical harness, figuring that a couple more knives and a grenade or two couldn't hurt, even if I didn't want his submachine gun.

"Terry? Was that you?" the voice from the back of the plane called again, so I grabbed Terry's head and pitched it toward the ramp with a nice overhand hook shot. It bounced a couple of times, then voices erupted in some creative profanity that would have impressed even Harker, and I heard several sets of booted feet storm up the ramp.

"You motherfucker!" the first voice yelled as he came after me. I guess throwing his friend's head at him was where he drew the line at acceptable behavior from someone he was trying to murder. Oh well, I hurt his widdle feelings. I was gonna hurt a whole lot more than that if the rough sketch of a plan I had rattling around in my head worked out.

I closed my eyes for the barest instant, just enough to confirm that the footsteps all seemed to be coming up the center of the plane, the biggest aisle in the stacked cargo bay. I retreated down a narrow cross aisle to the outer wall of the fuselage and squeezed my way between load rails and delicate electronic equipment until I reached the edge of the cargo ramp. I looked around for a button or lever or something.

Anything, really, that would raise the ramp, hopefully not so fast I couldn't run down it. After seconds of scanning the walls, I saw the big red mushroom button I was looking for—clear across the body of the plane.

"Of course it couldn't be that easy," I muttered. I looked around, seeing four heads farther up in the plane, all swiveling left and right, looking for me. Oh well, nothing for it but to do it, as my high school football coach used to say. I shoved my sword in the sheath on my back, tucked my head in, and sprinted across the open area by the ramp. Only one of the four goons turned around, but since he yelled at the top of his lungs right before he let loose a burst of automatic weapons fire in my direction, one was plenty.

I ducked behind another skid of refrigerated serum and tried to figure out a new plan. I couldn't just slam the hatch closed and try to shoot the plane down, because they'd seen me, so I'd never get out of the cargo bay alive. Also, I didn't really have anything to shoot down a plane with. But then I looked down at the harness I took off the guy whose head I chopped off, and realized I didn't need to shoot it down. Not if I could blow it up instead.

I tapped my comm. "I'm coming down the right side of the ramp. I need cover fire, so light up the middle and the left. And I mean *my* right and left, so it's opposite for you." Last damn thing I needed was getting shot by my own people because we got our rights and lefts mixed up.

"So cover you, but don't shoot you," Faustus replied. "Got it."

I pulled one of the grenades off the appropriated tactical harness, pitched it toward the nose of the plane, and took off for the ramp, slapping the "CLOSE" button as I went. The ramp started moving, the bad guys started shooting, Faustus started shooting back, and I started hauling redneck ass for daylight. I hopped down onto the ground, pulled the second grenade off my vest, chucked it into the hole, and turned to walk away.

I had the whole scene planned. I was going to turn to Faustus, say something witty just as the first grenade went off, then walk away without looking back as the second grenade took out all the cargo and hopefully the fuel tanks of the plane, making me one of the greatest movie badasses of all time, walking away from an exploding plane without even a backward glance.

Except I overestimated the distance between the cargo bay and the fuel tanks, and I never heard the second grenade detonate. Because as soon as I turned around, the first one exploded, in a very satisfactory *boom*. But that was quickly followed by the earth-shaking, eardrum-splitting, spleen-rattling explosion of a tank completely full of jet fuel blowing up less than a hundred feet behind me. It was like surfing, only the water is air, it's super-heated and full of flesh-rending debris, and you're on fire.

Yeah, I got blown up. Again. Damn Nazis. My last thoughts before I blissfully passed out from my face impacting the hood of the stolen pickup truck was *at least we got 'em. I hope Harker's team is having a better time.*

36

Harker

T here I was, in a barren concrete block hallway with harsh light blaring down and washing out any hint of texture the place might have had, looking for a pimple-faced baby wizard who needed his horcrux kicked. I dropped my Sight down over my mundane vision and looked around, hoping with all the magic he'd been flinging around, that Even Skinnier Criss Angel had left a little residue for me to follow.

Sure enough, there was a faintly glowing trail leading off to the right. I followed, continuing to look at everything through the hyper-colorized, slightly off-axis filter of the magical spectrum, where the wizard's footprints glowed a neon green against a deep brown background of floor. The green matched the color of the wards on a door to my left, and the footprints went through the door, so I switched back to the mundane view to blast my way through. There was a moment's disorientation that comes from switching spectrums, then I was standing in front of a gray metal door with a utilitarian knob and no visible locking mechanism.

I knew it was warded, but a quick slash across the surface with a silver-edged knife took care of that, while also setting off a shower of sparks that let me know the door was trapped physically as well as magically. I got a little shock through the leather grip of my knife, but nothing too bad. I stepped square in front of the door, raised my rubber-soled boot, and planted my foot right in the center of the door, pushing *hard*.

The door didn't open. No, it more imploded. The metal crumpled and bent around my foot, then the whole thing ripped out of the frame and flew across a familiar room, a room I never thought I'd see again in anywhere but my nightmares. It was another perfect facsimile from my time in France, but this was the large, leather-appointed office of *Unterscharführer* Brittlav, a Nazi I had multiple unpleasant meetings with in France during World War II, the last of which ended with both Brittlav and my fiancée, Anna Treves, dead.

This was a perfect replica of that room, only larger, with much more space between the furnishings, a massive desk and chair, a leather sofa and pair of matching armchairs, a roaring fireplace. Whoever had created this place even mimicked the scenery outside Brittlav's home, broad rolling lawns with the French Alps far in the background. This was all for my benefit, all to distract me, and for half a second, it even worked.

Then I remembered I was here to kill a motherfucker and called up a shield just in time to deflect the lightning bolt the aforementioned motherfucker threw at my face. "Cut it out, Baby Raistlin!" I shouted, looking around for the skinny little shithead. "What are you so pissed at me about, anyway? Did I kill your favorite demon or something?"

"You killed my dad and got my brother sent to prison, you nosy prick!" The scrawny young man stood up from behind the desk, his face flushed red with anger.

"You're gonna have to narrow the field a little bit, pal," I said. "I've sent a lot of assholes to prison, and even more to the cemetery. Did I kill your dad for any particular reason, or did he just try to swipe my parking spot? Because if it was a Saturday around Christmas, that's totally justifiable homicide."

"You sicced a demon on him! And not just any demon, you fed him to Asmodeus!"

"Oh! Now I remember your dad! He was a fucking prick. And your brother? He was worse! That cockmonkey raped a girl and implanted a demon in her, then acted like she didn't matter because she wasn't rich or White. Yeah, kid. I hate to break it to you, but you come from a family of assholes." His dad was Jacob Marlack, and I did in fact feed him to Asmodeus.

This was concerning not because I fed a human to a demon. If anyone ever deserved to be eaten by one of the Lords of Hell, it was Marlack. No, my concern was about *why* I summoned Asmodeus to kill the man. I needed the demon to take Marlack out because *I couldn't*. Jacob Marlack beat my ass like a drum the first time we fought, so the next time I didn't fight—I cheated. I called up Asmodeus, convinced him that one of his lieutenants was working with Marlack to overthrow him, and let him floss with the wizard's intestines for a while before sending him home to Hell.

Marlack's son was a piece of work, too. He was part of a group of frat boys playing around with shit they had neither the brains nor the mystical power to handle, and I'd worked with Luke's old Renfield to get him sent to prison on multiple counts of rape. I looked at the skinny kid who was calling up a massive fireball in his hand, preparing to fling it in my direction.

"*Cadere,*" I said, pointing at the fireball. It tumbled off the kid's hand and fell to the surface of the desk, where it did exactly what you'd expect it to do. All the shit on the desk went up in flames, the junior varsity wizard jumped back flailing his arms in the air like someone had just set *him* on fire, and I almost fell over laughing.

I did recover enough to point at the desk again and say, "*Aqua.*" A sphere of water about the size of a basketball materialized over the desk, then fell straight down, dousing the flames, and the skinny spell-slinger, in cold wetness.

"What the fuck?" the kid asked, glaring at me as he tried to focus enough to call fire again.

"I never have to worry about my fire extinguisher running empty,"

I said. "As long as there's water vapor, there's water. Now do you want to chill the fuck out and get out of here, knowing that you tried your hardest to avenge your dad but it didn't work out, or do you want to throw down for real?" I called power, surrounding my fists with spheres of purple energy to match the glow in my eyes.

"How about Option C, where I just shoot you in the fucking face?" the shithead said, reaching around behind his back and drawing a Beretta pistol. Or, mostly drawing a Beretta pistol, because as soon as I saw his hand move, I let loose with a blast of energy right in his chest and started moving across the room, not wanting to be wherever he expected me to be when he got his gun out.

My blast knocked him off his feet, and I heard a *crunch* and a muffled yelp as he hit the floor, but he still managed to yank his pistol out and pass it over to his good hand. He squeezed off a couple of rounds, but they either went wide or glanced off my hastily erected shield.

I looked over my shield and called out to him. "That the best you got, Junior? At least your dad was willing to actually fight. Until I fed him to a demon, that is. You just want to shoot me? Come on, we both know that ain't happening."

"I don't need to shoot you, asshole," Marlack the Lesser said with a sneer. Another one of those times when the bad guy gives you a look that's a lot less "I give up, I'm busted" than it is "I've got some sneaky shit up my sleeve."

He dragged himself to his feet, shaking his left arm to try to bring some of the feeling back into it. I was pretty sure he had a broken clavicle, given how he landed, and I knew that everything he did was gonna hurt for about the next month. Unless he died tonight, which I was giving about a fifty-fifty shot. I didn't *want* to kill him, per se, but I wasn't going to work all that hard to avoid it.

"I don't need to shoot you, I just wanted to distract you," the kid said, then raised both hands over his head with a grimace of pain and flung a lightning bolt at my feet. I dodged it easily, then dodged the next one, then the next, then pulled up an energy shield and planted it in front of me, letting the deadly electricity bounce harmlessly off.

The streaks of white fire struck my purple energy field and ricocheted off in all directions, almost like each bolt fragmented into a dozen smaller bolts on impact, then each of those arced up and slammed back into my shield, each of them breaking into even tinier little darts of power, whipping around and into my shield like a nest of angry hornets. Electrified, lethal hornets that moved at nearly the speed of light. They slammed into my shield again and again, individually not very powerful, but the cumulative effect was starting to wear on my shield and my energy level.

I reached out with my magic, feeling for a leyline to use to top off the tank, but there was nothing there. Nothing I could access, anyway. It was like what Liang had done in DC, blocking me off from the reservoir of power around me. I locked eyes with Marlack Junior, and his wicked grin told me everything I needed to know. This had all been part of his plan. Maybe his only plan—to keep me firing magical attack after magical attack, to hammer my defenses with annoying attacks that weren't powerful enough to do any real damage, but took power to defend against nonetheless. This little bastard's whole *raison d'etre* was to wear me down enough to need to refuel, then somehow keep me from doing so. Probably until the Master, or Chancellor, came out for the main event.

Which, judging by the fact that a door I could have sworn didn't exist ten seconds ago just slid open in the wall behind Marlack, must have been exactly what was happening at that exact moment. "Well, shit," I muttered. I tried to reach out to Becks through our link, to see if she could funnel energy to me that way, but there was nothing. I could sense her presence, but it was like I was hearing her on the other side of a cinderblock wall, and nothing could get through but the most muffled awareness that she was there, that she was still alive and fighting, but not able to help in any way.

Help me in my long-awaited battle against...a librarian? I was baffled at the image of the person coming through the door. He was a thin young man, almost frail in his build, with dark brown hair in a shag around his head. He wore round wire-rimmed glasses and a loose-fitting suit that seemed much more suitable for someone my age than someone who looked to be in his early twenties. Of course, I look like I'm in my thirties, and I dress like a college kid who spends too much time listening to jam bands, so I guess I should stop judging books by their covers. There was something familiar about him, about the delicate line of his jaw, about his big, round eyes...something familiar, but unidentifiable. Maybe I'd fed his parents to a demon, too.

With the Big Bad finally making an appearance, I decided it was time to end this charade with Marlack. I formed my shield into a V shape, took a few long steps across the room, and punched the gaunt little wizard right in the face. He spun around and sprawled on the floor, out cold, and I turned to the new arrival.

"I guess you're the Chancellor," I half-said, half-asked.

"I am," he replied, and his voice was familiar, too. Something in the back of my mind tickled, something about this room, this house, now this guy, standing in front of me smirking at me as I tried to figure out who the fuck he was. Then it clicked into place, and I felt my skin go pale as his smirk spread into a vicious grin.

"I am the Chancellor," he said. "But you can call me Edgar."

"Fuck me," I said as I looked in the eyes of the man who had spent the last few years trying to destroy my life and everything in it that I hold dear. The man who possibly had more cause to hate me than anyone on Earth. Edgar Treves, who I'd thought was killed in Auschwitz in 1942. Edgar Treves, younger brother to Anna Treves, who died in my arms in this very room. Edgar Treves, the Chancellor.

37

"Edgar?" I said, taking an involuntary step back. "How? You... they took you to Auschwitz."

"Yes, *they* did. After *you* gave up on looking for me. After *you* stirred up the hornets' nest of the Fürher's men in town. After *you* destroyed my life. *They* took me to Auschwitz, and you cannot imagine what happened to me after that." Edgar sneered at me, an ugly look across his handsome, almost cherubic, face.

"Then tell me about it, Edgar," I said, trying to stall. I needed backup, because I didn't think I could actually do it. I wasn't sure I could actually kill this kid, who I once looked at like my own little brother. I gestured to the heavy, leather armchairs. "Sit down, tell me what happened after they took you. I looked for you, but then he took Anna, and I..."

"You abandoned me, you worthless piece of shit!?" he yelled, a vein pulsing in his neck. "You left me there, in the camp, with no one. No family, no one I knew, just me and a bunch of French Jew children and Gypsy trash for the guards to play with. They all went after the skinny boy who played the piano. Your friend Brittlav made sure they knew I was a musician when he handed me over to them. That way they could be certain to target my hands." He held up his fingers, all six and a half of them. His left pinky finger was gone, along with half of the middle finger on that hand. His right hand was missing the ring and pinky finger. No matter how he lived so long, he could live forever and never be able to play piano like he had as a child.

"Edgar, I'm sorry," I said, but he silenced me with a slash of his arm.

"Shut up!" he screamed, and I saw red energy flicker around his fingers for a brief instant as he did. *Magic*. That explained why he still looked thirty when he was close to ninety.

But Edgar had no magical ability when I last saw him. I checked. After all, it wouldn't do to be living with a hormonal teenager, which is to say *insane* teenager, and have them suddenly manifest the ability to throw a fireball at your face. But there'd not been so much as a hint of magical power hiding within him as a boy. There was a theory that everyone had *some* magical talent, it just needed to be unlocked, but most of the people I'd heard talking about it had shuddered when they thought about the level of trauma required to unlock that potential. Then I thought about all the Magneto origin stories I'd read over the years. If anything was going to trigger a magical manifestation, Auschwitz would do it.

"They did something to you, didn't they?" I asked, trying to keep my voice low, my tone soothing, like I would if I were talking to a wild animal. Problem was, I don't usually talk to wild animals. Anything that comes at me, I blast it into unconsciousness and then go on about my merry way. Beasties get a little nap time in, and I don't get bitten. But this was not a case for my normal negotiating style.

"Not 'they,' Harker. 'He.' My *Übermeister*. The man who set my feet on the path to glory and righteousness. The man you murdered, Harker! The man you tore apart with your bare hands and bathed in his blood!"

Oh. Well, that actually did narrow the field quite a bit. I've killed more people than some less-ambitious Ebola strains, but ripping people apart with my bare hands is pretty rare. I blow a lot of people up, I shoot a fair number, although most of those live, and I blast a bunch of people with magical energy in one form or another. But there's only one person that I've literally ripped apart in recent memory. "Mengele."

"Don't you say his name!" Edgar screamed, spittle flying from his lips. "You don't deserve to say his name. You don't know his greatness. You're just—"

"I'm just the man who ripped his fucking arms off and beat him to death with them," I said, cutting off Edgar's tirade. He wasn't coming back from around this bend. He'd been broken in the camps by a man that invented new ways to destroy human beings for fun, and he'd been broken for a long time. Might as well keep him off balance as long as I could. My reserves of power were refilling, but slowly, so if Edgar wanted to stand toe-to-toe and throw magical haymakers, I wasn't quite equipped for that fight yet. "Mengele was a sick fuck who got off on torture and hid his fetish behind science, claiming that he was working to create the Fuhrer's *Übermensch*."

A lightbulb went off in my head. "Problem was, Mengele was starting from flawed materials—humans. So you started somewhere else, with cryptids, trying to use the similarities in their genetic makeup to blend them even more closely with humans, but only the traits you wanted your humans to have."

"Strength, speed, stamina, heightened senses, incredible endurance." Edgar ticked off traits on his fingers. For a brief moment he wasn't focused on killing me. Then he saw that he needed both hands to count to five, and then he wanted to murder me again. I saw his focus shift from sneering asshole bragging to his prey all the way over to murderous psychopath who wanted to bathe in my viscera in half a second, and had just enough time to dodge to the side as a ball of fire streaked for my face. "And innate magical ability. But that was already in all our subjects. We just needed to awaken it in them, like Father awakened it in me."

Father. Shit. "Mengele wasn't your father, Edgar. Mengele and assholes like him *murdered* your father, murdered millions of other people. They tried to murder *you*!"

"Herr Mengele was more father to me than anyone I'd ever known.

More than the wretched Jew that spawned me, more than you ever *tried* to be. No, Mengele may not have contributed to my creation, but he certainly had a hand in my evolution!" With that, he stretched both arms out in my direction, channeling raw energy at me in long beams of destruction.

I ducked and wove around the room as Edgar's energy blasts cut a swath through the walls of the building, setting bookcases alight and punching the glass out of the fake windows. I called up a shield and enchanted it to reflect power, hoping I could angle Edgar's beams back at him, but as soon as I lined up to try, he waved his hands and shifted his spell mid-casting, turning the brilliant white beams of pure power into rivers of fire streaking from his palms to wrap around my shield and engulf me.

Heat washed over me in waves, scorching my face and legs around the shield. I ducked my head to keep the blast off my face and protect my vision, then focused my energy on expanding the shield. I stretched it up until it neared the ceiling, then down to the floor, and used my will to curve the energy around into a big microwave dish-looking thing, which was finally successful in rebounding the power onto Edgar, but I'm pretty sure it took more out of me to divert it than it took out of him to conjure it in the first place.

I dropped my shield and sprang at him, knowing that I didn't have enough gas left in the tank magically to get into some big wizard's duel crap. But that's why I study martial arts—so that when clobberin' time gets here, I'm ready. Unfortunately, Edgar was ready, too. He snatched me out of the air like a bug and flung me into a bookcase. I slumped to the floor with a pile of books raining down on my head, but I wasn't even close to finished. I might have only had limited energy for spell casting, and no way to get more, but I was still the baddest motherfucker in the valley, and I was not about to be put down by some little shithead with daddy issues and a grudge.

Edgar let out a grunt as I slammed into his hastily erected shield, trying to concentrate enough to blast me into oblivion. But it's hard to focus when someone is basically setting off Roman candles a few inches from your face while they try their damnedest to beat your face in. I called up harmless but distracting bubbles of light and color, then flung them into Edgar's face. They smacked into the shield and exploded in a flash, but it was like having a bunch of multicolored camera flashes popping off at the end of your nose—painless, but a nuisance.

The punches and kicks I was throwing would not be painless if they landed, because I was putting all my strength and momentum into them, but the kid's shield held fast. I knew that eventually I could wear him down, but I didn't know if I could do it before he figured out that I was too close to defend if he just dropped his shield and blasted my face off. Spoiler: I couldn't. He got tired of dancing with me a couple seconds after I got close, and dropped his shield. Power flared around both his fists, and I knew he was calling up a baby nuke's worth of mystical energy, so I had to think fast.

Fortunately, while I've never been the best hand-to-hand fighter in the world, I've trained with some of them, and there's one thing they've all told me through the years. If you're trapped in a fight with someone who you can't beat clean, then fight dirty. So as Edgar called up power into his fists, keeping just a ghost of his shield wrapped around his face and chest, I shifted my focus downward and set his feet on fire.

No, really. I let fly a stream of fire that burned so hot it was almost blue, incinerating Edgar's shoes and probably burning off a fair number of his toes in one shot. He let out an ear-splitting howl of pain and collapsed to the floor, clutching his feet and screaming.

That's what happens to a lot of really strong people in their first real fight—they take one good hit and they fold. I'm sure his feet were pure agony. I know, I've been set on fire way more often than I like to think about. But you can't take your eyes off your opponent just because a couple of your appendages have been melted into candle wax. But since this little shit, who I thought had been dead for eighty years, had just spent a lot of time and effort into trying to murder me and everyone I love, I held off on the lecture and just kicked him in the face.

Or I tried to kick him in the face, that is. What really happened is that he dropped to one knee, screaming and clutching at his feet. Then I took a step back, lifted my right foot, and swung it forward with the express intention of kicking the shit out of Edgar Treves, then turning him over to Becks and Director Pravesh to find a prison to put him under. Except he healed from my magical fire almost instantly and was playing possum. So when I kicked at him, he grabbed my foot and gave it a big yank upward, dropping me flat on my ass.

So as I lay there counting the lights, Edgar peeled the smoking remnants of his ruined shoes off, tossed them aside, and stepped up to stand over me. "Well, this little family reunion has been truly lovely, but I have a few more people outside to kill, then I need to make sure that my shipment of super-soldier formula gets off the runway without an interference from your idiot friends. But don't worry. I'm not going to kill you. Yet. I'm going to tie you to a chair and make you watch as I peel the faces off every one of your friends and tack them to the wall of my office. Then I'm going to gut your little Black fiancée and cut off her head so I can hold it in one hand while I slit your throat with the other. What do you think about that, Harker?"

I don't know who taught this kid to fight, but whoever it was should have warned him not to monologue unless you've really got your opponent beat. I was just lying down recovering for a few seconds while he babbled, then I realized he was actually waiting for a response. "What, you actually want to know what I think about that little revenge fantasy?" I asked, sitting up and clambering to my feet.

I must have moved faster or just better than he expected, because Edgar stepped back as I stood up. "I think it's adolescent bullshit, spouted by some power-mad little boy who's pissed off because he was warped by a madman who manipulated his mind and body into some abominable patchwork of man and monster. I think you couldn't kill me with every henchman you've got standing right here between us, and I think I'm about three seconds from slapping the taste out of your mouth. That's what I think. Now shut the fuck up and let's dance."

38

Edgar had more magic than I did, on account of his tank being full. He might even have been physically stronger than me, on account of whatever tinkering he and Mengele had done to him. But what he didn't have was a century of experience kicking the shit out of things that are more powerful than him. That was my edge, and while it was thin, it was what I had, so I latched onto it and hung on.

I charged Edgar, letting fury show on my face. I wanted him to see how pissed off I was, so hopefully he'd think I was out of control. Unfortunately for him, I learned my coping mechanisms from Marvel superhero movies, so I don't get angry. I'm *always* angry. He slammed a shield down in front of himself, and I vaulted over it. I cut a front flip in midair, spinning myself around so I landed facing Edgar's back. I called up power, noting my dwindling reserves, and instead of trying to blast through his shield, I wedged energy *under* his shield, which was a sphere around him, like I suspected.

A lot of time if you create a shield that completely surrounds you, you just naturally complete the shape through the floor. It's actually easier to conceptualize a sphere that goes all the way around you, five feet from the center of your body, than it is to model the shape of the shield to fit the room, especially if there's any kind of uneven surface. So most people either make a flat shield in one direction, or a big hamster ball of magic, with themselves as the hamster. Edgar made himself a nice big ball of energy to hide in, and I wriggled my little magical fingers of power under it and threw the son of a bitch through the ceiling.

It wasn't easy, ripping out a chunk of floor and foundation and hurling a human being surrounded by energy into the air, but I was determined. I was also *pissed*, which probably helped more than being determined. Edgar flew off his feet, but wisely held his shield in place as the sphere slammed into the ceiling and walls, then crashed back to the floor, sending him to his knees from the impact. He let his shield drop, then stood up, shaking splinters and concrete dust from his hair.

"Impressive," Edgar said. "But how much more of that can you manage? Aren't you getting tired, after casting so many high-powered spells?" Then he flung a pair of fireballs at my head, followed almost immediately by a pair of ice spheres. I caught the fireballs by wrapping my shield around them, smothering the flames and very studiously not setting the entire place on fire. Yet. Once this shit was over, I was one hundred percent burning this bad memory to the ground.

"To quote yet another superhero flick, I can do this all day," I said, batting the iceballs to the side with a shielded hand. Then I lashed out with a stream of power from my left arm, wrapping energy around Edgar's feet like a whip. I jerked the whip back, and his feet flew out from under him, slamming his back and upper body into the floor. I dragged him close, then picked him up by the shirt front. "Edgar, I don't want to hurt you," I said, holding him in front of my face.

He spit right in my eye. "That makes one of us, Harker. Because I want to hurt you, very much." Then he slammed his forehead into my nose, setting my eyes to watering. *Goddammit*, I thought. *I taught him to do that.* I dropped him, which was exactly what I told him would happen when a bigger, stronger opponent picked him up and got too close, and he cut loose with a blast of raw energy into my chest that felt like it set all my internal organs aflame.

I screamed and fell to the round, calling up a shield all around me. Edgar stood over me, just blasting away and laughing maniacally. That was one part of Big Bad School he obviously didn't skip, because his evil laugh was on point. I screamed, partly because what Edgar was throwing at me hurt like a motherfucker, but partly to keep him from noticing my hand reaching around to the back of my belt. He remained oblivious until I drew my pistol from the holster at the small of my back and brought it around to level it at him.

He laughed some more, and just shifted his attack to defense, spinning his power into a large flat energy shield between the two of us. I fired twice, more to express my rage than out of any hope the bullets would pierce his shield. I was right, they flew until they were about six inches from his face, then smacked into a blue-tinged wall of air and dropped to the ground, their kinetic energy completely absorbed.

"Is that all you've got, Harker? If I'd known it was going to be this easy, I would have killed you years ago, and I would have done it all on my own!" Maintaining his shield with his left hand, Edgar closed his other into a fist and began to call power into his right.

That was the moment I'd been waiting for. I needed him distracted, and getting him to commit to keeping a shield up while he lashed out at me was the best way to divide his attention. He flung a bolt of power at me, and I swatted it back at him with my own shield, aiming for his feet and forcing him to kneel down to catch his own energy blast on his shield.

While he knelt, I fired off three pistol rounds at his face, grinning tightly as I saw the bullet slam into the hastily raised shield. Edgar fired another blast, but it was a weak, wobbly attempt, and I used the shield wrapped around my left arm like a ping pong paddle and scooped it up, then slammed it back in Edgar's direction. He got his shield in front of it, but this one hit him square, and he staggered back a couple of steps. I fired the pistol at his feet, and he hopped backward to avoid getting his toes shot off.

When his feet came down, my grin stretched even wider, because his heels were hanging out over nothing, and as he turned his head to look behind him, I dropped my gun and cut loose with an even bigger blast of power than I'd thrown at him before. It smacked into his shield and dissipated, but the impact did hurl Edgar backward another step, straight into the hole I made in the floor when I flung his shield across the room earlier.

It wasn't a deep hole, but I didn't need it to be. I just needed it to hurt a little and distract a lot, and it definitely did that. Edgar fell into the three-foot hole and slammed his chest into the far side. His shield winked out, and the fire around his hands also vanished. With no ready defense, and no energy blasts to fling, I had a chance to close out this fight even though I was running on mystical fumes myself. I jumped down into the hole, just a couple feet scooped out of the floor in a circle, and stepped to Edgar with a massive right cross.

That had practically no effect. Edgar grinned at me, then said, "Enhanced DNA, remember? The fae are remarkably durable, if their other abilities have proven difficult to duplicate." He reached out and backhanded me, almost like he was swatting a fly, and I spun completely around before dropping to one knee. I was quickly reminded that the fae are strong as fuck, too.

But pretty easy to hurt, if you know the trick, and I do. I ejected the magazine from my Glock and yanked another one out of my left back pocket. That's where I keep the cold iron bullets. I keep the white phosphorous "dragon" rounds in spare mags in my right back pocket. Important not to mix those up. By the time I reloaded, Edgar was on top of me, laying in heavy punches that glanced off my shield, but every impact took more energy to repel. Once I finally got a usable round in the chamber, I kicked out and swept the skinny man's legs out from under him.

He crashed to his side, once again slamming into the exposed flooring at the side of the hole we were fighting in, and I put three rounds in the center of his chest. It was a nice, tight grouping that should have pulped his heart and ended my two-year long nightmare, but the bullets simply thumped into his chest and stayed there, glinting copper jackets I could see through Edgar's torn shirt.

"Seriously?" I asked him. "A bulletproof vest. What kind of evil wizard are you?"

"The kind that believes in technology," he said, a hitch in his breathing from the pain of three nine-millimeter rounds hitting him from five feet away. The Kevlar kept him alive, but it didn't do jack shit to save him from the impact. But even with what must have been excruciating pain in his chest, he still dragged himself to his feet and started to call up more power. Energy swirled around his head, so dark purple and red it almost look black. He raised both hands over his head to call down something nasty onto my head, but I had other ideas.

Ideas like kicking the little shit right in the knee. His leg bent sideways with a sickening *snap*, and Edgar let out a scream as he went down. The energy whirlpool around his head siphoned back into his body, creating a magical backlash that I knew from experience would set every one of his nerves ablaze. He screamed again when the magic ran through him looking for an outlet, like electricity only less forgiving, and I stood up.

"You little motherfucker," I said, my voice low with pain and fury. "Do you know how much pain and suffering you've caused? You got people killed. Good people, irreplaceable people, people I cared about."

"People like me, then?" he said, and for an instant I saw the child he used to be in the hollows of his cheeks, in the bags under his eyes, in the delicate, spindly fingers. Then it all went away in a flash of rage, and he fired off a bolt of magic fire that caught me right under my ribcage on the left side, lifted me completely up out of the hole in the floor, and slammed me into the far wall of the room.

"I killed people you care about?" His voice wavered a little bit as he dragged himself to his feet. I could see the sweat beading on his forehead, from the exertion of handling so much magic in a short time, or just in the agony of having your kneecap kicked into another zip code. I wasn't sure which, and it didn't much matter. If he hit me with another blast like that, right through my shield and right through my body, I wasn't going to be the one limping out of this room.

"You killed *me*, Harker! You killed me as sure as if you had put me on that train yourself. You kept us in the dark about what you are, about everything you could do. You could have killed Brittlav long before he took me, before he ever laid eyes on my sister! You could have gotten us out of Europe, to America, or anywhere your rich 'uncle' wanted to go. But no, you had to stay and fight, fight your futile war against the Führer and the glory of the Reich. Do you see now, Harker? Everything you did, it means *nothing*! I've got my army of super-soldiers, and before long, I will enslave all of the lesser races and create the Aryan paradise the Führer envisioned! And then—" He cut himself off, like he almost let something slip.

Shit. It was all I could do to try and beat this motherfucker, now I had to investigate, too. "Then what, Eddie?" I asked, using the nickname he hated and putting as much scorn into my voice as I could muster while wincing from what was going to turn into a glorious bruise, if it didn't turn out to be broken ribs. Again. "Then you gonna build yourself a bunker and off yourself because you're too shit-scared to face the consequences of your actions? Because that's what your precious Führer did. He did it with a load in his pants in a hole in the ground, a bullet from his own gun lodged in his brain."

"That's not what happened! That Braun bitch betrayed him, and made it look like suicide to sully his great legacy. When he—" He cut himself off again, but the cat was out of the bag this time. I knew what his endgame was. I was just a step. An important one, and a very personal one to Edgar, but I wasn't the whole game. No, they were looking at a much bigger prize.

They had billions of Big Pharma dollars from years of jacking up prices and fleecing insurance companies. They had the formula to create superhuman troops that could mop the floor with any ordinary soldiers. They had people at the highest levels of the U.S. government, and I just assumed that wasn't the only country they'd infiltrated. They had all that, coupled with one incredibly powerful, batshit crazy wizard.

They weren't in this just to kill me. No, they needed to kill me because Luke and I, along with the tattered remnants of The Shadow

Council, were one of the very few groups of people with a snowball's chance in hell of understanding what they wanted to do and actually stopping it. Because they didn't want to create a Fourth Reich, like so many Nazi assholes had tried to do since the mid-40s. They had no interest in creating a new Reich, because they planned to bring back the Third Reich.

These crazy bastards were going to resurrect Hitler.

39

N ever again." We said it when we emptied the camps. We said it when we buried those murdered there. We said it when we remembered the lost. We said it, but we didn't *do* it. We didn't stop it from happening again. We didn't stop it in Russia, we didn't stop it in Cambodia, we didn't stop it in Rwanda. As a matter of fact, we said "never again" so often, and with such little action behind it, that people started wondering if it was anything more than "thoughts and prayers"—an empty platitude to help politicians survive the news cycle.

And maybe that's all it was to the talking heads on TV. Maybe that's all it was to the people looking at monuments, even to the people looking at yellowed photos of grandparents and great-grandparents they never had the chance to meet. Maybe that's all it was to a lot of people. That's not what it was to me. To me it was a reminder that in order to stop the terrible things, people have to stand up against the terrible people. It was a reminder that if people with power sat by and watched as those without power were persecuted, then we are as guilty as the ones committing the crimes. It was a reminder that sometimes, one person can make a difference, if they're willing to fight.

That's why I stood in the middle of a fake French chalet with a stabbing pain in my chest, aches everywhere else in my body, and barely enough magic to light a candle, and I stared down the brain-washed kid brother of a woman I once loved, another victim in this whole shitshow, but one that was way too far gone to save. That's why I knew I was going to have to kill him to stop him. And he had to be stopped.

"You get that I'm going to stop you, right?" I asked. My breath was coming easier now as I healed from the bruises I'd taken. I might not have had much magic left, but the physical gifts my unique heritage has given me were still very much in effect. The longer I kept Edgar talking, the more healed I became. "We stopped your pissant little house painter once, and we'll stop you idiots again."

"How do you think you'll do that, Harker?" Edgar's grin was vicious, pure predator. "We've got all the money! This time we didn't start at the bottom, in some stinking beer hall with the rank and file. No, we started at the top, with the men that own everything, and we showed them what we could give them if they just went along with our plans. They don't give a shit how many people die, so long as their pockets stay full. Then their influence trickled down to your so-called normal people until they're ready to start a fight over getting a vaccine or wearing a mask to a restaurant. We've got your people so divided they can't stand to look at each other, much less stand beside one another!"

"That's where you're wrong, Eddie. That's what your pals in the camps couldn't teach you, because they never understood it them-selves. It doesn't take everyone standing together. It just takes one person standing up. Well, I'm still standing, motherfucker. And you can't do a goddamn thing about taking over the world until you manage to take me down."

Eddie's smile stretched across his face, and the glow around his fists flared almost blinding white. "Happy to oblige, Harker." Then he brought both fists up and unleashed bolt after bolt of magical energy, straight at my chest.

I dove to the side and cartwheeled left, letting his blasts slam harmlessly into the wall behind me. I felt sheetrock shrapnel bounce off the back of my legs, and when I rounded back over to my feet, I launched myself across the room at Edgar, a human missile with big purple fireballs around my fists. I slammed into a shield and let my grip on the energy around my hands drop. I pounded on his shield with my fists, making flashes of light where I struck and mostly just working on keeping him contained while I tried to figure out what I could use to end this little shit. Out of the corner of my eye, something glinted over the faux fireplace, and when I recognized it, a slow grin crept across my face.

Edgar channeled another blast of power at me, but I leapt right this time, landing in front of the mantel as his attack blew a hole into the hallway and through the exterior wall. Moonlight streamed in, and smoke and dust began to filter out into the night air. I reached above the digitally imaged fireplace and snatched down a replica of the sword that hung in the original chateau in the French mountains. This one was off-balance, heavy, and very much not the magical sword of the Archangel Michael, as the original had been, but it was enough for what I needed.

I channeled the last of my magic into the sword, calling up my soulblade and infusing the cheap metal replica with my magic, with a part of my very essence. White fire lit up the length of the blade and blazed out of the tip. I spun around to Edgar, and pounced, my sword flashing down in a massive overhead strike meant to cleave his shield into splinters.

I connected with his shield, my entire body weight behind my stroke, and my magic flared up from tip to hilt. Edgar saw my attack coming and poured more energy into his shield, tying it directly to the root of his magic and feeding it straight from the source. My soulblade slammed into his power-engorged shield, and we both poured every ounce of magic we could muster into the collision. I felt the impact in my teeth, in my bones, in my balls. Magic flowed out of me like a firehose, and I could sense Edgar doing the same thing, channeling energy as hard and as fast as he could.

When we slammed together, energy *exploded* outward from us, blasting down doors and walls, sending the upper floors of the house high into the sky. The entire place turned to splinters and embers around us, like we were ground zero at a nuclear weapons test. When I blinked vision back to my eyes a few seconds later, I saw Edgar still in front of me, down on one knee, head hung low, panting. He had no shield left, not even a hint of magic around him. Just a big circle of devastation spreading out from where I stood, standing over him with nothing but the hilt of a cheap pot metal sword in my hand.

He looked up at me, a tiny rivulet of blood trickling from the corner of his left eye, and he laughed, a sickly, wet, coughing laugh that sounded as much like a hacking cough as anything. "That your best shot, Harker? Because I'm still here. I'm still here, you're cut off from your magic, and none of your weapons can hurt me. What are you going to do now, Harker? Because if you can't stop me, I'm going to walk out of here and send your bitch straight to Hell where she belongs, along with all the race traitors in this mongrelized, piece of shit country."

"Yeah," I said, my voice raspy with effort. "That's what you'll do if I don't stop you. You'll kill everybody I care about, then me, then you'll move on to everyone who doesn't look like you think they should look, or think like you think they should think, or love who you think they should love, until the whole world is boring-ass blond people who put raisins in their potato salad like fucking barbarians. So I think I'll stick to the plan where I stop your sorry ass."

Edgar stood up, his eyes beginning to glow red. "And how do you think you're going to do that?" he asked. "I just took your best shot, and it did nothing. Nothing! What else have you got left, Harker? What have you got?" He was screaming, frothing at the mouth, which made what I had to do next even more distasteful. But I did it. I took one for the team, even with the slobber.

I reared back and I punched him right in the mouth. Right in his white-flecked lips. I felt my knuckle split on his front tooth, and knew that meant I'd just cut the shit out of his lips, too. He took one step back, his hands flying to his face. I stepped in and punched him in the gut, doubling him over. "You think I need *magic* to beat your ass,

Eddie? Wake the fuck up, son. They don't call me the Wizard, or the Sorcerer Supreme, or any of that shit. They call me the fucking Reaper, and it ain't because I'm good at harvest time."

I grabbed one ear in each hand and slammed my knee into the center of his face, hearing a wet *crunch* from his nose. I snatched a handful of hair and jerked him up straight. Blood poured from his ruined nose, and he looked a little dazed. The red glow in his eyes was gone, replaced by fear. For the first time since we'd started this dance, he finally believed that I might be able to beat him.

Too bad for him that beating his ass was just the beginning. I held the back of his head in my left hand and punched him in the face with my right. One, two, three stiff shots and I felt something move under my knuckles as his orbital socket moved sideways. I didn't want to deal with eyeballs falling out, so I punched him in the midsection again, breaking a rib and hearing Edgar retch all over the floor at my feet.

"Never again," I said as I kneed him in the face.

"Never again," I said, slamming a fist into his jaw and spinning him completely around before he fell to his back.

"Never. Again!" I screamed it this time, straddling his body and wrapping my hands around his throat. I couldn't beat the son of a bitch with magic, but I could wring his goddamn neck. I felt his windpipe under my thumbs as Cassie's face floated up in my mind, then Joe's, then Gabby, then finally Jack. Poor stupid, arrogant, deluded Jack Watson, who murdered my friend and Luke's unrequited love for a promise no one could ever keep. I saw his face, the look of horror at what he'd done to Cassie mingled with the shock as Luke shoved the handle of Jo's hammer through his chest. The way the light went out of his eyes when he died.

As my memory of Jack faded, so did Edgar's struggles. All his training in magic, and they couldn't help him when someone bigger and stronger wanted to just choke the life out of him. I let go of his throat, gasping at the impressions my fingers had made in his flesh, and sat back on my heels. I moved over to one side, never taking my eyes off the body, but it didn't do anything. I slipped on my Sight, looking over the corpse in the supernatural spectrum, but there was nothing to see except the fading residue of magic flowing from his body into the earth around us, returning to the natural cycle.

He was dead. After two years of torment on my part, and eighty years of rage on his, it was over. An adolescent revenge fantasy that metastasized into a global conspiracy to resurrect one of the most evil men to ever live. But it was over now. There would be some cleanup to do, some other pieces of his conspiracy to root out, but with Edgar dead, at least I didn't have to keep looking over my shoulder, wondering who I was going to lose next. I could rest. I could mourn.

I stood, ready to walk away, this chapter of my saga complete after so long. I could almost feel Anna looking at me with her kind brown eyes, even as I stood over the body of her baby brother. I took one last look at the shattered body of the broken man that I first knew as a smiling, gentle, talented boy. He lay there, his neck twisted at an obscene angle, and I reached down to turn his face to the front. As I did, something glinted from around his neck, some kind of pendant, and I pulled it from beneath his shirt.

It was a locket, a small golden oval with a stylized H engraved on the front. It was battered, and scuffed, and obviously old, but somehow familiar, too. I sifted through my memories of the time I spent with Anna, trying to remember if it was hers, maybe something passed down from a mother or grandmother, someone with an initial "H." Nothing came to me, then a chill ran down my spine and a rock settled in my guts. Suddenly I knew where this locket came from.

I couldn't get it open with my clumsy fingers, and I didn't have enough fingernails to wedge in the seam, but a quick flip of the wrist with my pocketknife, and it was open, a familiar image, if one that chilled me to my core. There was a picture of a man in a suit coat, with a necktie and stickpin, his hair neatly combed and his face clean-shaven. I knew, though I couldn't see, that under the dress coat and shirt he wore a pair of rugged work pants and heavy boots more suited to unloading a barge than sitting for a photograph. Facing him from the other frame was a beautiful young woman, a blonde with high cheekbones, full lips, and a smile full of innocent cheek. She wore a peach dress, not that the photograph showed any color, and she shared a nose and a bit of the shape of her eyes with the man who gazed upon her. The man who looked at her with love, and with a protective eye, like all big brothers should.

I knew the man, and I knew what he wore because I remembered the day I sat for the photo, just a few days before I left London with Luke, Renfield, and the woman in the picture. A woman I hadn't seen for nearly a century, since she stormed out of my life in a haze of gun smoke and a trail of bloody footprints. I remembered where I'd seen the locket now. It had hung around my sister's neck from the day our mother died. My sister, who I last saw in Chicago in 1929, had given this locket to my first love's brother, the man who spent decades working to destroy me and everyone I loved. My sister, who had a quick temper and cold fury. My sister, whose last words to me were seared in my brain forever.

"This isn't over, brother."

THE END

ACKNOWLEDGMENTS

No book comes together in a vacuum, and this one was certainly no exception. I have to thank my amazing cover artist Natania Barron, and my awesome editor Melissa McArthur for their hard work in a year that has been pretty shitty for all of us. I couldn't do this without that pair and their hard work.

Thanks to Jimmy Liang for buying the right to die in this book for charity, and to John Scalzi for having a great sense of humor when I told him I wanted to blow him up in a book.

James Tuck is a real person and a really amazing tattoo artist and author asked in Atlanta. I fictionalized him here as Harker's tattoo artist, because he's the only person I'll let tattoo me nowadays, and I figure Harker would be at least as picky as me.

I owe a huge thanks to the following people who helped me out when I fell at a book festival this year and broke both arms (and eight bones in my face!). This bunch of yahoos showered me with Doordash gift cards, support, love, and ice cream. So a big thank you goes to the following:

Hope & Patrick Dugan
Misty & Todd Massey
Rick Gualtieri
Joelle Reizes
Jessica Nettles
Sarah J. Sover
Shael Hawman
Chris & Sheelah Kennedy

Curtis & Dr. Tracy Krumel
Emily Leverett
Marion Deeds
Wayland Smith
Gail & Larry Martin
Jeanne Adams
Jean Marie Ward
Nancy Northcott
Jim Nettles

And Dino Hicks, who in addition to sending me a gift card, unknowingly gave me one of the tools to my physical therapy, since he gave me a beautiful sphere of labradorite last year at ConCarolinas. I keep it on my desk as a paperweight, and I have used it as part of my physical therapy to get my arms back in some semblance of shape.

And I would be horribly remiss if I didn't thank Stuart Jaffe and Darin Kennedy, who were at the festival when I took my tumble, and helped load my truck, get emergency care, and then drive me to the ER. Darin even waited with me and drove me home at three in the morning! Yes, buddy, you really earned your "Ride or Die" merit badge.

Lastly, I have to give thanks to my best friend, my boon companion, and my familiar Puck. If you've signed up for my newsletter, you've seen pictures of the furry little bastard for a couple years now, either laying on my keyboard, laying on my arms, or crawling up on my shoulder to "help" me work. I had to say goodbye to him as we were finishing up work on making this book, and it's honestly the hardest thing I've ever had to do. His decline was rapid and unexpected, even though we knew it was inevitable as he grew older. I miss him more than I could ever say.

So please, if you have the chance to get or give a pet this holiday season or any time, look into an animal rescue in your area. Puck was a rescue, and he gave me fifteen years of snuggles, of purring into my microphone when I was recording podcasts, of putting his front paws on my leg and not leaving me alone until I picked him up and set him on my desk so he could "help," and all the love in the world. When I was injured and had to sleep in a recliner for a month until my arms healed, he slept on my chest every night, cuddling up to make sure I was okay. He was the best, the prettiest, the snarkiest, and the most "cat" I could have ever asked for, and I will miss him forever.

JGH
11/23/21

ABOUT THE AUTHOR

John G. Hartness is a teller of tales, a righter of wrong, defender of ladies' virtues, and some people call him Maurice, for he speaks of the pompatus of love. He is also the best-selling author of EPIC-Award-winning series *The Black Knight Chronicles* from Bell Bridge Books, a comedic urban fantasy series that answers the eternal question "Why aren't there more fat vampires?" In July of 2016. John was honored with the Manly Wade Wellman Award by the NC Speculative Fiction Foundation for Best Novel by a North Carolina writer in 2015 for the first Quincy Harker novella, *Raising Hell.*

In 2016, John teamed up with a pair of other publishing industry ne'er-do-wells and founded Falstaff Books, a publishing company dedicated to pushing the boundaries of literature and entertainment.

In his copious free time John enjoys long walks on the beach, rescuing kittens from trees and getting caught in the rain. An avid *Magic: the Gathering* player, John is strong in his nerd-fu and has sometimes been referred to as "the Kevin Smith of Charlotte, NC." And not just for his girth.

Find out more about John online
www.johnhartness.com

STAY IN TOUCH!

If you enjoyed this book, please leave a review on Amazon, Goodreads, or wherever you like.

If you'd like to hear more about or from the author, please join my mailing list at https://www.subscribepage.com/g8d0a9.

You can get some free short stories just for signing up, and whenever a book gets 50 reviews, the author gets a unicorn. I need another unicorn. The ones I have are getting lonely. So please leave a review and get me another unicorn!

ALSO BY JOHN G. HARTNESS

THE BLACK KNIGHT CHRONICLES

The Black Knight Chronicles - Omnibus Edition

The Black Knight Chronicles Continues - Omnibus #2

All Knight Long - Black Knight Chronicles #7

Lady In Black - Black Knight Chronicles #8

BUBBA THE MONSTER HUNTER

Scattered, Smothered, & Chunked - Bubba the Monster Hunter Season One

Grits, Guns, & Glory - Bubba Season Two

Wine, Women, & Song - Bubba Season Three

Monsters, Magic, & Mayhem - Bubba Season Four

Blood, Sweat, & Tears - Bubba Season Five

Shinepunk: A Beauregard the Monster Hunter Collection

QUINCY HARKER, DEMON HUNTER

Year One: A Quincy Harker, Demon Hunter Collection

The Cambion Cycle - Quincy Harker, Year Two

Damnation - Quincy Harker Year Three

Salvation - Quincy Harker Year Four

Carl Perkins' Cadillac - A Quincy Harker, Demon Hunter Novel

Inflection Point

Conspiracy Theory

Histories: A Quincy Harker, Demon Hunter Collection

SHINGLES

Zombies Ate My Homework: Shingles Book 5

Slow Ride: Shingles Book 12

Carnival of Psychos: Shingles Book 19

Jingle My Balls: Shingles Book 24

Snatched: Grandma Annie and the Cooter of Doom: Shingles Book 29

Deader Than Hell: Shingles Book 40

OTHER WORK

The True Confessions of Fandingo the Fantastical (with EM Kaplan)

Queen of Kats

Fireheart

Amazing Grace: A Dead Old Ladies Detective Agency Mystery

From the Stone

The Chosen

Hazard Pay and Other Tales

Raptor

Have Spacecat, Will Travel

FRIENDS OF FALSTAFF

Thank You to All our Falstaff Books Patrons, who get extra digital content each month! To be featured here and see what other great rewards we offer, go to www.patreon.com/falstaffbooks.

PATRONS

Dino Hicks
John Hooks
John Kilgallon
Larissa Lichty
Travis & Casey Schilling
Staci-Leigh Santore
Sheryl R. Hayes
Scott Norris
Samuel Montgomery-Blinn
Junkle